FIRE

By
Linda K. Rodante

Dedication

to Cindy and Robert Kerce

Thank you for lives well-lived, for your example of Christ, your faith and friendship. Nothing is more important in today's world than living for God.

And to my Lord and Savior, the Lord Jesus Christ. Everything I have is from you. You are my light and my salvation. You are the strength of my life.

Finally, my brethren, be strong in the Lord, and in the power of his might. Put on the whole armor of God, that ye may be able to stand against the wiles of the devil.

For we wrestle not against flesh and blood, but against principalities, against powers, against the rulers of the darkness of this world, against spiritual wickedness in high places.

Wherefore take unto you the whole armor of God, that ye may be able to withstand in the evil day, and having done all, to stand.

Stand therefore, having your loins girt about with truth, and having on the breastplate of righteousness; And your feet shod with the preparation of the gospel of peace; Above all, taking the shield of faith, wherewith ye shall be able to quench all the fiery darts of the wicked.

And take the helmet of salvation, and the sword of the Spirit, which is the word of God:

Praying always with all prayer and supplication in the Spirit, and watching thereunto with all perseverance and supplication for all saints...

Eph 6:10-18 KJV

Chapter 1

Put on the whole armor of God, that ye may be able to stand against the wiles of the devil.
Ephesians 6:11

Patriot didn't want to die.

Although that thought had crossed his mind more than once over the last few years. He took a breath, let his gaze sweep the parking area from behind the SUV's windshield. The church buildings stood behind him, the vacant lot in front of him. No, he really didn't want to die today, but GreasePaint's yell still rang in his ears, squeezing his chest.

"Don't come! Don't come!" the gang member, as close a friend as he'd had in the gang, had shouted over the phone. Then the shout morphed into a scream.

Patriot turned off the SUV.

He'd called the church and told Reece Jernigan to keep everybody inside. Then he'd phoned Detective Rich Richards and let him know what was up. Faster than a 911 call, and he didn't have to prove anything.

Before GreasePaint's shout, the conversation had already turned ugly. The gang wanted to talk—at the pond behind the church. Patriot had shivered at the mention of the church, shivered again when he overheard the argument with GreasePaint, and his heart froze at his friend's scream.

They wanted him, not GreasePaint. But Patriot hadn't shown at any of their appointed rendezvous over the last three weeks. So now they threatened to take their pound of flesh from someone he cared about.

He slipped the SIG Sauer from its holster and eased

5

from the car. Ahead of him, a field and jogging path stretched to the pond with its stand of trees. And the street behind that held families and innocent children. But until backup arrived, he was on his own.

He studied the bushes and trees at the water's edge. Nothing moved. The stand of trees could hide anyone.

"J-beck," he hollered. "I'm here. Just like you asked. Show yourself!"

A car pulled to a stop near the jogging path, and a young woman stepped out. Jogging pants, T-shirt and hair pulled into a ponytail. She put two hands against the car and began to stretch.

No!

"Get out of here!" Patriot yelled.

Her head jerked his way.

He waved his gun. "Leave! Get out of here!"

She froze. Patriot held the SIG higher. *Come on, lady. Go.*

A warning shout erupted from behind him even as his peripheral vision caught movement near the pond. He dove for the ground and his car's coverage.

Crack!

Dirt kicked up next to him. Whoever had shouted the warning fired a shot from behind him over his head to the bushes beside the pond. Someone hollered. Sirens joined the sound. Help was on the way.

Figures scrambled from behind the bushes and dashed for the stand of trees, disappearing among them. A man with a mohawk faced Patriot, hauling a limp male forward. Red splotches covered the man's shirt. GreasePaint. Patriot's gut clenched.

"Patriot! You want your buddy? Come get him." Mohawk sent a twisted smile then shoved GreasePaint into the pond before bolting for the trees.

Patriot rose behind his open car door and scanned the bushes. He threw a glance over his shoulder.

Behind the lone bush at the edge of the parking lot, Reece Jernigan sprawled on the ground in a shooter's prone position, Glock drawn and pointed at the foliage next to the pond. "Go, man. I'll cover you."

Patriot leapt to his feet and raced forward. He skidded to a stop at the water's edge then jumped into the shallows. Red fanned out around GreasePaint. Patriot grabbed his friend's arms and lurched back to bank. Mud sucked at his feet, and he stumbled.

"Here." The woman he'd seen near the jogging trail jumped into the water beside him. "I'll hold him. You get on land."

What?

But she shoved her hands in next to his, so Patriot let go and climbed up the bank. He turned as she hauled GreasePaint to the edge, and they manhandled him ashore.

The woman scrambled from the water and dropped to her knees. "Where's he bleeding from? Where..." Her voice trailed off as she yanked up GreasePaint's shirt. Multiple knife wounds crossed the man's chest.

Patriot's stomach rolled. The sirens had stopped. Footsteps pounded. Shouts followed. A hand grabbed his shoulder.

Reece dropped next to him. "The police are here. Ambulance on the way. Is he..."

"Barely," the woman said. "I need your shirt, Pastor."

Reece tugged it over his head and handed it to her. She covered the wounds and glanced at Patriot. "Need your hands, too. Both of you, until the EMTs get here. Apply pressure to as many of these cuts as you can."

***

The surgical waiting room had seen better days, but Patriot could care less. Reece lounged in a chair, but Patriot had paced for much of the last three hours. Nobody could tell him how GreasePaint was doing.

When the woman returned from wherever she'd gone—if she returned—he should tell her thank you, but really, she could have gotten herself killed. He looked at Reece. He must know her. She'd called him...

"Are you the pastor now?"

He bit back a grin at the look on the man's face. Horrified.

"Are you kidding? No."

"She called you pastor."

"Yeah, I heard that. They're forcing *Assistant* Pastor on me. Not wanting that either."

Patriot laughed. The man was an ex-gang member. He could understand how the title *Pastor* might rankle. "I understand."

"Pastor Alan's still there. And his wife, Daneen. She's fighting cancer, though."

"I'm sorry to hear that. From the one time I met them, both seemed very genuine. Very caring."

"They are."

The woman walked into the waiting room, nodded at Patriot, and stepped in front of Reece. "It's been touch and go, but they've given him blood and sutured the main wounds. None real deep." She glanced from one to the other. "Sliced rather than stabbed. A reason for that, maybe?" When neither man said anything, she nodded. "I think he'll make it. A good thing that water was so cold. Not something you think about in Florida in April, but March was our coldest month this year. Good thing."

Patriot took in her scrubs and what looked like just-washed dark hair—combed and hanging straight to her shoulders. It made her look younger than he'd remembered. Earlier, she'd brought him and Reece a pair of scrubs, too, then disappeared. And now she'd come in with more information than he'd received from anyone else. She must know someone or she worked here.

He stopped next to Reece. The man's wife worked at the hospital. "Hey, is Kati on today?"

Reece shook his head. "She would have been in emergency." He nodded at the other woman. "With Chloe. They're both off today. Kati will be here, though, as soon as her volunteer shift is over."

His focus skidded back to the other woman—Chloe. She could be dead right now, jumping in like she had. If things had turned out differently, he'd have another person on his conscience.

"Thanks for the help. GreasePaint needed it." But he couldn't help a frown. "You could have been killed though. Didn't you notice my gun or the fact that Reece was shooting at someone? That's usually an indication you want to leave, exit the premises, take off."

Her expression had gone from initial smile to surprise to a glare. "Thank you for recognizing that your friend needed more help than you could give. Didn't *you* realize that you could have been killed?"

"I'm with the police. I know what I'm doing."

"And I work in ER. I knew what I was doing—trying to save someone's life. If somebody needs my help, I'm ready to give it."

He stared at her and squelched the desire to roll his eyes. "All right. Glad to hear it, but you might have ended up dead."

She looked him up and down, green eyes narrowing. "Yeah, and you could have, too." She turned and stalked out of the waiting room.

Reece chuckled.

Patriot gave him a black look. "You know exactly what I mean. It can be a disaster having someone who doesn't know what they're doing try to help."

Reece rose, stretched, and grinned. "Yeah, but you've got to admit—GreasePaint might be dead if she hadn't been there."

A doctor strode through the door. Both men turned.

"I'm looking for Gary Lovett's family."

Patriot stepped forward. "That would be me."

The surgeon eyed him. "You're his brother?" At Patriot's nod, he continued, "I'm Dr. Stallings. Your brother has a lot of lacerations. Serious but not deep."

Patriot made a noise in his throat. *Because they wanted me there before he died, wanted me to watch him die.*

The doctor quirked a brow at him. "It's a good thing the water was cold and Ms. Swearingen was there. The loss of blood was significant. He needed blood transfusions and surgery. Next, we'll need to weigh his injuries and his overall wellness and decide where to go from here. I just wanted to give you an update."

The doctor turned away, and Patriot put a hand on his arm. "You're saying he's going to make it?"

"I'm saying his chances are better than when he came in."

The doctor left as two other people entered. Patriot sighed. Great. Detective Rich Richards and his partner. The day couldn't get any uglier. Richards had never given him a break, even when he had been Patriot's handler.

Chloe stepped in behind them and sent a glare Patriot's way. "I found these two detectives in the hall asking for you."

She whirled as if to leave, but Detective Richards cleared his throat. "If you don't mind, I have a few questions for you, too."

Patriot snorted. Of course he did. Richards headed up the gang unit and was so laser focused on the job that nothing else mattered.

The detective threw a glance in his direction. Chloe arched an eyebrow, and her gaze bounced between the two men.

Wonderful. He didn't need the woman any more involved than she was.

Reece cleared his throat. "We had some news about GreasePaint. He might make it after all."

Detective Richards's smile could be real. Patriot wasn't sure.

"That would be a miracle." The detective's glance took in his partner. She dipped her head in agreement. "One we hadn't counted on."

"God still does miracles." Reece's comment brought a nod from Chloe.

Rich Richards shifted back toward Patriot. "Tell me how this went down again. Thought you were out of state."

"I was. Don't know how they found me, but I guess they thought it was cheaper to have me fly back than to send three or four to Denver to kill me."

"You were in Denver?"

"If you didn't know that, then at least someone was keeping it close to home."

"But you came back? To testify at another trial?"

"Not this time, although one is coming up shortly. They sent me a video of GreasePaint. Nothing like he looks now, just a video of him sleeping at the crib with j-beck holding a knife next to his face. The message said if I didn't come back by today, the next video would be…" He glanced at Chloe. "Harder to watch."

"Why didn't you call the office?"

Patriot's gaze shot Reece's way.

Richards swung his head between the two of them. "What? You called Reece? Before you called the Sheriff's Office?"

Patriot's eyes narrowed. "Someone at the office had to tell the Gordones where I was. You've got a mole on the inside."

Richards's partner frowned, shifted, and crossed one arm over the other.

Patriot couldn't care less what she thought. His focus tightened. "*Someone* let them know where to find me. And gave them the number to my phone. I got instructions to head to the church and then they'd text me where to meet. I wasn't sure why they picked the church, but I figured Reece needed to know since he heads up security there."

Richards considered Reece. "And what did you do?"

"Got everyone inside and told them to hunker down and not come out until further notice."

"Like that would work with that group."

Reece straightened. "We have a lot of good people in the dorms and a lot of staff looking out for them."

"Yeah."

"But what we don't have and haven't had is contact with anyone from the Gordones for three years. The gang war decimated them. But what we heard is that j-beck is back and they're reorganizing."

Richards's head tilted. "I wonder who your source is?"

Reece said nothing.

"J-beck is back, and from what *we've* heard, he's looking to be captain," Richards said. "So far, though, he's managed to stay out of our reach."

"Why they're targeting the church though...."

"Oh, come on, Reece. You're harboring Luis—"

"Harboring?" Reece's voice edged up. "Luis served his time."

"For racketeering, but what about murder?"

"He wasn't charged with murder."

"Not then, but you know he killed the gang leader before him. How else would he get to be captain? And how many other people has he killed? You're harboring a murderer."

"Wow," Patriot said. "I'd heard you had a vendetta

against Luis, but I didn't quite believe it. Then."

"I'm just putting two and two together like you and Reece should have done. The Gordones are the ones with a vendetta. Luis is the reason their gang was decimated."

"As I remember, you were the one in charge of that whole takedown. You're the reason they were annihilated. A feather in your cap." Patriot couldn't keep the sarcasm, but also the respect, out of his voice. The man irritated him like a bad-fitting shoe, but Richards had formed an army of law enforcement within hours to bring down the Gordones and most of Luis's gang in one night.

The other detective cleared her throat and shot a glance Chloe's way.

, Patriot's head swiveled. "Chloe would probably like to answer your questions, Rich, and be on her way."

Richards's eyes widened. So, he had forgotten her.

Patriot wanted to shake his head but turned his gaze to Chloe. Her hair had dried, and it glowed where the sunlight from the window caught it. Her slim build looked good in the scrubs. She'd be a distraction in the ER. But he doubted her appearance was on her mind. The woman had received an earful of unsolicited information and looked like she was cataloging it all.

***

An hour later and the room had cleared. The detectives and Chloe Swearingen had left, and Reece had slipped outside to call Kati. Patriot put his head in his hands. The hum of the air conditioners played background music to his jumbled thoughts.

Why would j-beck want him back? Except to kill him. But it still didn't make sense. Since they'd found out where he was, why not send someone to Denver to do the job? Or come himself? That would have been more like it. Just show up on his doorstep and, when Patriot opened the door, put a bullet in him? Or a knife. Why tell him to fly back to Florida and meet at the church? Could Richards be right? Did it have to do with Luis Ramirez? And if so, what did he—Patriot—have to do with that?

Sounds at the doorway startled him. He jerked his head up.

A man in scrubs stepped inside. "You Patriot?"

"Yes."

"He's asking for you. Insisting. Won't rest until he sees you."

"Oh. Good. I'd like to see him, too."

Patriot headed down the hall beside the man.

"He's still recovering, still weak. They just moved him to intensive care. Whatever he has to say, hear it and leave. Don't try to discuss anything. It won't make sense. He's got a lot of sedatives in him."

Patriot nodded and slipped into the room, taking in the number of machines and the lines hooked to GreasePaint. The man's normal ruddy complexion had an ashen look that reminded Patriot of coals from a grill—ones that had burned down to cinders. His friend's 250 pounds looked fragile, too.

"GreasePaint?"

The man's eyes flew open, snapped back and forth, then rested on Patriot. A moment's hesitation and then he forced a smile. "You're still alive."

Patriot stepped next to the bed, "You are, too."

GreasePaint lifted his head and tried a laugh. He grimaced instead. "J-beck janked up. He could have smoked us both."

"Yeah. I'm wondering why he didn't. Look. You all right, man? You're not looking good."

The big man lowered his head and closed his eyes a moment. "I'm fine. I heard them talking when they thought I'd passed out. You have something they want."

"What? Who?"

"The Gordones."

14

"What do I have?"

"Not sure, man. Something. You don't know?"

Patriot shrugged. He'd left everything here when he'd taken off three years ago. And he'd never had or known anything important. The captain hadn't trusted him that far. Could be GreasePaint misunderstood.

"Look, they told me not to stay long..."

GreasePaint closed his eyes again. "Yeah."

The silence stretched. Patriot edged backward. GreasePaint's hand jerked. His eyes opened once more, and he lifted his head from the pillow.

"Don't let them get you. j-beck's planning a party, and you're the prize."

An alarm sounded, and GreasePaint fell back against the bed. His body shuddered.

Patriot stopped. Alarm shot through him.

No, Lord, don't take him. They're after me. You know they're after me. Not him.

A nurse ran in and shoved him out of the way. "Wait outside."

Patriot stepped through the doorway as a man in scrubs rushed in.

He leaned against the wall. *God, I have a deal for you...*

***

Outside the second floor waiting room, Chloe leaned over the balcony railing and inhaled the fresh air. She loved to escape to this place, surrounded by potted plants and with a magnificent view. Sunset hovered over the small town now, highlighting both palm trees and home-grown businesses. The Gulf Coast of Florida had beautiful sunsets. This one smeared the sky with tangerine clouds against a peacock-blue background.

She sighed. A long day. First, a man had yelled and

waved a gun at her, then gunshots rang out, and third, someone hurled a man into the church pond. It hadn't taken any thought to run forward and help, but the shock of seeing multiple knife wounds...

During her time in the ER, they'd had numerous grim situations. She'd been congratulated on her cool assessments and procedures. But today's direct involvement had caused an emotional roller coaster she needed to deal with. Plus, the man Patriot. Like she could have stood by and done nothing. Right. No wonder her tight shoulders sent pain throughout her neck and upward.

And GreasePaint... She shook her head. No, his name was Gary. Gary Lovett. A young man struggling for his life. In a gang. But what had he done that they would do that to him?

She stared into the melon-colored sky and forced her pulse to slow. Why had this shaken her? She taught classes at New Life Church for people with addictions yet had not felt this level of concern.

Or hadn't for a long time—not since she'd tried to help Alex with psychological problems and failed miserably. She'd drawn back then. Not getting involved with people meant she'd never have that guilt again. No, she wouldn't repeat that mistake. The ER suited her just fine. She could step in amid the physical trauma, do her job, and go home—leaving the follow-up to the hospitalist or surgeon or psychiatrist.

Her phone vibrated. She pulled it from her pocket.

"Swearingen." She squeezed the phone. "But he was on the mend when I left. Yes. Yes, I know. I'll be right there."

She sprinted through the second floor waiting room and rushed down the hall. The man had taken a turn for the worse. Why? And why had she left? She wasn't on duty. She should have stayed, kept an eye on him. Just in case. But she'd left, as she always did. She rounded the corner, skidding past another nurse, only slowing as she approached the doorway.

Her efforts, their efforts, couldn't be in vain.

Chapter 2

*Am I a God near at hand," says the L*ORD*, "And not a God afar off? Can any hide himself in secret places that I shall not see him? saith the L*ORD*. Do not I fill heaven and earth? saith the L*ORD*.*
Jeremiah 23:23–24 NKJV

Chloe entered the surgical waiting room and stepped in front of Patriot, her hands clenched at her sides so she wouldn't beat them against his chest. "You! You were in there. What did you do to him?"

He stepped back, eyes rounding. "Is he—"

"Alive? Yes, he's alive, but—"

"Miss Swearingen." A voice came from behind. She whirled as Dr. Stallings stepped into the room, his brow raised. "I think we need to let Mr. Lovett's brother know—"

"Brother?"

Patriot stared past her to the doctor. "Know what?"

"That he's had a setback. The nurse said you were there." The doctor's voice held an edge of inquiry. "With the blood loss, the transfusions, and surgery, his heart has undergone a lot of trauma. But he's young. *If* we can keep him quiet, he'll have the most likelihood of recovery."

Patriot dipped his head. The doctor sent a glance at Chloe, then exited the room. Silence reigned for a minute.

"GreasePaint, I mean Gary, is your brother?"

Patriot's gray eyes held coolness and distance. "As close as he has to one." He walked to the window overlooking a courtyard.

She stared at his back, started to speak then stopped. *All right, God, I haven't done this right. He obviously cares.*

17

Help me.

"I'm sorry. I shouldn't have come in like that."

Quiet again. She moved toward the door.

"He asked to see me. Insisted, they said. I didn't realize he'd get so excited."

She stopped. "Forgive me. I didn't know what went on. I just…want him to make it."

He turned from the window, shoving his hands into the pockets of the scrubs he still wore. "I do, too."

"He has no family? I mean…anyone we should get in touch with?"

"I don't know. We were in the gang together. Never talked much about home. Detective Richards will track the family down. If he has any."

Chloe dropped her head, studied the carpet. "I'm going to his room. See how he's doing."

Reece jogged around the corner. "Patriot."

The man swung in Reece's direction. "What's up?"

"We're out of here. They're sending a deputy to GreasePaint's room. Someone called the Sheriff's Office. She said they're coming for you both."

"She?"

"Yeah. Let's go. I need to get you some place safe."

Chloe glanced from one to the other, her heart leaping. *Oh, Lord, no. Please.*

Patriot pushed past Reece and headed down the hall. "We'll wait for the deputy. Not going to leave GreasePaint unprotected."

Reece caught up with him, and they turned the corner, stride for stride.

The urge to follow swelled in Chloe's chest, but her feet remained planted. It wasn't her business. Or was it? She bit her lip, dropped into the closest chair, and prayed.

***

Sunday morning. Lynn Richards scooted into the row of chairs after her husband. The head usher, Dennis Bowing, had found them a place in the packed sanctuary. Almost every seat was filled. Church membership had grown steadily over the last five years. She loved the church's ministry, IronWorks, to gang members or those struggling with addictions or just people needing a new life. People came to hear God's Word or find help with physical and financial needs. They received that physical help, but also prayer and friendship and Bible study. It felt whole and good. Jesus was here.

She and Rich, though, had arrived late for services the last couple of weeks. *I bet this is the last song.* Her heart dropped. She loved the praise and worship, but Rich took a longer time dressing in the mornings than he used to—even when throwing on jeans and a T-shirt, which most guys wore these days. She wouldn't mention it again. It would only intensify the tension between them.

Rich had never been an overly enthusiastic member, but he was solid. And the church needed his law enforcement point of view. She was proud of him and of the work he did, but these days...

Four rows in front of them and to their left, Becca and Luis stood together, singing. Her sister's mass of curly hair hung halfway down her back, and Luis's arm circled her shoulders. For Lynn, her sister's relationship with an ex-con rubbed her crossways, but she was trying. Unlike her husband...

Rich's antagonism toward Luis mystified her, but he dealt with criminals daily and saw a side of humanity she never would.

The music died, and quiet filled the sanctuary. Some people knelt at the altar. Others whispered prayers or simply bowed their heads. Lynn stood and closed her eyes, clasping her hands together.

Dear Lord, help.

It was all she could get out. Rich was stubborn, but he'd always been fun and loving, too. What had happened? He'd grown gruff and uncommunicative. Did it have to do with their inability to conceive? They'd held off having children the first few years of their marriage, and now, after trying for a year, she'd finally made an appointment with her gynecologist. Tears threatened. She swallowed and forced them back.

As the worship team began to sing, she lifted her head and her hands. *Lord, I surrender Rich to you, our marriage to you. Children to you. Please help.*

***

Chloe scooted the chair closer to the hospital bed. A Sunday afternoon visit fit into her work schedule. She'd have a few hours to sleep before being on call.

GreasePaint, no, *Gary Lovett* looked like life today. The first few days after coming out of ER, he hadn't. Her heart quirked, and she smiled.

The man smiled back. Man? Or boy? What had the paperwork shown? Twenty? Something inside her groaned. Her twenty-nine years made twenty sound young. At twenty, she'd had hopes of...

"Patriot said you jumped into the water and helped pull me out."

"Well, he needed some help."

Gary's smile stretched. "I'm a big guy."

"Yes, you are, and the bottom of the pond was muddy. I'm glad you're better. Did they tell you when you might get out?"

He shook his head. "I'm thinking they want to keep me longer than I want to stay."

"Do you have a place to go? Somewhere safe?" Her head indicated the door. "You still have a guard out there."

And the gang had never shown the other day. Thank

20

goodness. A lot of jabber, Reece said later. Just talk that the girl had taken seriously. Still, Gary needed a safe place, a place that could get him on the right road—one free of drugs and criminal activity. One that would introduce him to Christ. Her chest tightened. The dorms at the church were full.

"Yeah."

"Reece and Patriot were worried about you the other day. They heard the gang might want to finish what they'd started."

"Yeah. They want Patriot though. I'm just a side item."

"But why?"

He stilled. "You don't need to know any of that. Best if you stay out of it."

"From what I understand, Patriot's been out of it for three years, and it didn't help."

"He was a cop, a guinea pig and undercover. Then he comes back to testify against each banger arrested. They hate him. The cops hauled in a lot of members after the gang war. Patriot was in that. His testimony is putting them away, and they feel betrayed."

"But you don't?"

His forehead scrunched. "I feel it, too, but we were tight at one time. He saved me when I was on the menu—from some serious beatings. Lame stuff a couple of the guys cooked up against me. But I always knew he was different. Oh, he's no saint." Gary laughed. "There were women, but he didn't get into the stuff the others did. Or I did. He'd disappear when the skunk came out. The drugs, I mean. J-beck wasn't the only one suspicious. But Bear Trap—our captain—liked him. Patriot said all the right things, and he was useful. On the internet. Stuff like that. And always ready to help anyone, but especially the boss."

"He comes back from Denver to testify against the gang members?"

"I didn't know where he was. He had to pop-a-Houdini after the gang war."

Chloe frowned. "He had to disappear? He's in a witness protection program?"

"Yeah, I think. He's not with the police anymore."

"He's not?" Chloe straightened. "Really? I thought…"

"Nah. He told me he quit. I think it's been hard to testify against people he lived with. You know, we depended on each other. The gang is family."

Some family. One that tries to kill you. But she said nothing, just leaned forward. "Gary, what are you going to do now? After you leave the hospital?" They needed more rooms at the dorms.

Suddenly he looked younger than he was, and doubtful. "For one thing, gotta get used to people calling me Gary again. I guess I'll call my old man. See if I can go home."

***

Miss Eleanor forced herself up from her kitchen table. Her knees hurt, her back hurt, and her prayers seemed to be getting no place. She hadn't slept last night. Something was wrong, but she couldn't put her finger on it.

She closed her eyes. From somewhere inside herself, she reached up. *Lord?*

And waited.

Her hand gripped the back of the chair in front of her. She swiped a hand at something over her head.

"Get out! Get out, do you hear? I'm not listening to you."

No matter the aches and pains, she wasn't planning on giving up her prayer time. She turned and made her way to the living room on wobbly legs, sat on the couch, and reached for her Bible.

Weakness spread from her gut down into her legs and up into her chest. Some days were harder than others. *I'm ninety-two, Lord, and getting a little slower and a little tired. I could use some help.*

Her fingers flipped the pages to Hebrews 1:10, and she began to read. "'Thou, Lord, in the beginning hast laid the foundation of the earth; and the heavens are the works of thine hands.' You have made everything, Lord. You made me. Strengthen me. Strengthen me."

She read on, stopping at verse 14. "'Are they not all ministering spirits, sent forth to minister for them who shall be heirs of salvation?' I'll take an angel right now, Lord. I know Daniel prayed, and it took an angel three weeks to get to him because of some demon spirit over Persia, but I haven't got three weeks.

"I bind every hindering spirit that is trying to keep me down and trying to keep me from praying. I bind them right now. Lord, Your Word says that whatever we bind on earth shall be bound in heaven. Therefore I trust you to stop whatever is hindering me and to send someone to help me."

She inhaled, forced herself from the couch, straightened her legs and back, and walked back to the kitchen. God was good. God was faithful. She sat down in her chair and picked up her coffee. The warmth swirled through her.

Smiling, she leaned her head back against the chair and closed her eyes. And drifted...

The phone rang. She jerked awake, looked around.

Ring. Ring.

She snatched up the phone. "Hello?"

"Miss Eleanor?"

"Kati. Good morning. How are you?"

"I'm fine, but I wasn't able to sleep last night. Are you up? Can I come over?"

***

Rich Richards watched his wife come from their bedroom, long blonde hair tousled, short silk nightgown showing off shapely legs. A sigh coursed through him. He loved her despite their differences, and he was not looking forward to what would seem to her a declaration of war.

"Lynn." She looked his way and smiled. The groan went through him again. "We need to talk."

Her smile faltered. "That doesn't sound good."

She'd always clued into his tone. He picked up her coffee, set it on the table, and pulled out her chair.

She lifted a brow. "Definitely not good."

They'd had their share of fights. Squabbles mostly. But this would be different.

He slid into the chair opposite her. Although his time with God had grown less and less over the last couple of years, he'd lifted a quick prayer upward earlier. Yeah, he knew where he should be spiritually and what he needed to do, but somehow he couldn't seem to get there.

She stretched, and he waited before touching her hand. "I'd like to go to a different church."

Her eyes rounded. "A different church? What? Why?"

"Just to try some other churches. Find something not...so involved with...you know, all the...riffraff."

She withdrew her hand. "*People*, you mean."

He gave an impatient wave. Of course she'd object to the term, but it was nicer than others he could have used. "Yeah, people. The kind I run into daily, arrest daily."

She hesitated, then scooted her chair closer to his. "I know it's hard for you to see people that..."

He jerked away, stood up. "Don't placate me. We need to go to another church." He'd thought about it for a while and made the decision. If she was the "Christian" wife she claimed to be, she'd go along with it. He needed it. He needed to get away. *Hard* wasn't the word.

Lynn stood, too. She shoved waist-length blonde hair back over her shoulders and put her hands on her hips. "Where did this come from? How long have you thought about it?"

"Awhile."

"And you didn't think to discuss it with me?"

"Why? It would have been a fight from day one."

"Because it's my life as well as yours. 'We need to go to another church.' You mean, you do. I have friends at New Life, family..."

"You can have friends at any church. You can see family outside church."

"And I like the ministry they're doing. God is there."

Heat shot through his body. "What they're doing is allowing criminals a free ride."

Lynn's voice rose in response to his. "That's ridiculous. They're ministering to their needs, helping them get back into society. They're ex-gang members or coming out of prison, veterans with PTSD."

"I know what they do." His teeth gritted. "I'm on the board."

She crossed her arms. "You agreed with this when the church started the ministry. What's different now?"

He said nothing, and her brows drew together. "It's Luis, isn't? Ever since he got out of prison, you've been different. What's that all about?"

"The man's a menace. And everybody fawns all over him."

"He served his time, Rich."

"Yeah. Time served for racketeering. Three years out of ten. Big deal. I need a church where I don't have to look at his face every week."

Lynn whirled, marched to the sink, and set her cup in it. "Sharee and John are coming home."

"For a visit?"

"No. For good."

Sharee and John. Lynn's best friends. Home. After six years as missionaries to Indonesia.

"I can't believe it. Finally." Amid all the craziness, John might be the one person he could talk to. "When did you find out?"

"She texted just before I came out here. You know they'll come to New Life Church."

The shard of hope inside Rich died. Of course they would. New Life was home. He turned away, moved toward the bedroom and his clothes. "Doesn't change anything. I need a new church. One I can relax in. You can come or not."

***

Patriot paced from one end of the suite to the other.

How many times could a person compromise himself and still live with it? What he'd done undercover haunted him even after three years. Yeah, he'd been there to stop evil, stop further criminal activity, to be a witness. He could justify everything he'd done. But could he continue to live with it?

He ran a hand through his hair. Being cooped up here didn't help. Too much time to think. These digs, the men's dorms across from the church, provided a safe place for him. He hoped. The dorm housed twenty men who met the resident requirements of Bible study, work, and counseling. But he was here incognito, waiting to testify at the next and final trial.

He'd spent three years flying between here and Denver to testify against the Gordone gang and the individuals that he'd known undercover. No wonder they hated him.

But his life now consisted of this second-story suite, nighttime prowling with the aim that no one would see him, and talking with Reece, Pastor Alan, and Luis. No one else knew where he was. It left much to be desired. He grimaced. Hiding. That was what he'd done these last few years, too.

His mind swirled, and he snatched up the dumbbells from the desk and worked the bicep curls. He'd hated undercover work, and he hated what had happened to GreasePaint. If they could nail j-beck for attempting to kill GreasePaint, it could break up the gang completely.

White supremacists. He glared into the mirror. Blond hair, blue-gray eyes. No wonder the Sheriff's Office had asked him to go undercover. He looked the part. He brought both hands up over his head and slowly lowered the weights behind it. A tricep extension. One, two, three. Again. Again.

When he finished the reps, he shifted the weights, leaned over, and turned on the radio to hear this Sunday's worship service. It had started a while ago, but at least he could catch Pastor Alan's preaching. The man pulled no punches

An engine revved in the parking lot. Tires squealed followed by the sound of the car racing down the road. Patriot stepped to the window and flicked back an inch of curtain.

Nothing. The car was gone. No one standing in front of the church. He shrugged. Let the curtain drop, then flipped it open again.

What had caught his eye?

A light, a flash of yellow at the right corner of the building. There. It jumped again then ran along the ground next to the building until it made a sudden leap at the doors.

He stared. No! A second later, he spun, dropped the weights on the bed, and grabbed his phone. Where would Reece be? He jabbed Speed Dial. Inside for sure. Observant, but no way could he see the trouble outside.

"Yeah?" A muffled answer.

"You've got fire at the front doors. Yeah, *a fire*. It's moving fast. Like someone used an accelerant. Take everyone out through the back. Hurry. Don't let them panic. Don't let them come this way. I'll call 911."

He jammed his feet into his boots, grabbed a towel from the bathroom, soaked it in water, and threw it around his neck. He snatched his jacket, pulled it on, and dialed 911. He ran out the door yelling information into the phone. Except for him, the dorms were empty—all the men were inside the church, along with those from the women's dorm…

His focus shot to an attached building. The nursery! A man flew out the back of the church and sprinted to the nursery doors. Patriot thanked God for Reece's quick thinking.

The front doors were already a mass of flames, and the fire had crossed to the other side of the building. He gritted his teeth. Definitely accelerant.

Chapter 3

For we wrestle not against flesh and blood, but against
principalities, against powers, against the rulers of the
darkness of this world, against spiritual wickedness in high
places.
Ephesians 6:12

Chloe sat in her regular seat, a third of the way down and in the middle of the pew. The music ministers had moved across the stage and were well into their second song. Many in the congregation now stood with hands raised, singing, worshiping. Pastor Alan made his way to the platform.

She let her gaze travel over the packed church. For the last year, there'd been talk about building a new auditorium, but Pastor Alan had nixed the idea a couple of times. No one understood why. Their Gideon, three-hundred-strong congregation had outgrown the church.

Her focus shifted from the song to Lynn Richards who stood a couple pews in front of her. Lynn stood next to China and China's husband, and although she sang with the rest of the congregation, she threw a look over her shoulder every few seconds. Sad. That was what hit Chloe. Lynn looked sad. Rich wasn't here, but he often missed because of his job. Being a detective came with a lot of weird hours and a lot of stress.

Chloe tried to concentrate on the song again but heard a small voice behind her. She swiveled in her seat, smiled at her friend Isabella and grinned at six-year-old Manuel. The boy was a constant delight—inquisitive, fun loving, and respectful to adults. She could picture herself with a son like him. One day. Hopefully.

She'd noticed Reece earlier at his usual location,

standing with his back to a side wall. He could watch the front doors that way. Several years ago, some gang members with AR-15 rifles had paid a visit to the church. She'd never heard the whole story about that, and for a person who liked to stay informed, that had proved hard. But Reece was always at the side wall, always alert.

She glanced his way again in time to see him touch his earpiece, his face tightening, followed by a quick exchange over the mic. He headed toward the narthex doors where another security person met him. Chloe twisted around. Her gaze followed them.

A teenager in the first pew stood and looked at the closed doors, frowning. He leaned forward and said something to Reece. Others surrounding them turned, too. What was the problem?

Reece said something to the teen, then turned to the security guard. Both men walked quickly up the aisle. The guard disappeared through the doorway next to the stage. Reece mounted to the platform and whispered to Pastor Alan. The man's body straightened. After a quick question and answer, he nodded and made a sign to the worship leader. A moment later, the music died.

Alan turned to the congregation. "Quiet. I need everyone quiet." He waited a moment as the chatter died. "Listen, and do not panic. Am I understood? Listen. Do not panic. There is fire at the front doors of the church."

A collective gasp and immediate conversation followed the announcement.

"Quiet, please." The pastor's voice stayed even and calm. "Line up in the aisles. We're going out the back, past me, past the stage, and through the two doors in back." He pointed behind him. "Do not try to go out the front. That is where the fire is. Come this way."

Chloe's heart jerked. *Fire?... No.* Once in her life was enough. Having Alex's house catch fire had been enough. Even if... Her heart flipped. She pushed the emotions down.

The church held a lot of people. They needed to get out without delay.

Around her, people surged to their feet and began moving into the aisles. Her row rapidly emptied except for herself and a young couple who were waiting to get into the aisle. People bunched together. Voices scattered across the sanctuary, rising in volume.

Pastor Alan spoke again. "Please stay calm. Let Miss Eleanor and the other seniors out, as well as the children. Let parents get in line with their children. Someone is already at the nursery getting the babies out. Don't worry about your little ones, but move swiftly. No shoving. Two lines. Here and here." He pointed. "We have two back doors. Don't push. Don't panic."

Chloe looked around. Isabella and Manuel were edging toward the aisle, too. They should have gone first. Children first, Pastor Alan had said. And their parents.

She scrunched her nose against the sudden smell of smoke and twisted to see the narthex doors. They seemed to move, to breathe in, and an orange glow appeared through the crack between them.

A church member twisted to look and reached for one of the handles.

"Don't open those doors!" Reece hollered.

But the man had already pulled the door part way open. The sight of dancing flames in the narthex yanked a shocked gasp from those close by.

"Close that door. Get in line. Exit through the back." Reece's voice took on the command of authority.

Chloe's heart settled as she heard it. People filed forward, hurried but calm. Down front, one of the youth put an arm around Miss Eleanor and led her forward.

"Those with children get up here. Two lines everyone. Use the doors behind the stage on the right and left. Hurry. Don't run."

Chloe turned to Isabella. "You and Manuel go first."

She stepped aside and waved Isabella and her son forward.

Relief flooded Isabella's face. "Gracias." She pushed the boy ahead of her. "You are always so kind, Chloe. Manuel loves you."

Chloe leaned down. "Thank you, Manuel. The feeling is mutual."

"Is it a real fire?" The boy's voice jumped, eyes bright.

Chloe straightened and looked at the doors. Flames had started eating the bottom, their red light and crackling sound sending an ominous warning up her spine.

"Yes, Manuel, and it's serious. Go with your mother."

He shoved a stuffed elephant under his arm and shifted closer to Isabella as she inched down the aisle.

"Move!" Reece's voice jumped an octave.

The lines were moving, people passing the platform, heading for the outside doors. The smell of smoke wafted over them.

"Hurry," a woman said.

"Come on. Keep going." An irritable voice rose.

"We'll all be fine if you don't panic." Reece spoke once more.

Gray smoke circled them, and Chloe covered her mouth. Surely someone had called the fire department. Where were they?

She let others pass her. Children and seniors and families. She only had to worry about herself, and the two lines were halfway down the aisles now. She would be fine. Everyone would get out safely.

Thank you, Lord. She glanced around. *If anyone needs help, God, please show me.*

A man who usually sat by himself was having trouble moving forward with his cane. Chloe had talked with him several times. He was a veteran, an amputee. Other members crowded him, and he needed space. He'd pulled aside and stepped back into the pews. Sweat beaded his forehead. Another man said something to him, but he shook his head.

Chloe edged her way forward. He might not want help, but he might need it.

"Chloe, what are you doing?" Kati, Reece's wife, caught her arm. "Get in line."

"I think Mr. Hernandez needs help."

Kati glanced toward him. "Yes. He needs to get back in line, too." She said something to the woman in front of her, who moved so Chloe could get past. Then Chloe climbed over the next two pews.

"Mr. Hernandez, can I help you?"

Frustration played across his face. "I'm fine. You need to help someone else."

"How many people did you help during the war? You were in Afghanistan, weren't you?"

A man next to them in line raised his head. His gaze met Chloe's entreating one, and he stepped back, then reached a hand to the veteran. "She's right, Carlos. Step in here."

The man nodded. "All right. Thank you."

Chloe turned toward Kati with a smile in time to see the back doors move and fly inward. Flames, smoke and heat poured inside. The woman beside her screamed, and then someone else. People pushed against one another, and the line surged forward.

"Move!" someone yelled. "Don't stop!"

***

Patriot sprinted to the back of the church. He grabbed the handle of the first door, but it was locked.

"Come on, Reece. Get them out of there. You've got too many to waste time."

He searched the area for a hefty piece of wood in case he needed to break the stained-glass windows.

Then both back doors flew open and people stumbled out. Children, elderly men, and women. Patriot released a held breath. Families exited next. Then the women and men from the dorms.

Luis Ramirez, his arm around Becca Stapleton, emerged and called out to Isabella. She and Manuel ran up to him.

"Move back." Patriot gestured with his arm. "Make room for everyone to get out."

An older man with a cane and distinct limp exited. Dennis Bowing, the head usher, stepped forward from somewhere behind Patriot and assisted the man.

At the end of the line, the woman Chloe exited. He started. He hadn't expected that, but he should have. It made sense. She must attend here. She hovered near the doors as if expecting someone else.

He twisted around, easing away from the doors himself but keeping an eye on Chloe. "Is there someone else?" He threw the words at Pastor Alan over the rising voices. The scream of sirens sounded, too. Good. They'd have help in minutes.

Pastor Alan stared at the burning building. Flames spiked at the roof. "Reece. I haven't seen Reece.

"What?" Patriot felt a jerk go through him. No. He shot a look from one door to the other. No one appeared. He started toward the building, almost stumbling over Luis, Becca, and the others as he did.

Reece ran out the left doorway. "That's everybody."

"Okay then." Patriot's gut relaxed. Everybody was out. Excellent. He turned toward the mass of people behind him. "Back up. Get away from the building. Make room for the fire trucks."

Reece and Alan backed a few feet, as did the others, but everyone's focus centered on the burning church. Flames ran across the top of it, and black smoke swirled and mounted against the turquoise sky. Patriot's senses took a hit. He knew the congregation felt it more. But everyone was out…

The flashbacks didn't happen as much as they had that first year, but the fear was still the same. He tucked it down and turned toward the crowd.

"Come on. Move back. The trucks will need room. Get away from the sparks."

A woman screamed. Heads twisted toward the sound. A child raced for the church's back door. A woman scrambled after him. Patriot rushed forward but collided with Luis as the man darted after the pair.

The boy ran past Chloe and into the building.

"Manuel!" Luis shouted.

Patriot grabbed his arm. "Get his mother. I'll get the boy."

"No." Luis shoved him. "My nephew. I go."

"*I'm a firefighter.* I'll get him."

Both men raced for the back door.

Chloe started after the boy. "Manuel!"

The boy's mother reached her, and Patriot yelled at them both. "Stop! Don't go in there. Luis, stay with them. I'll go."

The mother whirled on him, eyes wide, striking out. Patriot pulled back, and Luis pinned her arms.

"*Él quiere el elefante. Se le cayó el elefante.*" Her words sounded frantic.

"*Está bien. Déjalo ir, Isabella. Él salvará al niño.*" Luis's voice rose over hers.

She grabbed Patriot's arm, but he pulled free in time to see Chloe run into the church, shouting the boy's name.

No. Not again.

He pushed the woman toward Luis and sprinted into the building. A few feet ahead of him, Chloe disappeared into the smoke. It's black-and-gray signature already filled most of the building. Patriot pulled the wet towel across his face. The woman wasn't prepared for this, but neither was he—no helmet, no turnout gear, no airpack. It didn't matter.

Her cough reached his ears. *Get low.* He dropped to his knees and hoped she had enough sense to do the same.

34

Chloe tried to yell Manuel's name, but the smoke grabbed her throat, closed it. She coughed. Patriot looked like he was going for the child, but Isabella had grabbed him. If Chloe could just reach Manuel before he went too far...

Chloe fell to her knees and lowered her head. "Manuel! Stop! Come back!"

As the smoke swirled, he appeared just ahead of her. She yelled again, and another voice hollered from behind. Good. Patriot or someone else *was* coming. She crawled forward, but the six-year-old ran ahead and disappeared into the churning blackness. She could guess where the boy was going, back to where they'd sat. But why?

She crawled forward, coughing. The smoke roiled above her. Was she moving in a straight line? Yes. The pews were on her left. She shouted his name. How could he disappear so fast?

The sudden roar of flames overhead stopped her. She shot a glance upward but saw nothing but the curling darkness. The fire had intensified. She scuttled ahead.

A crash from the front doors dropped her to her face. Flames and heat gushed out. Sparks spun and lit the dark smoke. And then miraculously, they parted, and Manuel stood there, eyes wide, the elephant clutched in his arms.

Chloe pushed herself to her knees, grabbed him, and tucked him next to her. As they crawled away from the burning embers, the boy began to cry.

"Shush, Manuel. They're coming for us."

She stopped. Had she headed in the right direction?

The boy coughed. "I want *mamá*."

"I know, Manuel. I know."

A cracking sound above them sent Chloe diving under a pew, Manuel tucked under her as far as she could get him.

Thank You for the wooden pews Miss Eleanor insisted on. They don't have metal frames so hot that they would burn us. Just please get us out of here.

The heat built around them. Above them, the fire roared. The boy whimpered.

"They'll find us, Manual. They'll find us."

They would, but would it be too late? A song from the morning's praise and worship slammed against the tumult of the fire. God was faithful. God was a light in this darkness. He sought and saved those who were lost.

Relief surged through her, but with the heat intensifying, she knew she had get out. A shout brought her head around, and a face appeared below the smoke a few pews away. Patriot scrambled up the aisle toward them.

Thank You, Lord!

He gestured for her to come his way.

She moved her mouth to the child's ear. "Manuel, we have to move. They're coming to get us, but we need to get out." The boy buried himself farther into her chest. "You want to see your mom, don't you?"

A hand grasped her arm. She jerked her head up, and it slammed against the wooden seat. Light pulsated before her eyes.

"Take my hand." Patriot's voice sounded rough.

She rolled her shoulder back to expose Manuel. Patriot's surprise faded quickly, and he reached forward. In one swift move, he grabbed the boy and pulled him free of Chloe's arms. The stuffed elephant rolled away. Manuel screamed. Patriot tucked him against his own chest. He tore a towel from around his neck and tossed it to her.

"Put this over your head and shoulders and follow me out." He crawled toward the aisle. The boy's screams quieted.

Chloe forced herself forward. The aisle now had hot spots that burned her hands and knees. How was Patriot making such speed with the boy in his grasp? The smoke seemed lower with a mix of colors—black, white, even tan. Patriot clambered on. She coughed and tried to keep up. Her lungs hurt, and tears streamed from her eyes. Above her something cracked. A moment later, with a swoosh and flying sparks, an object fell behind her. She scooted forward, then stopped and looked back.

"Don't stop!"

Patriot's shout caught her off guard. The cracking came again. She scrambled up the aisle, still on all fours, glad for the wall on the left that kept them oriented.

To her right, more debris from the ceiling fell. Her intake of breath caused a fit of coughing. Tears ran from her eyes, and she couldn't see. Where had Patriot gone? The towel had fallen back. She pulled it tighter around her head, covering her hair, mouth, and nose.

A figure stepped out of the smoke. A firefighter. Relief leapt like a gazelle through her.

The man leaned down. "Hold on." He lifted her, turned, and headed back down the aisle.

Seconds later, she inhaled cool air. The fireman lowered her gently next to Manuel and Patriot, who had his arm around the boy. His gaze met hers. The relief flooding through her was mirrored in his eyes.

The firefighter glanced over her. "How's your breathing?"

Chloe coughed. "I'm okay, I think."

He frowned and glanced past her. "Stay here. The paramedics will be here in a minute." He walked toward the firemen who were pulling hose from one of the trucks. A ladder truck drew forward. Several sheriff's deputies and Rich Richards were cordoning off the area around the church.

Isabella rushed to her son's side, smothering him in a hug.

"He's probably got some burns." Patriot's voice sounded hoarse. He coughed.

A paramedic bent beside him. "Hey, kid. How're you feeling?"

Manuel said nothing. His eyes rounded.

The paramedic smiled. "I need you to talk to me."

"I'm okay."

"Does your throat hurt?"

Luis leaned over. "*¡Manuel, estas bien! ¡Gracias Señor! Regresaste al fuego. ¿Que estabas haciendo?*"

"I wanted my elephant."

Luis straightened, glanced around. "He went back for the elephant?"

"He dropped it when we were in line, and I wouldn't let him get it." Isabella stroked the boy's hair as the paramedic continued to examine Manuel. "I didn't want to lose our place in line."

Luis put his head close to hers and mumbled something, then he looked from Chloe to Patriot and back. "It was my birthday present to him. I took him to the zoo, and that was the animal he wanted. I would have bought him another. I would have bought him five if he wanted." He clapped Patriot on the shoulder. "*Gracias, amigo. Gracias.* I owe you. You saved my nephew."

Patriot pointed at Chloe. "She found him." He glanced at the paramedic. "Check her out."

Chloe shook her head. "No, if you hadn't found us, we wouldn't have made it."

"The firefighters were on their way."

"But the ceiling was coming down." She cleared her throat. "I've never seen fire like that. It spread so quickly."

As if in exclamation, a crash from the burning building made Chloe jump. Smoke surged into the sky, sparks shooting upward. She swallowed.

Pastor Alan pushed through the crowd behind her and ducked under the crime scene tape. Rich Richards walked forward to catch his arm.

"Alan, stay behind the line."

"I know it's just a building, Rich, but it's a place God gave me. There's been a lot of ministry here." He glanced to his left at the men and women's dorms. "A lot left to be done."

Reece, holding Kati close, stepped up next to him.

They all stared at the fire.

Chloe's heart squeezed. It was hard to watch. *Oh, Lord.*

Orange flames shot from the roof and into the air like satanic fingers tearing at what they prized most, mocking them. She wrapped her arms around herself, no longer feeling the heat, only the cold chill of demonic forces.

She blinked. Had she really thought that? Felt that?

The ladder truck pulled forward, and a minute later, a firefighter ascended the rungs. The stream of water from the hose looked small against the leaping flames, but then the smoke increased, curling and masking the blaze.

Chloe shook herself. "The sides look untouched. It's mostly the roof."

"You can't see the front."

Patriot's voice startled her. She glanced his way. Soot smeared his face, his clothes, and through the blond hair. No doubt about where he'd been. She must look similar.

The paramedic caught her attention. "You have any burns?"

"I...uh..." She glanced down at her palms.

The woman nodded and searched her bag. "How's your breathing? Talk to me a minute."

Beside her, Kati sniffed, and Chloe lifted her gaze. Kati's tears glistened. *Yeah, Kati. Me too.* Chloe looked away from the paramedic and at the church. Pastor Alan, backed by the rest of the congregation had inched forward, watching.

"We've set up a perimeter." Rich's voice had softened but still held authority. "I need everyone behind the yellow tape to keep them safe and preserve evidence. We are going to want to find whoever did this."

A murmured agreement rose from the crowd. Chloe found herself nodding, too.

She glanced around, ignoring the woman trying to bandage her burns. Besides herself, Patriot, and Manuel and his family, only Pastor Alan, Reece, and Kati were in front of the tape.

Murmuring erupted from the crowd. A multicolored glow lit the ground beside the church. The fire backlit the stained-glass windows and radiated light and color outward.

One of the firefighters shouted something.

"Watch out!" Patriot threw his arm toward Manuel, shoving him to the ground. "Get down. Cover your head."

Chloe dropped her head and covered it with her hands. Those near her did the same just as the windows exploded. Shards of glass flew their way and scattered in the grass in front of them. People cried out, and the congregation surged backward.

Questions and answers ping-ponged back and forth through the crowd. Chloe's gaze bounced from Kati and Reece, to Alan and Rich. They seemed okay. To her left, Manuel sat up. Isabella snatched him to her, and Luis enfolded them both in his arms.

His head swiveled back to the crowd. "*Becca?*"

The young woman had been standing not far away. Now she slipped under the police tape and ran to him.

Rich whirled and waved the congregation back. "*Everyone* behind the tape."

Luis caught Becca's hand and moved from Isabella's side to Alan's. "Pastor, God can work in any place." He indicated the smoking remains of the church. "He is not limited by this. He is not defeated. We will rebuild."

Pastor Alan nodded. "Yes, Luis, we will."

Chloe swallowed. She could have been in there with Manuel and Patriot. Her focus settled on Patriot. His eyes met hers, and the jerk of her heart surprised her.

"*Gloria a Dios*," Isabella said as she lifted Manuel into her arms and headed toward the yellow tape. "Glory to God. We will triumph."

***

A third paramedic squatted in front of Patriot as he settled on the ground a few feet behind the line.

"You have burns?" the man asked.

Patriot held out his hands palms up. Yeah, the hotspots on the carpet had left some burns, as had flying cinders from the ceiling beams. And maybe the glass. He glanced toward Chloe and the boy and thanked God the glass had fallen short. He wondered about Chloe's long hair. Glass might have caught there, but he didn't see anything. The fire had curled it, though, in some places. He winced. If the flames had caught there, her face would have burned, too.

Most people had no idea what fire could do, how fast it spread, how fast it could kill.

The paramedic crouched in front of Manuel said something that made the boy laugh.

Patriot watched the team with the hoses, watched them melt the flames with the silver water. A precious commodity during a fire.

Once the injuries were treated, the paramedics left, and so did the adrenaline. Perhaps he wouldn't have found Manuel in time. He wasn't sure. People did foolish things during times of crisis. And people died. Why had Chloe run past him to try and save the child? What if they'd both been lost? A woman and a child. Again.

He turned his head. "Why did you rush in there? Didn't you see I was going?"

Chloe's face registered surprise. "No, I…well, you and Isabella were arguing. Someone needed to get him fast. I thought I could grab him inside the door."

He looked down before shaking his head.

"What was I supposed to do?" Chloe's voice inched higher.

"I don't know. Wait one second?"

Her hands flew out. "Wait?"

He let out a breath. She was right. And he'd done the same thing. Chased after her and the boy.

Still, he couldn't control the dread inside him. She could have died, and the boy, too. "You always jump in when someone needs help?" His angry tone made sure she didn't think he was complimenting her. She'd had no idea what she was doing. The same way she hadn't known what was going down that day at the pond.

Heat leapt into her green eyes. "Do *you*? Was I supposed to sit around and do nothing? Wring my hands?"

"No, I—"

"And what about you? Don't tell me you're a firefighter, too."

"I am."

She leaned away from him, clearly disbelieving what he'd said. "Kind of like you're in law enforcement—only you're not?"

Man, the woman was irritating, but she had him again. Someone had obviously mentioned his status. "Okay. You're right. I'm no longer in law enforcement. I got out a few years ago, but the other day, I was acting in that capacity."

"Oh. Right. I get it. You step back in when you feel a need."

"You wouldn't understand."

"No, I wouldn't." She rose.

He did the same. "But I am a firefighter. I work with the Denver Fire Department." He'd had to do something when he'd arrived there three years ago. Something that would make him feel respectable again.

Her gaze dropped to his feet and rose back to his face. "Perhaps I'll wait and have that confirmed."

She stomped off, and he halted the sudden urge to pull her back, yank out his ID and prove himself. Instead he shook his head. He'd deserved her censure. But the pain of amateurs getting involved and getting killed had raised welts all over his psyche that might never heal.

Chapter 4

*For the word of God is quick, and powerful,
and sharper than any two-edged sword,
piercing even to the dividing asunder of soul
and spirit, and of the joints and marrow, and
is a discerner of the thoughts and intents of
the heart.*
Hebrews 4:12

Chloe pulled into the church parking lot. No way would she miss the work party today—their third this week. Work had started on Monday after the fire, and today was Wednesday, so she was a couple days behind. But her work in the ER had interfered.

She stepped from the car and stopped. The white walls, shattered windows, and roofless building trapped her breath. The gables standing at each end of the church made the scene worse. They held up...nothing. Men, women, and equipment spread over the area encompassing the burned-out husk of the church, the nursery, and the church offices.

Her heart stuttered. She flipped her ponytail on top of her head and tightened her hands around it.

Oh, Lord.

A professional crew worked on an area at the right of the church, but the others were church members or volunteers from the community. She'd seen that on the news. The public had stepped forward to help. Some offering their services, some offering finances. *Thank You, Lord.* They needed it.

She straightened her shoulders. It was April. Resurrection time. Yes, they would rebuild.

Okay, find the person in charge and offer to help. But

first...

Someone had decided all these helpers would need food. Smoke curled from a large metal barbecue to her left, and the aroma from the grill caused Chloe's mouth to water. Pastor Alan had probably come up with the idea, then found someone to get groceries and to cook. After working all night and sleeping until noon, lunch had taken a back burner to getting here. Her stomach clenched at the tantalizing smells.

She walked that way. Becca was helping Luis at the grill. *Luis?* The ex-gang leader cooking? Hmm...

The scent of peppers, onions, and sausage enticed her. The Florida State Fair had the same drawing card, and she could never resist it. Could she get something to eat before being assigned a work detail?

"A chef?" Luis sounded indignant. He waved a meat fork at the food on the grill. "I only do this to help Isabella. She had to take Manuel to a birthday party."

Becca leaned toward him. "But I can tell you've done it before. It smells *delicioso*."

"Yeah, it does." Chloe stepped beside them. "The workers are going to swamp you soon."

"One o'clock, I tell them." Luis stabbed sausage links and slapped them onto the cutting board next to the grill. He skewered them with a fork, then slashed them into smaller pieces. Juices ran and splattered onto the hot surface, spitting and sizzling.

Chloe raised a brow at Becca and edged back. "Don't let me get in your way,"

"Isabella and I learn together from our uncle. He worked at this meat shop and would bring home slabs of meat, and we cook it." The fierce profile of his face gave way to a mocking grin. "We liked to eat."

"You must have learned a lot." Chloe eyed the buns, meat, and veggies. "I just got here. Any hopes of getting one of those before I start work?"

Becca held a bun out for Luis, and he flipped a sausage

into it and piled it with peppers and onions.

"It is our secret, senorita."

"_Sí_. _Gracias_." Chloe grinned and walked away. She bit into the sandwich, and her taste buds danced. Now, to find the person in charge...

***

"_Lynn?_"

"Who did you think they'd put in charge of cleanup? Reece?" Lynn tossed her waist-length hair over her shoulder.

Chloe giggled. "Not in his line?"

"I'd like to see him find the right cleaners for this project."

"I imagine Alan gave him the insurance adjusters."

Lynn grinned. "He could have his Glock on the desk when they came in." Her hand slapped against her mouth. "Oh no!"

"What?"

"His gun! And his desk."

"Oh my goodness, I never thought... The office files."

Lynn's eyes rounded. "All the data on everyone who lived in the dorms and have been through the program. All the legal stuff."

"Surely they had fireproof files. And hard drives for backup."

"It's a church. Half of our stuff was donated. Are hard drives fireproof?"

"I don't know. Some are, I bet, but the office wasn't completely destroyed, was it?"

Lynn let out a loud breath. "No, it wasn't. I've avoided that area. Rich is still investigating, and I'm staying as far away as I can."

"I don't know how you do that."

"You learn not to ask questions."

"Do they think it was the Gordones?"

Lynn shrugged. "Rich heads up the gang unit with the Sheriff's Office, and he's here, so… But your best bet is to talk with Pastor Alan or Daneen."

"Daneen's here?"

"She and Alan have been here from sun-up to dusk the last two days. And Reece, of course. The guys and girls from the dorms all pitched in, too. When Daneen called and asked for assistance with the cleanup, I couldn't say no."

"How is she doing?"

"You wouldn't know anything is wrong." Lynn's face reflected the somberness that Chloe felt.

"She has a deep faith in God. I admire her." Chloe pulled on her ponytail. "All right then. What can I do?"

"Could you tackle the windows in the nursery? Everything's covered in black soot. There's someone in there washing the walls, but don't disturb him. Just do the other rooms. We've taken the toys and beds and everything out to wash. We vacuumed." Lynn turned to the Jeep Grand Cherokee parked on the grass and kicked her foot out. The lift gate opened.

Chloe grinned. Lynn loved her cars. The more gadgets and widgets the better.

She grabbed the bucket Lynn handed her—filled with cleaning supplies. "Okay. I'll stay out of his way."

"Just a second. Wear the gloves, keep the door or a window open, and wear a mask if you feel you need it. There are instructions in the bucket and a ladder in one of the rooms. You'll need it, as the windows are pretty high. I'll send someone else to help as soon as I have an extra hand."

Chloe gave a mock salute and headed to the nursery. She opened the first door. A lone figure with a long-handled brush and a bucket of sudsy water turned her way. Even with a mask covering his mouth and nose and a ballcap on his head, she recognized him.

Patriot's eyes narrowed, and he returned to work.

"And how are you this fine afternoon?" She didn't wait

for a reply. The look in his eyes let her know she wasn't welcome. "Don't worry. I'm not here to disturb you. I'm cleaning the windows in the other rooms."

She shut the door and stepped to the next room. Whew. What a fun guy. Too bad his attitude didn't go along with his apple-pie-and-baseball good looks.

As she surveyed the windows and walls in the room she'd entered, her own attitude flagged. Wow. How did the walls and windows get so much smoke on them? She set down her bucket and attacked the glass panes.

**

Patriot finished washing the walls, but he couldn't paint until tomorrow after they had dried. He stood and listened. Evidently, Chloe hadn't finished the windows next door. If he cleaned the walls in the third room now, he could start on the second when Chloe left; but that was such a gutless move he wouldn't consider it. *Not running any more.* He lifted the bucket with one hand and the long-handled brush with the other and headed out.

When he opened Chloe's door, she was teetering near the top of the step ladder—arms swirling like a whirligig. He dropped the brush and bucket and leapt across the room. Thrusting his right hand against the small of her back, he used his left to catch her arm. She still swung the other in a tilt-a-whirl fashion. A second later, she leaned forward and grabbed the top of the ladder. He kept hold a moment longer.

The air in her lungs came out in a rush. "Oh. My. Goodness. I was so going to fall. Thank you!"

She tried to back down and bobbled. He caught her arm again and held on until she was off the last step. She slid to the floor and dropped her head into her hands.

Well, there was no place else to sit. He stepped away and studied the top of her head and bit back laughter that threatened. The gyrating copter thing she had going when he stepped into the room had to be the funniest thing he'd seen in a long time.

She glanced up at him before he could tame the amusement. Her look changed. "You're laughing?"

"I'm trying not to, but…that whole whirligig image of you is still here." He tapped his head.

"*Whirligig*? What? I almost fell." She shoved herself to her feet and stabbed her hands to her hips.

He tried to straighten his face. "Yeah, I know, but…"

"*But*?"

He laughed then. He couldn't help it. And he kept laughing.

"All right. All right." She waved her hand at him, sounding indignant, but a corner of her mouth turned up. "It wasn't that funny."

"If you say so."

She shook her head, ponytail flying.

He walked over to his stuff. A chuckle threatened, but he swallowed it. Amazingly, the bucket stood upright. Nothing had spilled.

He cleared his throat. "I thought I might tackle the walls, but I can start on the other room if that's better for you." When he picked up the brush, he glanced at her then eyed the step ladder. "If you stay off the ladder. What's it doing here, anyway?"

"Someone knew we'd need it. And I do need it to finish the windows."

His raised brow drew a narrowed-eyed look from her, but that twist to her mouth remained.

She tilted her head toward his bucket. "If you want more soap and water, there's a bathroom over there. Cleaning stuff, too. And you won't bother me. I'll be finished in a few minutes."

Okay. So, he'd stay. Better than working in the other room and wondering how she was doing. He felt the grin start again as he headed for the bathroom and the clean water.

A moment later, she climbed halfway up the ladder and reached for her phone on the top step. As he filled the bucket, she fiddled with the phone, and then music swept through the room. A Christian song he knew. Was that what she was doing when she'd almost fallen? Finding music on her phone?

She grabbed a rag from the ladder's shelf, leaned over, and began work on the window.

He walked across the room and set his bucket down. She looked like a sixteen-year-old in her cut-off jeans and T-shirt. At the hospital, he'd pinned her age between twenty-five and thirty. Now he wasn't sure. He watched for a moment then dropped his gaze.

Keep your mind on business, man. You've got too much or your plate for anything else.

Then the image of her swirling arms rose again and the amusement. How long had it been since he'd laughed like that? Much too long.

***

Chloe twisted her head one way and then the other. Her neck was tight, along with other assorted muscles. Well, what did she expect trying to keep up with Patriot all afternoon?

She'd washed windows as fast as an automatic car wash cleaned cars, since he wouldn't leave until she finished and stepped off the ladder. Sheesh. She didn't need that much oversight. Although the hours spent working with Patriot had left a slight humming inside. One she stuffed down when she stepped into Miss Eleanor's small living room.

Her gaze slid over the group of prayer warriors who had come tonight, all crowded together here rather than spread out in their meeting room at church. This would do for a while. Everyone passed hugs around and talked about the fire, praising and questioning.

After a few minutes, Miss Eleanor asked for quiet.

"Kati had a question earlier this week. The same one

most of you have." She gestured at Kati.

"Me?" Kati lifted her brows.

Chloe grinned. Kati liked being inconspicuous in a group unless she was showing off her kickboxing, and she only did that to get others interested.

"Okay, but...I don't want to sound as if I'm questioning God, but I am questioning. I'll step out there then. We prayed. Miss Eleanor and I had a time in prayer. God had put something on both our hearts even though we didn't know what it was exactly. And still the fire destroyed the church."

Miss Eleanor nodded. "You're right. We did pray, and I do believe it was about this. I believe God had others praying, too." Her glance scanned the group. "Am I right? Did other people feel an urge to pray before the fire?"

A number of people nodded. A couple said yes.

"And yet we have questions. No one was hurt—including Manuel and Chloe and that man who came from nowhere and went in after them."

A man carried in a chair from the kitchen. "He was the one in the gang shooting earlier this week. I heard him talking to Reece. I think Reece called him Patriot."

Heads turned toward the speaker. Questions followed.

Miss Eleanor put up her hand. "Reece and Pastor Alan are keeping that situation close to their chests. Let's honor that and drop the subject. We can pray in a general way later.

"But let me address the fire. I think you all know that not every battle, whether physical or spiritual, is won without hurt or casualties on both sides. Sometimes we think that because we're God's children, nothing should happen to us, but that's not truth. Far from it. In order to win the war for our souls, Jesus had to go through the crucifixion. Remember that. But we have the final victory. We've read the end of the Book. Or we should have." She looked around at the group.

"I have." Isabella put a hand up. "I read through the whole Bible last year."

"Me, too.

"And me."

Chloe nodded. Pastor Alan had challenged them to do it and given out a reading plan.

Others murmured in agreement.

Miss Eleanor grinned. "This group always makes me proud. So, you know the end of the Book. As I said, we win. We win the war, but in the meantime, there's middle earth." She smiled. "Not really, but if you know the story, you understand what I mean. We're in a battle. We have weapons—the Word of God, the name of Jesus, praise and prayer, and God has given them for a purpose."

"The blood of Jesus and our testimony," inserted the man with the kitchen chair when Miss Eleanor paused.

"Oh yes. Excellent. And we use these weapons to stand against the Enemy and in the gap for people and situations. We're helping people on the front lines in physical or spiritual combat. And we help others—our loved ones and friends. They might not see the enemies surrounding them, but we're praying for their discernment and protection. Angels are sent because of our prayers, just like they were sent because of Daniel's."

"I believe that, Sister Eleanor." Isabella's voice jumped. "I believe in angels. I prayed all the time for Luis when he was in the gang and in prison."

Several others agreed.

"Good. The book of Hebrews tells us that angels are ministering spirits sent to serve those who will inherit salvation.

"Now, I have two scriptures I'd like you to go home and think about. When we meet next week, I want to take a short time to discuss them. A short time. Because the work we do here, the warfare in the Spirit, is important.

"The first scripture is Matthew 11:12. It states that the kingdom of heaven suffers violence, and the violent take it by force. Think about that."

Chloe pulled a little notebook out of her purse and

wrote down the reference.

Miss Eleanor held up her hand again as the group began to talk. "The second verse, or actually two verses, are Daniel 10:12–13. Here, an angel tells Daniel he was sent to answer Daniel's prayers but was held up for twenty-one days by the prince of Persia—which Biblical scholars tell us refers to a demon over that country. And then it says that Michael, some say the archangel Michael, was sent to help him get through to Daniel with the answer. You might want to read all of Daniel 10 to understand that better.

"In short, we're in a real war, a spiritual war, and our prayers make a difference. We'll discuss this next week, but right now we have a lot to pray about."

Two hours later, Chloe stood next to Kati as they watched the others leave. Reece had dropped Kati off but was playing basketball with some of the guys from the dorms, so Chloe had volunteered to take Kati home.

She gave the older woman a smile and a hug.

"You're tired tonight, Chloe?"

"Yes, but I'm so glad others weren't. We had a lot to cover in prayer."

"More than I realized. You know this person Patriot?"

"A little." And maybe after this afternoon, she might want to know more. Well, no. He'd mentioned heading back to Denver soon. Ah well...

"I felt the need to pray for him when you mentioned him."

"Yes, I did, too. And others did obviously, along with prayer for Luis and Rich. And the IronWorks ministry."

Miss Eleanor reached to give her a hug. "It's good when the people of God are sensitive to the Spirit." She glanced at Kati. "I've tried to be an example of prayer during our meetings through the years, but I haven't actually taught. God impressed that on me this week. I need to teach more. The prayer meetings from now on will begin with some teaching. A short teaching because the prayer we do is important."

Chloe murmured her agreement but watched Miss Eleanor. Her eyes had not left Kati.

"Kati, you and I, we've prayed together numerous times. Just the two of us. You see the spirit world better than most. God moves on you to pray, and you do it. I won't be here forever, and someone has to take over the leadership role. The IronWorks ministry is important. It shouldn't be left without intercession, without prayer covering, if something happens to me."

Kati stared at her. "I know that, but..."

"No, buts, Kati. Pray about this. I'm not leaving Chloe and all the others out. I'm just saying someone has to take up the mantle."

"But I have a job, and I volunteer at the anti-trafficking house, and Reece and I want a baby. Someone needs to head up the prayer group if something happens, Miss Eleanor, but that isn't me."

Chapter 5

Behold, God is my salvation; I will trust, and not be afraid:
*for the L*ORD *J*EHOVAH *is my strength and my song; he also is*
become my salvation.
Isaiah 12:2

Chloe parked her car and headed to the portable building for the Sunday morning church service. A week since the fire. Seven days. How was everyone feeling? How was she feeling? Her scramble to save Manuel had replayed in her mind all week. The flames, the smell, the heat. The fear.

Maybe Patriot was right. She tended to jump in to help before thinking sometimes. It worked well at the ER, maybe not so well other times. Hmm… She knew what she was doing in the ER. In most cases. She was trained, had experience. That could make the difference.

The burn that still aggravated her knee might help her to remember. She grinned at the memory of Patriot's laughter Wednesday. Laughter was good, and since he'd been so growly before, it had thrown her.

She said hello to Dennis Bowing as he held open the door of the temporary building. Wow. Someone had worked overtime to get these buildings up for the service. Chloe stopped and let others pass her. Chairs filled the sanctuary instead of pews. Quite a few people had wanted to replace the pews with chairs anyway. Well, they got their wish. The place was packed. What were the occupancy requirements?

Dennis motioned her forward. His smile seemed forced this morning.

"You okay, Dennis?"

"Just wondering about this." He waved his hand. "I

can't believe how many people are here. You'd think they would be afraid of something happening again."

"I think it's a case of we're not going to let anyone—gang or person—stop us from coming to church."

He grunted. His sharp chin seemed even sharper under the stress. But she understood that.

"Well, I hope the fire department doesn't show up. To count heads this time."

"Yeah. Is there a lone seat somewhere, or should I stand like some of the others?"

"I'll find you a seat, Chloe. Don't worry."

Up front, Pastor Alan stood between ornamental plants and the worship group. Her heart spasmed. Everything looked different. Their church was gone.

Alan moved forward and motioned to someone. As Chloe took her seat, Miss Eleanor stepped forward. One of the youth helped her up the short flight of stairs to the platform. She took the mic Pastor handed her.

"I just want to say something this morning. Many of you have called this week, and we've talked. I understand where you're coming from. Last week was hard, but you need to know—there's no God like our God. The Enemy tried to burn us down, but he missed! He might have burned a building, but the church is not a building. It's the body of Christ. It's me and you. And all Satan's done is make me mad. What about you?"

Some of the congregation cheered in agreement. Another person whistled. Chloe grinned. Luis, Becca, Isabella, and Manuel sat in front of her. They stood and clapped.

"There's no God like our God. He's going to do something with this—something good. Wait and see." Pastor Alan beamed.

"*Gloria a Dios!*" Isabella shouted, then Luis joined in, lifting his voice, shouting praises to God. The worship group started a praise song, and Becca pushed past Luis and strode into the aisle. With hands raised, eyes closed, she twirled and danced.

The atmosphere changed, become heavy with expectancy. Chains were falling. Her own, too.

She'd pressed on at work, telling herself everything was okay, but the involvement with GreasePaint and Patriot followed by the fire had disturbed her more than she knew—until now. Tension seemed to melt from her shoulders. And her worry over GreasePaint? Useless. He'd left the hospital before she could say goodbye. She'd have to trust God with that, too.

The worship leader slipped into another song, the words ministering to her soul, telling of God's faithfulness. She lifted her arms, moved into the aisle with Becca, and began to sing. She needed this time of worship and freedom. God inhabited the praises of his people, and the atmosphere vibrated with His Presence. Even after all that had happened, God was good—God was greater.

Kati and Isabella joined them, and then others moved into the aisle or filled the front of the sanctuary. On the platform, Miss Eleanor danced her own unique ninety-two-year-old dance. Chloe grinned.

Pastor Alan laughed and stepped forward. The music quieted. "This is the sound of freedom, of dry bones rising and coming together, and the Holy Spirit breathing on us. If you feel Him moving on you, don't resist. Let Him have his way."

A minute later, he returned to the front. "I'm laughing at the Enemy. You should, too, because what Satan meant for evil, God will use for good. Don't let this fire get you down. Think about it. No one was seriously hurt. The dorms weren't touched. Neither were the counseling offices. We're going to build another church. We're already receiving money from the community. And we had the building insured. We can expand. Reece and I wanted larger offices, anyway." Laughter followed. "Satan made a mistake when he pushed someone to start a fire here."

Miss Eleanor reached for the mic. Alan chuckled and

handed it to her once more. "You know who the real Fire is, don't you? The Scriptures call God a consuming fire, and when the apostles were filled with the Holy Spirit, fire sat on each of them. Think of it—fire represents God and the Holy Spirit, and God makes His ministers a flame of fire."

Pastor Alan grabbed his Bible from the pulpit and flipped it open. "Listen to this. Ezekiel 1:27. Ezekiel saw a vision of our Lord, and he says, 'from…his waist up, he looked like glowing metal, as if full of fire, and that from there down he looked like fire; and brilliant light surrounded him.' We want the fire of God to consume us."

"Yes!" Luis shouted.

"God is described as a fire from the loins up and the loins down, and we are tried by fire. First Peter 1:7 tells us that the trial of our faith is much more precious than gold, though it be tried with fire "that it might be found unto the praise and honor and glory at the appearing of Jesus Christ." Our faith is being tested. We have a ministry that has grown over the last four years. Will we let a fire from the Enemy tear it down, or is God's fire, his Holy Spirit, big enough to overcome this?"

"We will overcome, Pastor!" Luis's voice again.

Chloe turned her head. The men and women from the dorms stood and shouted in agreement.

"Thank You, Lord. Thank You!"

***

Patriot stretched at the end of his nighttime run. A sliver of moon cast its buttery light around the church's jogging path. He was glad of darkness, but staying hidden all day—the sheriff, Rich Richards, and Reece had all advised him to lay low—was becoming as much a bore and burden as he'd imagined.

At least at night he could get out and run and pretend the church really needed a nighttime security guard. Something to keep his mind and body occupied. The small apartment Reece had moved him into under cover of darkness was his hideaway until they captured j-beck. He had to give one last testimony in court stemming from his time undercover. A month away. If nothing else happened by then, whether they caught j-beck or not, he'd head out. Back to Denver? Or start over someplace else? The job with the fire department in Denver had started to feel like home before this...

He walked toward the front of the temporary sanctuary only to stop in the shadows. Maybe *pretend* security wasn't the right word. He narrowed his eyes. Someone else had stopped in the darkness, with their gaze fixed on a window watching the Wednesday night service. The sounds of praise and worship drifted to where Patriot stood. Whoever was standing there could hear and see the congregation even as he could. But why would someone stand and watch from the outside?

He noted big, fuzzy hair just as the man spun and darted toward the front parking lot. He carried a container in his right hand. Patriot sprinted after him.

The church door opened, and Chloe stepped out. Patriot swerved around her.

"Whoa!" Chloe's voice arced.

He raised a hand but didn't stop. The man had reached a Ford Explorer and yanked open the door.

"Hey." Patriot lifted his voice. "Hey. I'd like to talk to you."

The stranger whipped his head around. A silvery face stared at Patriot. One backward glance, and he dove into the car, started the engine, and backed up. Patriot jumped out of the way and grabbed the door handle. Locked. The car tore forward, yanking his hand free, and squealed out of the lot.

He tried to see the license plate, but the streetlamps were too low. No overhead light had come on when the man opened the door. But Patriot had seen enough. Clown hair and a painted face were an obvious disguise.

Chloe ran up beside him. "What's going on?"

"Not sure." Whatever it was, he didn't like it. He'd catch Reece later and let him know. He started for the dorms, but Chloe caught his arm.

"You're chasing someone who obviously didn't want to be caught. And he's carrying something suspicious, and you're just walking off? I don't think so. What are you doing here? I thought you were headed back to Denver."

Just what he wanted everyone to think. Reece and Kai had passed the word around. He ground his teeth. He'd acquired a good idea of her persistence the other times they'd interacted—even with the window washing. If it had been anyone else, he might have fobbed them off with some story, but he didn't think it would work with her.

His mind raced. Could he put her off? "Look, do you have time off tomorrow evening?"

"No."

"Friday evening?"

"Yes. Why?"

"Because if you want to know what's going on, we need a safe place. Not here. Not now. You jog, right? Let's meet at the beach Friday evening."

"The beach?" Her eyes narrowed.

Great. Did she think he was a pervert or something?

"Yeah. Bring Kati if you want. Pass-a-Grill, at the Twenty-First Avenue beach access. Far enough south, I think, nobody will recognize us. Say seven thirty. It will be dark soon after. And don't mention to anyone that I'm here."

That narrowed-eyed frown hadn't left. "Okay. I'll bring Kati."

"Good." He headed toward the other parking lot. Better take this security detail a bit more seriously. Maybe he could get Reece's wife to give an explanation to Ms. ER without him there at all.

***

Kati sent her gaze around the portable office trailer that was now office space for Reece, Pastor Alan, and China. China had waved when Kati entered but then indicated her rental desk piled with files. Kati's friend had charge of restoring the office, the paper files, the computer, and whatever else could be recovered. The fire had roared across the church's roof and over the offices. Brick construction had left walls and some contents intact. Smoke and water damage had nearly finished it off, but China's determination was performing miracles.

Kati walked into Reece's office and leaned across his desk. "Babe?"

The ER had been busy last night, and she'd slept most of the day. The rest of today and tomorrow, she'd help at the church. Well, as soon as she got some attention from her man.

He looked up from the papers scattered across his desk. "We've got drawings for a new church already. And an estimate."

"Umm." She leaned a little farther, tilted her head, and aimed for his mouth. Right before she got there, he shifted forward and met her kiss with his.

"Come around here." He caught her hand and pulled her around the desk and onto his lap. "You get some sleep?"

"Plenitude."

"That's not a real word."

"It is."

He rolled his eyes. "Not one you want me to remember?"

She laughed and snuggled her face into his neck. "My six months on night shift are almost over."

"That I'm looking forward to."

"I thought you might be. Are these the plans?"

"Yeah. Dennis Bowing brought them by today. He wanted me to go online, but I asked for paper copies. Alan and I might need to make some constructive changes."

"Well, if you get some drawings you like, you can always tell Dennis or whoever what you'd like to change."

"So he said. Alan and I haven't had time to talk yet." He shot her a sideways glance. "We don't even have a committee yet."

Kati grinned. "That's when you'll need your Glock."

"Yeah. A committee for a new building. With a hundred decisions to make. Scary."

"Did you know Dennis owns that construction firm?"

"He mentioned it."

She studied the plans for minute. "I don't know much about this, but it looks big." She indicated an area. "What's this?"

"The atrium? The narthex? What do they call it? The area outside the sanctuary."

"Is this set up for one of those coffee houses inside the church?"

Reece chuckled. "You clued in on that fast."

She elbowed him. "It's just that…is that us?"

"As in?"

"We're not a megachurch, and a lot of our members don't have money for expensive coffee drinks."

He nodded. "Yeah, that was my thinking."

"We could do free coffee and donuts like some churches."

"That's a committee decision."

"I know you want to be in on that one. But really, how big is this sanctuary? I mean, how many people is this supposed to hold?"

"Dennis said seven hundred."

"Seven hundred? Wow. That's more than double what we have." She stared at the drawings, trying to analyze the emotions that swirled inside her. "Should we plan for this many people?"

"Not unless you have the money." Pastor Alan's voice jolted her.

Her gaze shot to the doorway, and she pushed up from Reece's lap. Alan waved her down.

"Stay where you are. I like to see you two still acting like honeymooners." He stepped into the office, his smile morphing into seriousness. "I just finished talking with the insurance adjuster. He wasn't very forthcoming about an estimate at first. You know the church offices and nursery were add-ons when the building was remodeled years ago. Before I got here, in fact. Way before you two got here. Basically, we've been making insurance payments on the sanctuary only. The nursery and offices are not covered."

Kati stood. "Oh no."

"Yeah. Oh no. We won't be able to rebuild what we had, much less make it bigger."

***

Icing filled the Long John, and powdered sugar covered the outside. Chloe licked her lips. Best thing next to a cream horn—which they didn't have. She didn't binge like this often, but the cases in ER last night had kept them all running like squawking guinea hens. An early morning stop at Publix was just what she needed.

When she climbed into the car, she took the plastic knife they'd included and cut the Long John in half. It had been a long night. She just needed *something*. When she picked up one half, powdered sugar scattered over her T-shirt.

Arg.

Oh well. She licked off the icing that had adhered to her fingers. Messy, but so good.

She'd parked way out by herself, knowing she'd be eating before she got home. In this case, privacy was a good thing. But as she took a bite, a car pulled up in front of her and stopped. The driver looked her way. A moment later, he still had not looked away. Creepy.

Uh. The whole parking lot is about empty, fella. Why

park here? She put the Long John back in its plastic container, brushed her fingers off on the included napkin, and turned on the ignition. She drove over a few aisles, closer to the store, and parked next to a truck.

After glancing around to make sure the man had not followed her, she lowered her visor. More privacy. Her next bite of the Long John melded the powdered sugar and icing in sweet deliciousness, although half the sugar dusted her shirt again.

Her view of herself in the rearview mirror caused a shake of her head. White sugar all around her mouth. *Lord, I don't need to see anybody I know right now.*

A man rounded the back of the truck. Jeans and a pale blue T-shirt were all she could see. At the edge of the truck, he hesitated. She straightened, every nerve on edge. Was this the man from the car? Had he followed her?

The blue shirt bent down until his face showed through car's front windshield. Ball cap turned backwards, dark sunglasses, a heavy beard. She pushed back into the seat, her mind jumping.

Start the car. Now. Drop the Long John. Start the car.

"Chloe?"

A familiar voice. "Patriot?"

Was it? In disguise?

Powdered sugar dropped once more when she shifted to watch him walk to her side window.

No! Go on. Leave.

He bent down again, looked at her, puzzled. She rolled down the window. *Lord, are You there? I've got powdered sugar and icing all over me.*

"Chloe?" The repetition sounded like a befuddled ninety-year-old.

All she could do was nod and watch the tension drain out of him. Then a slow smile showed through the beard.

"What are you doing? Hiding the goodies from your husband?"

"I don't have a husband."

His smile transformed into a grin. "Then just eating dessert before breakfast?"

She tried to put the rest of the Long John down without making a mess. Was the powdered sugar around her mouth as messy as a moment ago? "No. I...I...it was a long night."

Laughing. His eyes were laughing, although he said nothing. Why was this happening again? She did not appreciate being the source of his amusement.

Inspiration came. Redirect the man's attention. "Besides, I was trying to get away from Mr. Creep back there." She waved in the other car's direction. "He pulled up beside me, and I just felt like I should move."

Patriot's face changed. He jerked upright, his focus on the parking lot. "What kind of car? What color?"

Oops. She hadn't meant to do that. Unless he was as edgy as she was. She hurriedly brushed sugar from her mouth. "Black. Older model. I don't know cars too well. He was older, too, well, middle aged or something. It was probably nothing. I shouldn't have mentioned it." She brushed off her T-shirt—or tried.

He leaned down. "But you were leery enough you moved to another parking space?"

"I, yes...but...well, I'm overcautious like that. Nothing's ever happened. To me, I mean."

"But to someone you know?"

"Knew." The familiar catch tightened her throat. *Five years, Chloe. Don't make a big deal of it.*

He studied her. "I'm sorry to hear that."

"Yeah, well..." She dropped her eyes, brushed at her shirt again.

"I think you're going to have to wash that."

Heat shot up her neck and filled her cheeks. "Yeah."

"See you later today. At the beach." He headed back to his truck and lifted a white bag from the bed.

Yeah. The beach. And a good thing it would be dark

soon after they got there. Humiliation red was not one of her better colors.

***

Patriot handed the bag to GreasePaint as they headed down the road. "Breakfast."

GreasePaint's face skewed, but he reached for the bag. "I almost didn't recognize you." He pulled out a donut, bit into it, and muttered through a mouthful, "Good thing you took off the glasses."

Patriot shot him a sideways glance, smirked. "Your powers of observation are well known."

"Not as well known as my love of donuts, but you remembered."

"Well, I ran into someone else this morning who might rival you there."

"Oh yeah?"

Patriot nodded but changed subjects. His mind had been on the ER nurse too much today. "When we get to the church, I'll drop you at the office, but you're on your own then. Like I said, I'm—"

"In hiding." GreasePaint finished the donut and started on anther. "You okay with that?"

"Hiding?" He stared down the road. No, he wasn't okay with it, wasn't okay with having run three years ago, wasn't okay with any of it right now. "If j-beck finds out where I am, then it could endanger others. He hasn't contacted you?"

GreasePaint swallowed the last bite. "What? Are you crazy? Why would he do that?"

Patriot knew others it had happened to, others that the gang had beat up so badly they almost died, but they'd come back when the gang had reached out again. Like a woman going back to her abuser or letting him come back home again. Repeatedly.

He sighed. "They'd tell you it was my fault."

"It was your fault, man. If they hadn't known we were friends, if you hadn't saved me from their beatings…"

Patriot slid a look his way again. "Yeah?"

"Yeah."

Quiet reigned. A caution niggled inside him. GreasePaint had called him, had said it wasn't working with his old man, said he needed an out, wanted Patriot's help. If the gang had contacted him again, if j-beck had convinced GreasePaint into thinking Patriot was to blame…

Patriot glanced in the rearview mirror. Nothing. Good. But he slid his hand down to clasp the gun he'd slipped into the pocket on the door. Just in case. He wasn't going to get taken out because he'd forgotten everything he'd learned in the gang…

GreasePaint laughed. "Shkee, man. J.K. I ain't that stupid. If they did contact me, it would be to get you. Still."

Patriot checked the rearview mirror again, waited.

GreasePaint leaned back against the seat. "What about the girl?"

"What girl?"

"You know. The one at the hospital. The one that helped pull me out of the pond."

That one. A picture of her on the ladder, reaching for the window, ponytail swinging, rose immediately. "What about her?"

"Well, I don't know. She came by to see me. Could have been prospecting."

Patriot grinned and loosened his hold on the gun. "You think seeing you all cut up interested her?"

"Could be, man. You never know."

Patriot shrugged and wondered what Chloe would think of that. "No way to know. You get her name?"

"Nah. I was out of it mostly."

"Yeah. Well, too bad."

Should he warn Chloe? GreasePaint was going for his interview and application today. If he made it into the program, they'd be sure to run into each other at church.

Yeah, he'd better tell her. Another reason to contact her once Gary was accepted into the program. Why did that decision leave a warm feeling inside him?

He growled under his breath. *Get your act together, man. This is no time for distractions.*

Chapter 6

Is not my word like as a fire? saith the L<small>ORD</small>*; and like*
a hammer that breaks the rock in pieces?
Jeremiah 23:29 KJV

Chloe threw a frazzled look at her hair. The fire had
not burned it so much as singed it. She had tried to find an
attractive way to wear it today but settled for a messy bun
instead. She huffed and scooted to the front door.

Why had Patriot changed his mind and insisted on
picking her up? And why was he early?

She needed to deep-six her slippers and put on some
lipstick, but instead she threw open the door. And met his
smile.

Smile?

He stood there in T-shirt, shorts, flip-flops and a smile.
Chloe couldn't find her voice. He was good-looking enough
without the smile. Not that being good-looking meant
anything, He was a grouch. Even though last Wednesday's
workday had gone smoothly enough. Obviously because
neither of them said much. They'd just worked and listened to
music.

His gaze dropped to her pink bunny slippers, and the
smile broadened. Why did her cheeks feel hot again? For the
third time. He was on her blacklist, for sure. And pink bunny
slippers with the black shorts and green T-shirt she'd pulled
over her swimsuit wasn't that weird. Or was it? She huffed.

"Sorry I'm early."

Feeling off balance against the warmth in his eyes, she
waved him in. They were enemies, right? Or at least

antagonistic coworkers.

She indicated the living area. "Have a seat. I'll be ready in a minute."

"No rush. We'll get there. Reece and Kati are meeting us at the restaurant."

Hmm. Another surprise he'd thrown at her. Eating out. Together.

She scurried to her bedroom, kicked off the bunnies, and slipped into a pair of her own flip-flops. Too bad on the lipstick. She didn't use much makeup anyway. The ER wasn't the place for it. She grabbed her card-carrier and phone and headed back.

He still stood by the door. The smile returned. "You're fast."

"Yes, well, I have what I need right here." She waved the small card-carrier at him.

He ushered her out the door and gave a hand to help her into the truck—one she didn't need, but...His hand was warm on her arm. She let a breath out and settled back against the seat. Why was he being nice?

He grabbed a baseball cap from the dash and pair of dark glasses and put them on. She studied the stubbled jawline, straight nose, and deep-set eyes. All added up to her feeling and idea that he could handle himself in any situation. Tough. Well, she was tough, too. She straightened, put her shoulders back. At least, they told her that in the ER. She handled situations there without thought or worry. Just dove in and did what was needed. How was this any different from that? Why was she nervous?

Patriot's gaze shifted her way, and she turned her head and inspected the Dodge Ram he drove. It looked new.

"A rental?"

He looked her way. "The truck?"

"Yes."

"It is. I needed something while I was here."

"Then you're not leaving like we thought."

"You were supposed to think that. Reece's idea, with Detective Richards's agreement, to keep me safe. But let's talk about that with Kati and Reece."

"Okay." She studied the scenery outside the window. To keep him safe? He'd mentioned something like that Wednesday night, too. "But Kati's on call tonight, so we'll need to get through early."

"Got that. It's why we're meeting earlier."

"And you're okay with that and the restaurant?" Although with the dark glasses and backward baseball cap, he did look different—although not the same as the disguise this morning.

"Pass-a-Grille is far enough away from the Gordones' territory that I should be fine."

Hmm. "Okay. Tell me why you're in a good mood."

He slid a look her way. "That bad, am I?"

"Let's just say, Mr. Congenial you're not."

A lift of his mouth. "There are reasons. And I won't say I was wrong in what I said—about someone untrained getting themselves…killed—but I apologize for the way I said it."

She studied him. "Okay. I'll take the apology if you tell me something about yourself."

He kept his eyes on the road. His mouth straightened.

"Something innocuous. Anything."

After a moment, he nodded. "My brothers and I are football fans. Two brothers. One went to Florida State and the other to Florida at Gainesville. Florida Gators."

"Where did you go?"

"The University of South Florida. But there's a whole lot of rivalry between Florida and Florida State that USF has never seen. I usually hang with the brother whose team looks like the underdog. Of course, that creates more wrangling. It's always fun."

"And your parents?"

"Alive and well and living in Tampa."

"When you were undercover, that must have been hard for your family."

"Yeah."

"So, are they glad you're back?"

Silence stretched between them, then he cleared his throat. "They don't know. And I need to keep it that way."

"Oh. Okay, but what if you run into somebody you know?"

"I knew you'd have more questions than I could answer the other night."

"I'm sorry. I—"

"I'm taking a chance. When I had to leave before, I couldn't tell my parents or brothers where I was going or when I'd be back. I sent a message every so often that I was safe. Over three years. That was difficult for all of us. I don't know what's going down this time or if I'll have to disappear again. It's better for everyone if my presence here is secret." He paused. "We should be safe enough tonight, or I wouldn't have suggested this. But if I tell you we need to leave or move tonight, do it immediately."

Chloe caught the look he threw her. The man was serious. She bit her lip, and a ribbon of fear wove up her spine.

***

"Dennis." Pastor Alan's voice held that gentle but firm tone Kati knew. One she respected. Dennis Bowing and his friend might not realize it, but the time of negotiation had ended. "We need to wrap up this discussion for today. Reece and I will talk about what you've said. We will bring it before the board and let you know."

Kati wasn't sure what she thought of Roger Cummings, the man who had accompanied Dennis to this meeting. Confident, affluent. She hadn't met him before, but she knew the name. One of the church's chief donors.

The other men stood, and so did Kati. Why had Pastor

71

Alan asked her to attend? She had added nothing, simply listened. Reece had done much the same, only put in a question here and there.

Roger Cummings shook Alan's hand. "Thank you for your time. You understand I am putting forth this offer because I have profound respect for the work you are doing here." He nodded to Reece and Kati. "That you all are doing. I think, however, more would be accomplished if the church and the ministry were divided. That way the ministry would attract donors that are not, shall we say, religious. And the church could be the church without these unnecessary...distractions. Dennis's plans are excellent, and my company would help with that, too. We are here to help on both fronts."

Alan smiled and nodded. "I appreciate all you're offering, but we need time to think and pray, and as I said, talk with the board about it. Give us a couple of weeks."

Kati lost the rest of the conversation and stood silent as the men disappeared. Alan and Reece returned to the office after walking the two men to the door.

Alan stood behind his desk, and Reece moved next to the chair he'd sat in. No one said anything for a moment, and then Alan cleared his throat. "Anyone want to weigh in on this? It's just the three of us. Say whatever is on your mind."

Kati lifted her head and looked from one to the other. "*Divided*. He used that word. Jesus told us that a kingdom divided against itself will not stand. I think dividing the ministry from the church, taking it away from the message of Christ, will kill it. Or more importantly, it will cease to be effective. The offer to build a bigger church and newer and larger dorms somewhere else, away from here, will ultimately lead to the end of a Christ-centered mission."

Pastor Alan dipped his head. "You've put my concerns in a very neat box. Reece?"

Reece moved next to Kati and hugged her. "You see why I married her."

72

"But will the board, will the congregation, see it the same way?" Alan asked. "People love growth. The idea of a bigger church, more people coming, newer dorms."

"And people giving money who don't see the need for Bible studies or...religion, as he said." Kati clenched her hands. "It's so easy to get away from the vision God has for this church and go the way of the world. We're being attacked."

"Which is why I wanted you here, Kati. I wanted your feel of the situation. You see the Enemy's attacks in a way others don't. We need serious intercession in the weeks to come. Satan is trying to undermine what God has done here. The news media is playing up the attack on Gary Lovett and the fire. They're already questioning whether the church and the ministry go hand in hand. We know they do, but if Satan can bring uncertainty, if he can cause fear and doubt..."

"Especially when someone is willing to hand us a great deal of money to rebuild..."

Reece slipped an arm around her waist and squeezed. "With a whole lot of conditions attached."

"Too many conditions." Kati lifted a brow at Alan. "How long has Dennis been a member here?"

Alan smiled. "He's a good man, Kati. He means well. Dennis joined back when John and Sharee Jergenson were here. Before they married, in fact. We had trouble back then, too. A baby's kidnapping. So, about ten years ago."

"But Roger Cummings mentioned Dennis's vision. If Dennis is telling people he has a different vision for this church than the one we think God has, we'll have problems."

"The problem's already here. And we're getting more applications to the program all the time. In fact, we have two women from the jail applying this week. One Hispanic, one white. Both about thirty. Both advised by the judge—either here or jail." Reece's voice held a quiet conviction. "We need to pray. Starting now. Ask God for wisdom."

Kati glanced at her watch. "We'll have to cancel our

plans with Chloe and Patriot."

"Chloe and Patriot?" Pastor Alan's voice climbed. A brow lifted. "How did that—"

Kati waved her hand. "Nothing to worry about. She was outside Wednesday when Patriot chased whoever was here to their car and wanted an explanation." She grinned. "You know Chloe. She wouldn't have stood for any fly-by-night explanation, and Patriot clued into that right away, so he asked her to meet him tonight—with us as chaperones."

"Chaperones?"

The question in his voice made her laugh. "Not like that. Chloe was a little uneasy about meeting him on her own. I mean, all she knows about him is that she saw him waving a gun at her before the GreasePaint incident. And, of course, he did help at the fire. But I think they've had some words since."

Alan's glance bounced between them, then settled on Reece. "Speaking of which, somehow that man in what Patriot described as clown hair and makeup doesn't fit my idea of gangs."

Reece nodded. "Rich and I discussed it. Could be we have someone else who wants to stir up trouble. J-beck needs to prove himself. He won't be playing. He wanted to kill Patriot and failed. Probably wants to kill Luis, too. Maybe why the church was targeted. Rich could be right there. And they could be after Rich, too. He's at the church, involved in the ministry, and he's the cop that led the gang war that night. If j-beck wants leadership, he needs to bring down one if not all."

Kati stared at him, her heart jerking. "You mean they want to kill all three of them?"

"I'm sure that's their agenda, but a gang has lots of agendas that never pan out. However, j-beck needs to make one of these happen if he plans to be captain."

Pastor Alan sat on the edge of his desk, the line between his brows prominent. "Reece, your saying this so matter of factly is…scary. These are people we know you're talking about."

"They all understand this, Alan. Because we haven't brought it up doesn't mean we haven't discussed it between us. They're all smart and seasoned." He glanced at Kati. "Not everyone needs to know what these men are dealing with. In fact, it's better people don't know."

Kati tamped down her concern. They'd talk about it at home. "Is Patriot okay at the beach?"

"He should be. It would be a freak thing if someone from the Gordones saw him. He's far enough out of their territory. And he'd lose them in a minute. They wouldn't be expecting to see him."

"Chloe's meeting him."

"They'll be okay, babe."

She closed her eyes and sent a request to God. "I'll call Chloe and let her know Patriot is a straight-up guy. That we won't make it, but she'll be okay. She'll have her own car, too, so when Patriot gives her whatever explanation he's decided on, she can be on her way if she wants."

***

The early dinner of seafood and crab salad and sweet tea while watching the waves from the Gulf of Mexico curl into the beach had calmed Chloe's response to Kati's call and her initial chill to Patriot's words in the truck. Good thing, because his quick explanation of why he had chased the man Wednesday night had raised her qualms again.

What was going on?

But that was what Patriot, Rich Richards, and Reece were trying to find out. Right? The Sheriff's Office was investigating the fire and the incident with Gary Lovett. Sounded like enough people doing that. She'd leave it to them.

Patriot had asked if she wanted to walk on the beach. A walk? Really? But the water's reflection of the sun's descent, the liquid feel of the air, and the wind tossing her hair as they stepped outside drew her quick agreement.

She glanced up and down the shore. Only a few bathers dotted the beach. The lull in tourist numbers between spring break and summer added to the beach's attraction. She'd love a walk. And maybe a swim... No, talk of ridiculous.

"How did you and Reece get to know each other?"

"After the gang war, I was in the hospital for a while, and Reece visited. Reece wanted to thank me for going undercover and for letting Rich know about the firepower the Gordones had. It helped pull in the FBI and others to back up the Sheriff's Office that night. We struck up a friendship and stayed in touch while I was in Colorado."

The wind increased and ruffled the waters. Light danced across the waves.

"The beach is beautiful this time of year."

"Yes." His smile formed. "I've loved being in Colorado, but you do miss the beach when you've lived here all your life. Nothing quite like it. Of course, the mountains where I live now..."

"Are gorgeous. I know. I've been once. Would love to go again sometime."

They strolled across the soft sand. When they reached the harder sand near the surf, they turned to walk alongside it.

She chanced another look at him. He'd moved all the way to Colorado to escape things here? The way he talked about his family didn't sound like he was a loner. Undercover work must have been hard for him. The danger and the loneliness. So why...

"What made you get into it?"

His head turned her way. "Into what?"

"Undercover work."

"Something *innocuous*, you said."

"Oh, I...sorry. I've been accused of insatiable curiosity or asking hard questions or something like that."

The wind tugged at her hair and pulled long strands from her hair bun. She pushed it behind her ear to see him better. His look changed, and memory burst across her mind—

the way he'd yelled at her at the pond to go, to leave. Perhaps she didn't want to know...

He stopped and stared at the waves, the rush and withdrawal adding background noise to their moment of quiet.

"I'll try to make this quick and short. The Sheriff's Office knew the Gordones were bringing in drugs. They weren't your regular white supremacist group—as if that wasn't enough. This group went deep into the drug business."

"Wait. White supremacist? They only want white, Caucasians of European descent to lead the country. Is that right?"

"Close. Basically, they believe white people are superior to people of other races, especially blacks, Hispanics, and Jews. Different groups highlight different races, but they reject mainstream conservatism, wanting politicians that embrace their ideas."

"Okay. Sorry to interrupt. So, some are into criminal activities?"

"Yes, and the Gordones definitely were. The sheriff wanted someone on the inside. I...volunteered. I look the part, after all. White, blond hair, blue or blue-gray eyes. And I knew what they espoused. After months of living with them, BearTrap—the captain—finally trusted me enough to brag about the drugs they were getting in. And selling. He was into the criminal activity more than any belief in white supremacy. My gig was the opposite. When I joined, I let it be known I was a fanatic for white supremacy, even though I'm not. Not by a long shot, but you do and say what you have to. That helped when I told them I didn't do drugs. Didn't help the night they almost killed this African American kid who crossed our path. I managed to keep them from killing him, came back later to find him, but he was gone."

The sudden harshness in his voice raked across her heart. "You hated it."

"Of course. I joined the Sheriff's Office to stop that type of stuff. I wanted to call in backup and arrest them all, but that wasn't what I was there for that night."

"But why go undercover? I realize law enforcement needs that, but why you?"

"The Gordones' territory includes the beaches north of here, and I didn't live at the beach. I lived across town. Think about it. You can't go undercover where you live. Or shouldn't. Too many people know you. Someone's liable to out you at any moment. It still could have happened. But drugs were showing up at the beach. A lot of drugs. The Sheriff's Office here needed proof about who was receiving them, so they asked us if someone could go undercover from our department. They asked me. *Asked.* Yeah. There wasn't a good way to say no. I wish I had." He turned and started walking again. "It does something to you, to your soul, to be involved in that day after day."

His stride lengthened. Chloe jogged to keep up with him, straining to hear over the wind and his pace.

"The night we planned the war with Luis's gang, I knew I had to tell Rich the Gordones had serious ammunition. And j-beck heard me talking. He hated me anyway. I'd pulled him off a young girl he'd kidnapped weeks before, fought him for her, then got her to that anti-trafficking group Kati volunteers with. After that, things were raw. And I still didn't know how the drugs were coming in. BearTrap hadn't trusted me that far. But my time was up. I knew that. I had to get out or get killed. j-beck ratted me out the night of the war."

"But this guy, j-beck, wasn't caught?"

Patriot's jaw tightened. "No. He got away in the melee. My fault. I should have taken him down, but he had a knife, and…managed to get free. We lost him."

Managed to get free. Chloe heard the unsaid words. "You said he had a knife."

"Yeah. I've got a pretty nice scar across my chest. Not making any of those firefighter calendars for sure."

He'd tried to soften it, but Chloe heard more than what he'd said. A knife wound. "Sounds more serious than

GreasePaint's, and *he* almost didn't make it. How long were you in the hospital? In therapy?"

"Doesn't matter now. After I got out of the hospital, I ran. I'd had a guard most of the time in the hospital, but I knew better than to go home where j-beck and the others could find me. Oh, I called the captain and let him know where I was. Only him. He pulled some strings, got me a new name, a new life. We both knew I needed a place to hide for a while. I came back for the trials. Hoped enough of them would end up in prison that I'd be able to live my life again."

His sideways glance and smirk showed how ridiculous that was. And she knew enough to know that if they wanted, someone could put a hit out on him from inside the prison.

"So, you got a new name and a new career?"

He'd slowed to a walk again, and she could hear him better. "The captain helped me get a foot in the door at the fire department. Fighting fire is different than fighting people, but you sometimes come home with the same scars. When I went to Denver, I told myself I'd get back into church, wash the dirt off, and start a new life. One I could be proud of. It's been a struggle."

The sun had dropped lower, had smeared the sky with liquid fire.

His last sentence anchored inside her. He'd faced a struggle even in Colorado. She examined his profile again and saw the same austere look she'd seen before.

"What happened?"

He shook his head.

God, this is what I'm so bad at. I know there's something there, something that's hurting him, and I want to help. But I messed up bad the last time…

The question rolled around inside her. They moved on in silence, the waters battering the shore, the sea-life smell alive with every inhale. And yet…

"It's why you didn't want me at the pond or in the fire, isn't it?"

She had long ago removed the stretch band from her hair, and long strands whipped across her face. She had to grab it and pull it back to see him.

"Is this good in the ER? Stubborn persistence?" His words sounded gruff.

"Yeah. I guess it is. Never give up."

He stopped again. Way down the beach, a couple walked, but he stared out at the Gulf. It took a moment. "Okay, yes, it was. It is. Not long after I got through firefighter training, we were called to a house fire. Just as we got there, a mother ran in after her child. Neither made it out."

Chloe felt the hit in her chest. "I am so sorry. How horrible. I..." She let it trail off. What could she say to that?

"It was a two-story house. Everything blazing when we got there. Someone yelled that there was a child inside. You never want to hear that. Especially in that kind of blaze. The mother came from nowhere, ran past us and into the house. Two of our men took the first floor. The lieutenant and I took the stairs. Smoke pouring down, hard to see, and hot as... Anyway, we had no idea where she went or how she even got past the front door. We got partway down the hall on the second floor, and the lieutenant called a stop."

"What?"

"Yeah. I would have gone on, but the lieutenant's in charge. I was a rookie. I argued with him, of course. He said later we might have made it into a room and hauled a body or two out, but we wouldn't have made it back. The fire had too much control. It's his responsibility to make sure there's no more deaths than need be. The ceiling buckled and crashed in as the lieutenant came out. Because I'd argued with him—if only for a minute—the roof almost came down on him. He was right. We wouldn't have made it. But I still couldn't get it out of my head. A girl and her mother died."

Chloe touched his arm. "I'm so sorry. I have no idea what that's like."

"It ate at me."

She put her hand on his, squeezed. It was all she could do. She wanted to put her arms around him, to somehow erase the pain she heard in his words.

He stared at the waters. Chloe did, too. The waves gathered and dropped and rushed to shore. The sun rested lower on the horizon, and rays of light flashed off the ruffled surf so intensely it hurt to look.

"Afterward, the investigators told us she'd made it to her child's room. Impossible, really. But there they were— together." He cleared his throat. "I couldn't handle it. On top of everything that had happened here, then running and trying to put together a new life, I just didn't handle it. I hadn't made friends in the church yet. I was cut off from my family."

Chloe felt that. "You were alone."

"It felt that way. I did text Mom with a message to pray for me." His mouth half-lifted. "We still touch home when we need something, don't we? Anyway, that night I dreamed I'd walked into the fire. That I'd died with them. I wished I had."

"No."

"It would have been easier than living with myself."

"That's a lie of the Enemy. You know that, don't you? He wanted you to kill yourself."

"I tried."

Chapter 7

For God has not given us a spirit of fear, but of power, and
of love, and of a sound mind.
2 Timothy 1:7 KJV

Rich sat at his desk, fingering the coffee cup head down, staring at the papers in front of him. He should have left for home an hour ago, but he couldn't help but look for leads. Leads to a killer...

Luis's old gang was down to about nothing. Just as he figured. Luis had been the catalyst for whatever was going on

The real threat these days was the white supremacist group. J-beck's attempt to reorganize was pulling others in. From what they could determine, about five or six members of the Gordones survived the gang war between the two groups three years ago. They hadn't been able to get their hands-on j-beck then, but the grapevine said he'd been seriously injured after the fight he and Patriot had. The man's grudge against Patriot pierced deeper than the knives the man used. Rich had heard he was back about a year ago—looking to get the gang together, but it had taken getting Patriot back here to ignite the others. Only j-beck had slipped through their fingers again. Rich sighed.

"What's going on, Partner?"

The woman coming through the door had proved a help and a distraction—an experienced detective who nevertheless had let him know she found him attractive. He almost smirked. One woman in his life at a time was all he could handle.

Balancing Lynn's reaction to attending another church

and wondering what j-beck had planned would keep his life busy. Two balls in the air. He didn't need Lori's flirtatious attitude today.

She sat on the edge of his desk. Too near. He moved his hand from its closeness to her derriere and sat back in his chair.

After a brief hesitation, she stood. "We have one witness—that's Patriot—to what happened at the church the day of the fire, and even he can't say who was in the car or give us more than a cursory description of it."

"You'd think his years in law enforcement would have kicked in and he would have got us more info."

"Sounds like his firefighting skills kicked in."

"Yeah. And let's keep that information under wraps. No one needs to know he saw anything or that he's a firefighter now."

She leaned forward. A smile teased her face. "I have some news for you though."

He caught the serious edge in her voice. "All right. Let's hear it."

"Joe thinks he saw Luis at a restaurant with one of his former gang members."

He straightened. "What? When?"

"Earlier. When he was coming to work."

"Luis can't do that. He's on parole." Man, if this proved true, Luis would be back in prison—and it would be his own fault.

Rich shoved his chair back and grabbed his keys. "Let's pay him a visit."

***

Chloe froze. "But you—"

Awe edged Patriot's voice. "No. *But God.* I put a gun to my head and pulled the trigger."

Her heart jerked.

Not again. Not this again.

Everything in her tightened. She caught the glint of light as his gaze slid her way.

"Nothing happened. I checked the gun. Ammunition in right. Everything right. I put it to my head again and stopped. God had done a miracle. Maybe he still had a plan for my life. I put the gun away."

Something inside her somersaulted. *Thank You, Lord!* Satan had tried to end his life, to stop him from coming back. God did have a plan, and the Enemy was out to destroy it. How well she knew. She forced herself to stay quiet. She wanted to blurt it out, but this wasn't the time.

Just let it be You if I do, Lord. Not me. Please.

"With the video of GreasePaint"—his voice grated now—"I should have known they'd hone in on him. He was the only one I didn't testify against, and he got off. But all the man ever did was hang at the crib and do drugs. Why he ever joined the gang, I don't know. I tried to tell him to leave and start over someplace else."

"It's not your fault."

"I should have done more. Done something, anything, but I took off."

Chloe's heart hurt for him. The setting sun would usher in the night, but she didn't want that for an epitaph of today. *Lord, there's so many things I could say, and yet…should I say anything? You know how I messed up with Alex. Don't let me mess up again. Please.*

The words leapt from her mouth. "I have no idea what it is to live with all that, but I do know one thing—God is for you. Not against you. And his forgiveness is real."

He remained silent and disengaged his hand from hers. The sunset splashed the sky with salmon and tangerine and burnt orange, but her brain spun. She'd botched it again. Said too much. Why couldn't she keep quiet?

"I'm a coward, Chloe. After the gang war, I ran. Tried to kill myself."

"And you're going to beat yourself up over it for the rest of your life?" What was she doing, jumping in again? "And you didn't run just because of j-beck, you know. You ran because you'd forgotten who you were in Christ. Whatever happened during those days is forgiven."

"I know."

But she couldn't leave it alone. "Do you? Are you bigger than God then? Not forgiving yourself?"

She couldn't make out the look he gave her, but she took his hand again. She kept her head up, defiant, standing against the unseen Enemy that had lied to him. *God, give him eyes to see and ears to hear what You are saying to him. He is Yours. Let him know it.*

After a moment, his hand turned, grasped hers. "They try to prepare you, but they can't. The evil is so prevalent."

"You know, if you *hadn't* been upset with yourself *then* you could worry."

"I knew I needed to find a church and get some counseling when I first went to Colorado. But I couldn't afford it."

"Surely there's something out there for free."

"There are groups that ex-law enforcement or veterans have started. Once I get through this, perhaps I'll check those out."

"What do you have to do here?"

"This last court appearance. Testify against one more gang member. And when they pick up j-beck, I'll testify, too."

A shudder went through Chloe. "He's not going to wait for you to do that."

"No, and if I look at this in the natural, I'm dead. So, you're right in the things you've said, because they all point to one thing. Trust God. He can work an end to this. He's the one that does the impossible." And suddenly, he shook himself, as if shaking off the impossibilities and the hardness. "Listen, I'm getting hot. You've got a swimsuit under that T-shirt, don't you? I saw a strap that looked like a suit. Let's take a swim."

She turned, startled at the change, but then grinned. "Sure." She untwined his hand from hers, gave him a hard shove so that he stumbled sideways. His face showed his surprise, then he regained his footing and lunged for her, but she took off for the water.

Before she reached it, she heard him behind her. She swerved left out of his grasp, then right, and plowed into the waves. The cold shot up her legs, and she stumbled. She hadn't expected that.

It was up to her knees when he caught her. In the next instant, he swung her up against his chest.

"What was that for?" The growl only half-covered his amusement.

"Just thought we needed to move on."

He waded into deeper water. The clouds climbed in colors of coral and crimson and rose. She shifted her head back to look at him. His gray eyes held the laughter she'd seen before.

"Well, I'm glad you think so because…" And he tossed her into the waves.

She came up sputtering and shivering, with her hair plastered to her head. It wasn't her best look, but the grin on his face was worth it.

***

Rich parked the Porsche in the church parking lot and waited for Lori to exit. The dorms looked quiet. Rich knew the routine. During the week, morning classes included Bible study, counseling, English, and job training. The afternoon classes offered many of the same courses. Nighttime activities consisted of trips to a gym, basketball courts, or select movies. The movies picked were free of violence and overt sexuality. Rich had been proud to be part of the program.

He sighed and looked for the apartment with Luis's number. Men and women were drifting back from dinner already. He leaned against the car and waited. Lori stood nearby. Most of the residents knew him. A few waved. He waved back.

"They like you here?" Lori's voice jumped an octave.

"I attended church here. This program helps get their lives turned around, helps them get jobs, gives them a solid foundation in Christianity. In other words, being productive and doing good instead of what they've done before."

"You think the Christian stuff works?"

He slid a look her way. "It's proven. Christian programs like Teen Challenge have a recidivism rate much lower than other drug, alcohol, and abuser programs. They teach a different way of life than the residents have lived and to accept responsibility for their actions, to make right decisions. And to depend or something—Someone—greater than themselves."

"Well, it doesn't seem like Luis Ramirez made such a good decision—seeing an old gang member."

"You said Joe *thought* he saw Ramirez with a gang member. Let's find out for sure."

"Right. But where is he?"

Rich nodded toward the church's fellowship hall. "Dinner's served in there. Let's check it out."

When they stepped inside the dining area, laughter echoed from the kitchen. He nodded toward it and headed that way.

Luis stood at the sink, a pile of pots and pans on his left, and his hands gathering soap bubbles from the sink. Next to him, Manuel stood on a chair. Luis blew the bubbles his way, spraying his nephew's face. Manuel leaned back but laughed gleefully.

Isabella had her back to them sweeping the floor. "If you two don't stop, we'll never get out of here."

Luis glanced over his shoulder. His eyes met Rich's, then jumped to Lori, and he straightened.

"*Hola*, Rich. What can I do for you?" He shook off his

hands and grabbed a towel. Manuel twisted in the chair, his smile fading.

Isabella whirled, her gaze jumping between the two men.

"We'd like to ask you a few questions."

Luis nodded. "Okay."

"Is there somewhere we could go?" Rich looked pointedly at Manuel.

Luis turned to Isabella. "I'll finish here. Take Manuel home. *Te llamo más tarde.*"

Isabella's gaze darted between the two men again. She put the broom in a closet, lifted Manuel from the chair and with a nod, and left.

Quiet filled the room.

Rich moved forward. "Is Isabella working here now?"

"*Sí.* Pastor Alan said we needed a cook, and Isabella is a great cook."

Rich moved farther into the room. Lori stepped up beside him, crossed her arms over her chest. Luis's interaction with his nephew threw Rich, but he reminded himself that all criminals had good points. That did not make what they'd done any less a crime. He tightened his jaw.

"Can you give us an idea of your timeline today?"

Luis's eyebrows rose. "Timeline?"

"Yes, what did you do today?"

"You know the routine here. Bible study, classes, lunch, more classes, counseling."

"And that is what you did? Nothing else?"

"Ah." He paused. "I see. No, before classes, I had permission to meet a friend for breakfast."

"What time was that?"

"Early. 7:30."

"Where?"

"At Casa Linda's, over on the Southside."

"I know where that is. Whom did you meet?"

"My cousin. Why? What's going on, Rich?"

"What's your cousin's name?" Lori dropped her arms.

Luis shot her a glare. "Alberto Torres."

"And he was in your gang before you left for prison?" Lori's voice stayed even.

"*No.*"

Rich noted the heightened accent. He studied Luis and wondered how much it would take for him to lose his temper. Should he push? Lori had jumped out with the question too early.

"You know that would break your parole."

Luis's eyes narrowed. "I saw my cousin. That does not break my parole."

Rich watched him for a moment. "We heard your cousin's in a gang. Part of your parole is not to be in touch with gang members."

"Alberto is fourteen. My aunt wanted me to talk with him, tell him the dangers, what it's like in prison. He's acting out at home, but he's not in a gang."

"As far as you know."

"My aunt would know. She knows what to look for."

"Have you talked with any of your former gang members?"

Rich saw anger flare in the other man's eyes. "No. I know what I need to do for parole. You will not have to worry that I violate it."

"Because then you would be serving out your ten-year sentence." Rich wanted the reminder to irritate him. Perhaps he'd say something they could use, but Luis said nothing.

Lori's hand rested on her gun. "We're still investigating the disappearance of Marcos Suarez."

Luis's eyes flickered, but he remained quiet.

Rich almost smiled. The man had learned a lot in prison—or some would say he'd learned a lot since becoming a Christian. Luis's hair-trigger temper seemed under control.

"I assume you know who that is." Lori tilted her head, smiled.

"I have heard the name. There are a number of people with that name in the Latino community."

"And that's all you know?"

Luis shrugged.

Rich studied him. Luis was lying now. Evading. He slammed his fist on the counter. "Of course you know the name. He was your *capitán.*"

Luis stared at him, the muscles in his jaw standing out. "Perhaps he was, Detective. What has that to do with me?"

"We were wondering that, too—since you became captain after he disappeared."

Luis's gaze flicked from one to the other. "Are you accusing me of something? Are you arresting me?"

Rich said nothing. He'd arrested him before, three years ago, but now...no, they had no proof.

"*No? Bueno. Esto se acabo.* I'm through." He threw a glance at the unfinished dishes, then walked out the door.

Lori smiled. "We riled him."

"Yeah. Not sure I wanted him to know we were investigating Marcos's disappearance though."

She shrugged. "It'll give him something to think about. Perhaps he'll run."

Rich stared at the doorway Luis had gone through. The man was definitely guilty, and as much as Lori irritated him, she was as convinced as he was.

***

Chloe gazed at the night sky, the black expanse littered with hundreds—no, thousands of stars. The swim in the Gulf at sunset had washed her through with happiness. They'd lain on the beach afterward to dry off, talking of nothing significant. Just finding out a little more about each other. Laughing at family stories. He liked his work as a firefighter and had several stories with good endings to balance the hard one that had caused him so much anguish.

Warmth bathed her insides. She felt close to him. His openness about what he'd been through, his acceptance of the things she'd said. And the swim and lightheartedness over the last hour. Wow. What a change. She liked that he cared for others, that their pain touched him, and that he would sacrifice himself to help others. That was huge. And he was a believer. Even bigger. The sun had set, and night had fallen, and in that time, her whole perspective of him had changed.

Lord, what am I to do with this?

The wind's constant movement cooled her bare skin. She shivered. Her bathing suit had dried a while ago, but it would be nice to have her clothes right now. She'd waded ashore to take off the wet shorts and shirt during their swim, and they lay in a wet heap nearby.

"You're cold?"

"The wind's cool."

"Come on then. Up. Let's move a little."

He drew her to her feet. "You want to dance?"

She stared up at his shadowed profile. "Dance?" Where had that come from? "Dance?"

He chuckled and slipped an arm around her waist. "No one's on the beach but us."

And the waves make their own music. But still…

He lifted her other hand and waited a moment. Then they were moving over the sands, gliding, dancing, kicking up liquid starfire. Who would have thought…

She laughed. Felt a happiness she hadn't experienced in a long time. He liked her? She hadn't messed up with what she'd said?

The air swirled and eddied around them, and the warmth inside was too much. She needed to be closer, wanted the contact, and she laid her head against his bare chest. He'd thrown his soaked T-shirt onto the sand earlier, too. She'd seen the scar then—an eight-inch line of roughened skin that trailed from his left arm down and across his chest. Her head rested against it.

So, the man had a romantic streak. Who would have known?

Lord, don't let me fall for this guy. This is too quick. He's going back to Denver sometime. He lives dangerously. This would never work.

And yet...

"Chloe?"

She looked up but couldn't see his eyes. His face was close. She tried to say something, but words wouldn't come. Butterflies...not quite. Horses stampeding. Yes. That. And then his mouth was on hers, turning, moving, his arms tightening around her, and the entire beach disappeared. The sound of the waves lost to his kiss and the roar of longing in her heart.

***

Patriot paced the room.

He'd been out of his mind. No other way to describe it. Dancing in the moonlight. Yeah. That was a good one. He could still taste the salt on Chloe's mouth, feel her body pressed against his. Two days of telling himself how crazy he'd been hadn't lessened the feeling of her in his arms. He couldn't quarantine those feelings—the way she'd looked and laughed, the clean feel of being around her. As if the time in the gang had never been.

But what had he done? Even when he joined the church in Denver, he didn't get close to anyone, wouldn't trust himself to a relationship. He needed his head straightened out, his life in Christ back. And what if j-beck found him? That aspect of always looking over his shoulder had kept him alone. He'd dated a few times but put an end to it quickly. He couldn't put others in danger.

The time with Chloe had been a mistake. A big one. He'd let down his guard.

He closed his eyes for a moment, then picked up his

weights. Did the reps.

The heaviness gave way to a grin as he replayed Chloe's smile. It lit her whole face, her eyes joined in, and it fired something inside him. She seemed free of the ugliness he'd seen, and it felt good. It hadn't hurt that the last few times he'd seen her, she'd had him laughing until his facial muscles hurt. He'd laughed all the way to GreasePaint's house that day. Yeah, he needed that.

But the woman was naïve. She didn't see danger. Yes, her work in the ER brought the serious side of life to her, but she wasn't personally involved. In fact, as much as he'd opened up with her, she'd skipped away from any serious discussion of her own. He mulled that over for a few minutes. Had something happened in her life? Something that made her afraid of being vulnerable? If so, he could empathize.

Patriot moved to the window and stared out. The confinement here had stretched him to his limits. He needed a plan. Something that would draw j-beck out so he could get on with his life.

He grabbed his shirt and pulled it over his head. Maybe a talk with Reece. It wasn't quite dark, but China and anyone else should have gone home. Reece always put in an extra hour or two. He'd slip over to the office and ask Reece to help devise a plan, something to present to Richards and the captain. Something that would work. He took a step toward the door and stopped.

Even though he'd put off calling Chloe, she'd be expecting it, expecting something. The groan inside almost made itself heard. Who was he trying to fool? He *wanted* something, too—wanted to see her, talk with her, hold her again…

But he'd have to tell her he couldn't see her. Nothing could come of this. He had too much on his plate. Life was too dangerous.

His chest squeezed at the thought of that, but he jerked his head up and opened the apartment door. He'd deal with it.

As soon as possible.

He had to.

***

Miss Eleanor sat back in her chair, eyes closed, examining the symptoms. Chest pain, shortness of breath, weakness in her body.

Father, am I having a heart attack or indigestion? There are plenty of days where I just don't feel the way I use to. Low energy. Not much determination. I need some help here. If I have to go to the hospital, okay, but don't let the Enemy send me. Only You.

She reached for her phone. *I could call Alan. No, he has enough problems.* Daneen's chemo was ending, and she'd been totally exhausted. *You know she shouldn't have been at the church, Lord. She worked too hard.*

I could call Kati. Yeah, I might do that. If I need to go to the emergency room, who better than Kati to take me? She grinned. And Reece.

She loved that man. It had taken some time. Loving an ex-gang member with tattoos all over who carried a gun to church...well, it had taken her a while to get past the prejudices she thought she didn't have.

I know I'm no better than anyone else, Lord, but You just keep showing me. And then You show me Your love for me, too.

That love was mutual. God was her Father, her husband, her friend.

You know that I love You, Jesus. Like Peter. Telling You three times because he didn't understand what You were saying.

She stilled.

Are You saying something to me, too?

She bowed her head and listened. The unsettled feeling inside wouldn't leave. Neither her heart nor indigestion had woken her from her nap. This was something different.

A minute later, her prayers began, tumbled forth, lifted. The physical symptoms subsided, melted into forgotteness. Only she, the Holy Spirit, and the prayers remained.

Chapter 8

*Submit yourselves therefore to God. Resist the devil, and he
will flee from you.*
James 4:7

The church parking lot held a few cars, and Chloe pulled in beside Reece's black SUV. It was "girls' night out." Or would be. She, China, Becca, and Kati. The four musketeers. Yeah, it had been three, but—like the movie—they had let her in.

Her eagerness amused her. Should she mention Patriot or not? How many times had she told herself this wouldn't work? That she couldn't go through this again? Wouldn't go through it again.

And yet... She grinned.

She couldn't help herself.

He hadn't called, but only two days had passed, and he'd mentioned lying low. No one was supposed to know he was still in town.

She groaned. Well, that was the answer to her question. She couldn't tell the others anything. Although they might guess something was going on. She could barely keep the grin from her face.

She hadn't been in a relationship in years. She'd held on, waiting on God...wondering...if... Was it too much to hope...

A relationship.

Wow. Was she overstepping. A few hours of moonlight and dancing and she was higher than the stars the other night. Get hold of yourself, girl!

Chloe climbed from the car and glanced at the portable

office building. Behind it, a lone pine tree towered black against the tangerine sky. Everything was beautiful now. It beckoned her to take a picture, and she did. *Evening Sky with Pine.*

She headed toward the steps.

The office door opened, and Patriot stepped out.

Chloe stopped, heart soaring. He looked so good. Serious, brows drawn together some, but good.

Patriot started down the steps, lifted his head, and met her gaze. He stopped. The preoccupied look disappeared. His eyes widened, and then his face stilled.

Joy surged through her. Her face jumped with a mile-wide smile. She felt the dimensions of it right before it froze when he looked at her so impersonally.

"Hi." Her voice wobbled. She tried to catch it back, but it was impossible.

He nodded and made as if to walk by her. Her heart crumpled. *No.* This was impossible. He wouldn't. He couldn't...

The impersonal mask faltered, and he stopped. "We need to talk, but this isn't the time. Or the place. I'll call."

"Okay." *Hold it together, girl. Hold on.*

He looked as if he wanted to say more but instead walked past her.

She turned and stared after him, her insides caving and crashing as the waves had on the starlit beach two nights ago.

He strode toward the dorms, then disappeared behind them. The roaring reached from her gut to her throat.

Oh my. Stars in my eyes. Big time. He regretted all he told me. They hardly knew each other, anyway. Why did it matter? Why had she read so much into it? It was just a kiss. Well, two. And a whole lot of information he wished he hadn't shared, obviously...

She stood there unmoving, not able to get past the overwhelming hurt and disappointment. How could he...

Process it, Chloe. Just process it. Clearly, the other

night meant nothing to him—or not anything like it had meant to you.

Yep, relationships stank. She knew that. That was why working in the ER suited her. She could step in for a minute, do her job, and then get out of there. Go home. Leave this kind of stuff to someone else.

She yanked the office door open, waved at the three girls waiting for her, and marched into Reece's office.

"Hey, what's with Patriot? Something up?" Like he'd tell her. But she had to do something, anything to get the emotions under control.

Reece glanced up from his studying. "Hey, Chloe. No, he's just got a lot on his mind these days."

"Ah." She nodded as if she understood all that implied and forced her face into a noncommittal look. Or tried.

Reece pushed back in his chair. "I know you two didn't hit it off at first, but he's a good guy."

"Yep." The word caught, hitched. "Sure. Good guy."

He straightened. "You had dinner the other night and talked?"

"Yep."

A brow lifted, his eyes seeing more than Chloe was prepared for him to see. He leaned forward. "Even though I'll vouch for him, you don't want to get mixed up with Patriot right now. He's dealing with a lot. You should pretend the other day at the pond or…at the beach…never happened and go on with your life."

She started to protest, and Reece shook his head.

"They're on a manhunt for j-beck. Patriot can identify him, and he needs to watch his back. Until they catch j-beck, any relationship would cause problems. Serious problems. It wouldn't be you but how they could use you against Patriot. The way they used Gary Lovett."

Her gut clenched, and she could see again Gary's bloody chest as Mohawk—j-beck?—tossed him into the pond.

"Yeah. It's survival, Chloe. We've had some quiet

years. The ministry has grown. People are being saved, walking free of addictions. We couldn't expect Satan to lay low forever. It's time to put our armor back on—if we've taken it off—and I think some of us have."

***

Lynn exited the gynecologist office. How could she not be pregnant? Again. *Not* pregnant. Her shoulders drooped. The home test had been inconclusive, and she'd been so upset that she'd made a gynecologist appointment for today—less than twenty-four hours after the home test—to find out for sure.

She dropped her head onto the steering wheel of her Jeep. She'd been so sure this time. Body aches, nauseousness, no energy. And she was late. *Lord, how many times can we do this? Each test, each month...*

Tears fell, and she let them come, rolling down her cheeks, over her hands, dripping onto the steering wheel. It took a few minutes before she straightened and reached into the glove box for a tissue. Stupid. *You're stronger than this, girl. So many people have waited longer. Straighten up.*

At least she hadn't said anything to Rich. He was so hair trigger these days. But she wished she could tell him, tell someone...

Sharee.

What she'd give to have her best friend here. Now. Not in some faraway place, halfway around the world. With her two children. Two. Lynn shoved the envy away. No. She would not be envious of Sharee for having kids. How could she even think it? It had been a tough six years for them in Indonesia. Blessed, as Sharee always said, because they were doing what she and John felt God had called them to do, but hard.

However, they were long overdue for a talk. A call to Indonesia was just what Lynn needed. She tugged her smartphone from her purse and pulled up the number.

***

Kati stood by Reece's office door as Luis entered. She gave a quick nod. "All right, I'll get out of your way. The two new girls are checked into the dorms. Tomorrow one of the volunteers will go over the program and the rules, and then they can see a counselor before starting classes the next day."

Reece leaned back in his chair. "Thanks for picking them up at the jail."

"Sure, but you owe me."

"Do I?" He grinned and threw a glance at Luis. "We'll talk about it later."

She shook her head. "You men."

Luis's mouth twitched. *"Hola,* Kati. How are you?"

"Lo estoy haciendo bien. ¿Cómo estás?" She managed the words haltingly.

Luis grinned. *"A mí también me va bien. Tu Español está bueno."*

"I'm trying. Reece is a good teacher."

Luis's eyes crinkled at the corners. "But not as good as I, *señora.*"

Reece's head rose. He pushed aside the papers on his desk. "Do I hear a challenge there?"

"If only the program allowed some extra time, there would be."

"Excuses. You have from midnight until seven in the morning."

Luis laughed. "You have summed it up, brother. We cannot get into trouble because there is no time."

"I think that might have been Pastor Alan's idea when we formed the program. Or Rich's."

Luis sobered. "The man I need to talk to you about."

Kati picked up her purse. "I'll leave, guys, and you can talk."

"No, no." Luis waved her toward a chair. "Please. I think having two people might be better after all."

Kati studied him a moment. Luis had made an appointment with Reece, and she didn't want to hamper whatever he had to say. Sometimes the *mano a mano* talk worked better. She shot a look at Reece, who nodded. Okay, then. She slid into a chair.

Reece settled back in his. "Shall we pray before we start?"

Kati murmured agreement. Luis dropped his head. Kati loved the way her husband prayed. No flowery speech, just him and God and their needs lifted up, or, at times, just thanksgiving and praise.

When he ended and their heads rose, Reece focused on Luis. "You said you preferred not to wait, and you mentioned Rich. What's up?"

"The man came to see me the other day. With his partner. Someone had reported me talking with Alberto."

"Your cousin?"

"*Si*. They think he is in a gang."

Reece sat forward. "That isn't true, is it?"

"Not that I or my sister know."

"Good. Your parole…"

"I know. One of the conditions is that I have no contact with any gang members. But there is something else."

Kati glanced at Reece as Luis stopped. They waited.

His jaw worked for a minute. "There was a point before I went to prison when Becca asked me if I had ever killed a man…"

***

The long workday had tightened every muscle. Chloe twisted her head back and forth and tried to loosen the knots in her neck as she climbed from her car.

She surveyed the structure ahead of her. Pastor Alan

had rented portable modular buildings, put together with enough space for a sanctuary and offices. Chloe was okay with that. A necessity for now, but he also thought the congregation needed some fire-safety training—as soon as possible. Chloe understood, but trying to make one of the three times he'd scheduled for the class had proved hard. Dinnertime today was her only option. Sheesh. After a double shift.

She'd decided to pick up a few more hours in the ER this last week. Hours that would keep her, her mind, and, yeah, her heart busy. Stupid to have let it go so fast, anyway. She hadn't hurt herself this bad in a while.

Metal steps led up to the building. A few others jostled her.

"You coming from or going to work, Chloe?"

She held the door for the older woman who'd asked the question. "Just left."

"And now you're here." Amusement twinkled.

"Yeah." Chloe grinned, followed the others down the aisle, and found a seat near the front.

Two firefighters in uniform, their backs to her, stood talking with Pastor Alan. She said hello to a few people, then grabbed her phone and sent a text to Kati, teasing her about having to work and promising to give her all the needed info Reece would probably forget to tell her—like how hot the firefighters were. She smirked to herself. Yes, there were plenty of fish in the sea, as her mom always said. She tucked her phone away and looked up—right into Patriot's eyes.

Her heart jumped, went wild, then thudded. She shot a glance off to his left and tried to stuff down the shock. He was in uniform, a firefighter's uniform, the helmet tucked under one arm. What was he doing here? Were they doing some role-playing? Could she get out unnoticed?

She swallowed hard. Who was she kidding? She'd sat near the front...of all places. Her eyes edged back to where he stood. One of the "hot" firefighters she'd just texted about. He turned back and listened to the other men talk.

Chloe groaned inside, and her heart cracked again. Yeah, he was hot and so not interested in her. He hadn't called for that "talk" he'd mentioned a week ago, hadn't made any contact—and he certainly knew where she worked.

Lord, this is not fair. I have to be here and watch him... Yeah, she was whining, and she wasn't a whiner. She forced her shoulders straighter, put a smile on her face, and turned to talk to the person sliding into the seat next to her.

"Miss Eleanor! It's so good to see you..."

***

"What in the world is your problem?" The tone of Lynn's voice spun him around like a child's toy.

All the typical marital things Rich had ever heard jumped to his mouth, but he clenched his jaw shut, leaned over, grabbed his tie and jacket from the kitchen chair, and headed for the front door.

"Rich!"

He hesitated, then reached for the knob.

"Please." Her voice caught. "I know you've got to go, but can't we have a minute?"

"A minute for what? Fighting?"

"No, I..."

He took a breath, turned.

She stood, pleading with her eyes, unhappiness woven into the beauty of her face. He could leave or pretend. Neither felt right. He knew exactly what she referred to. He'd forced down a steak-sized sermon at last week's new church—alone. Not a comfortable way to hear from God. Maybe it was time for him to man up.

"What do you want?" *Good response, Richards. Warm, enthusiastic, loving reply from her husband.*

She edged closer, taking the little he was giving. "I just want to know what it is. What's eating you."

"Luis."

She knew, of course. They all knew. Her face went through a cascade of emotions. He waited, steeling himself for the argument. But she surprised him. She swallowed and said nothing.

"What? Aren't you going to tell me how much he's changed? How he accepted Jesus into his life? How great he is?"

She shook her head. "But I don't understand. You've given grace to others coming out of prison. What is different with Luis?"

He looked past her, wondering why it still felt like a knife in his chest. "He killed Marcos."

"Marcos? *Your brother-in-law?*"

Chapter 9

The thief does not come except to steal, and to kill, and to destroy. I have come that they may have life, and that they may have it more abundantly.
John 10:10

Lynn's hand flew to her chest. "But...I...how do you..."

Rich stepped forward, took her by the shoulders, and walked her back into the kitchen. They'd been married five years now, but Marcos was before Lynn's time. How would she see this? Would she believe him?

She dropped into a chair and shoved waist-length hair back over her shoulder. "Luis killed Marcos? Your best friend?"

He tossed his tie and jacket on another chair, turned a third one around, and straddled it. Yeah, he and Marcos had been best friends, but Marcos had changed. Rich had tried to turn him back, to get him on the "old straight and narrow," but he'd failed. That failure only multiplied when Rich couldn't find evidence to bring his murderer to justice.

He shifted his underarm holster and the SIG Sauer. "Marcos got involved with a gang. Left my sister while she was pregnant."

Lynn's eyes rounded. She shook her head. "That's horrible. How could he do that?"

Rich shrugged. "He wouldn't be the first, but this was my sister. I exploded."

"Naturally."

He smiled at her tone, then sobered. "You get with a

gang, and they own you. At first, it can feel good, like family. Only it isn't. Nowhere near."

"I knew he'd left your sister, but you never said why. So, that's why you joined the gang unit?"

"One of the reasons."

"Was he in Luis's gang?"

"No, Luis joined *his* gang. Marcos was captain at the time."

Another surprise for her. "Captain of a gang?"

"Yeah. Marcos got in deep. I think that's what he wanted all along. People to order around, to do his bidding. He liked control."

"Sounds like a fun guy."

"Yeah. So, Luis is with the gang six months, and suddenly, Marcos disappears. Vanishes. I haven't seen or heard from him since."

"You looked for him, of course."

"Yeah. The department helped. I knew Luis killed him. It's the only way he could become captain in that brief time span. I'd seen Marcos a week earlier. I kept up with him, working on him to reform him. Everything seemed as normal as it got with him. Then he disappeared, and suddenly Luis was captain."

"When was all this?"

"Before you and I met."

"That far back? Why didn't you tell me?"

"Embarrassed, I guess. My brother-in-law. My best friend. And neither my sister nor I was enough for him. The studies say those joining gangs want a family. That wasn't the case with Marcos. He had a family. He wanted excitement. He was always wild. We were in a lot of trouble growing up because he had this streak—always trying something dangerous, just on the edge."

"That sounds like you."

"Yeah. I liked the adrenaline, but I chose being a cop, doing something worthwhile. He didn't want the rules of being a cop. He was looking at joining the Marines—"

"Talk about rules."

"Yeah, I know, but they were elite, so he thought he could put up with it. But he had a health problem and couldn't get in. During that time, he and Tammy got married. They'd always had this on-and-off-again attraction, but she didn't like his need for excitement. They'd gone together a couple of times, but after he didn't get in with the Marines, he was depressed. I think Tammy felt sorry for him, and then she got pregnant." He stopped. Remembering when she'd come to him, telling him about the baby, asking about an abortion. "I told her, why don't you just marry him? You two have been hanging together forever. He'll settle down if you get married and there's a baby. That's what I thought, anyway."

"But he didn't?"

Rich snorted. "For about three months. I didn't know he wouldn't like a wife—my sister—so pregnant."

"He thought she was unattractive." Lynn's lips compressed.

"Yeah. I never caught on to the fact that he was so into women's looks. Tammy's attractive. You know that. But when she was about six months along, he started looking at other women, and I laid into him one night. He had a temper. I knew that, too, but I didn't understand how much it drove him. He almost killed me."

Lynn leaned forward, eyes rounded. "But you…"

"Won. And he hated it. We drifted apart. Well, it started when I joined the Sheriff's Office. The fight just made it worse. Next thing I knew, he's hanging with gang members."

"But are you sure about this? You know Luis killed him? It just seems…"

He watched her trying to wrap her head around it. "I can't prove it, but I know."

"What if Marcos just left or someone else killed him, and Luis moved in to take the empty space? What if there was an accident?"

He glanced at his watch and pushed up from the chair, feeling lighter. Relief lifted one-hundred-pound weights from each shoulder.

Lynn stepped in front of him. "I trust you, Rich. Your instincts. You know that. If you think Luis did this..." She sighed.

"I do."

"But you can't prove it?"

"I haven't been able to, but I haven't given up." He picked up the jacket and tie again and settled his shoulder holster back into place.

"I understand why you want to go to another church. If you believe Luis killed Marcos, then it's too hard looking at him each week. I should have known you had a good reason."

He touched her chin. "Yeah, you should have."

She stood close to him, her hand resting on his sleeve, and he could feel her warmth. He closed his eyes and drew her to him. Why hadn't he told her sooner?

Her head rose, and he looked down into blue eyes intent upon his. "Just don't let it become a vendetta. Don't let it change who you are."

A sharp jolt went through him, as if a sword had sliced his gut. If it hadn't already...

***

The fire chief was finishing up. Listing the things to do or not do during a fire. Patriot stood off to the side. He'd given the first half of the lecture. A new volunteer, the Chief said, on hiatus from his regular firefighting job, the one who'd suggested this training to the pastor.

Hmm. No wonder Alan had pushed it through so quickly. Patriot was behind it. Wasn't he supposed to be in hiding? Chloe had missed the last part of the introduction. She'd tried forcing her attention to anything but Patriot. The uniform looked too good on him.

"Plan what you would do during a fire. How would you escape? Make two or three exit plans. Remember, don't break a window unless you have to get out. That creates a draft and brings smoke and flames your way. If it's a kitchen fire, a grease or pan fire, don't throw water on it. Instead try to smother it with a metal lid. Do not try to move the pan. You will burn yourself and spread the fire."

A child's hand went up. "My mom always says that if my clothes catch fire, I should stop, drop, and roll."

The fire chief smiled. "She's right. Don't run. Stop moving. That spreads the fire. Stop, drop to the ground, and roll across the ground or floor."

Chloe shifted in her seat and closed her eyes. The talk had brought back images of the burning building, the heat, and the fear. She'd run after Manuel, but she'd had no idea what she was doing. She opened her eyes only to stare into Patriot's gray ones. Her heart kicked, and she dropped her head. It had been all she could do to sit through his part of the class.

What was he doing here? What had happened to lying low?

The Chief continued his wrap-up. "One last thing. If there's a lot of smoke, stay as low to the ground as you can. Get on the floor and crawl toward an exit. Travis? What have I forgotten?"

Travis? Chloe straightened. Travis? She'd missed that earlier. Was that his real name or something he'd made up? Did anyone else in here know him? Or know him as Patriot? She glanced around. Not many. Miss Eleanor and the prayer group, of course, but he'd lived in Denver for three years and before that with the gang. Reece had addressed him as Patriot. Wasn't that where she'd heard the name?

Patriot stepped up. "If you use an extinguisher, always aim for the bottom of the flames, not the top." His eyes sought Chloe's "And never go back into a burning building. Leave it to the experts."

She bristled. Even though he was right, he needn't single her out. The man was irritating and arrogant and...

Miss Eleanor's hand touched hers. "You did a good thing, Chloe. I'm sure he didn't mean for you to feel guilty for trying to save Manuel. If you hadn't, Manuel might not be here."

"Thank you, but I think he did mean that."

Would this be over anytime soon? Darkness was falling outside. The thirty minutes of fire-safety instruction had been followed by another ten of how to exit a burning building, and now they were going to practice it.

What?

Well, this might be good. She had already decided on *her* exit. As soon as she got outside, she was gone, out of here, vamoosed, absent, AWOL, not here...

Forty-five minutes of Fire Chief Thompson and the "new" volunteer, *Travis*, trading the stage for fire prevention and safety tips had her edgier than a wildebeest crossing the crocodile-infested Nile River.

She stood with everyone else, executing the line, the non-panic exit, and then the crawl.

The crawl?

"If the smoke is thick," the Chief said, "get as close to the ground as possible. That's where the air is. Yes, we're going to practice crawling. I've found that if people have actually had to get down on all fours, they remember it when it's needed."

No. This was too much.

She headed for the nearest exit. But before she could escape, others lined up in front of her, waiting for instructions. Giggling and laughter rose around her.

How did Patriot get in front of the line before her?

He moved them toward the exit, then instructed a young child on getting on his hands and knees. Others followed. A minute later, he helped one of the teen girls up and laughed at something she said, the sound rich and low. It did something inside Chloe, pain ricocheting back and forth. Then he turned and helped another person.

A few people hung back. Their stance told the rest that they were not doing this. Chloe would have grinned if her attitude hadn't been the same. Was there any way she could get past Patriot and out the door?

Miss Eleanor stepped in front of her but walked toward Patriot with a smile. "Young man, I am not doing any crawling today."

He bowed to her. Bowed! "Ma'am, I wouldn't think of asking you."

"Good for you."

He held out his arm and escorted her to the door.

Chloe suddenly wished she was ninety years old. But she imitated the couple behind her who were already on hands and knees, crawling. If Patriot—or Travis, or whatever his name was—thought she'd wait for any instructions from him, he could rethink that whole scenario. She'd be at the door and out before he returned.

But from her lower vantage point, she spotted his boots walking quickly back her way. Heat—no fire needed—surged into her face as she started to rise.

He stooped down, head next to hers, amusement in his voice. "You're doing good, Chloe."

She jerked her head up, words hot on the end of her tongue, but his eyes stopped her. Warm and concerned. Right. She'd buy into that when the Sahara Desert froze over.

He pulled her to her feet, held her just a fraction longer than necessary. "I hoped you'd be here. I'll be in touch."

The words were so low she wasn't sure she heard them, but then he directed her out the door. Pastor Alan waited, grinning, with the others. Everyone was laughing and joking.

Oh yeah, fun.

She ducked her head and glanced back. Patriot reached for the next crawler and lifted her to her feet. He did not look her way again.

***

"Miss Eleanor called another prayer meeting." Kati dropped her phone onto the table, trying hard to keep the tiredness from her voice. Sometimes prayer took so much out of her, and last night at the ER had already drained her. She needed some sleep, and she wanted time with Reece. He seemed to be gone too much these days. Besides, she needed to clean her house or maybe wash her hair. Or just curl up on the couch. Argh....

Reece pushed aside his dinner plate. "Tonight?"

"Yeah. Let me read you her text message. You're part of it. 'Come for prayer tonight at seven thirty. Our enemy has set up a well-coordinated attack that we need to counter. A man was almost killed on church property. Reece used his gun again—that he hasn't used in three years. The Gordone gang is trying to reorganize, and someone burns down our church. It's time to stop reacting with surprise and get ahead in this game. No, it's not a game. It's war.'"

"She's got it down except for the insurance money and Rich leaving the church."

"Yeah. But I'd rather not go tonight. You think she'll understand?"

He shrugged. "I'm in the office these days and don't get to talk with her as much as I'd like."

"You spend a lot of time there."

"Too much. I'd like to be out in the community more, on the streets."

"You've said that for a while."

"Witnessing on the streets, being where people live, and helping those in the dorms. That's more my style. The church stuff—finances and meetings and how to grow the congregation—that is not me."

"Your gifting is in witnessing and meeting people where they are. Have you talked with Alan about it?"

He grabbed her hand. "Leave the dishes. We can do them later."

She let him lead her to the sofa and curled up next to him, leaning her head on his shoulder. He slipped his arm across hers.

"So, what's this about? Not wanting to go to prayer. That's not like you. Just tired?"

"Yeah."

"Nothing to do with what you said the other day about Miss Eleanor wanting you to take over the group?"

Kati punched him. "How do you do that?"

He chuckled and pulled her up into the center of the room. "Let me show you something."

"Ah, we just sat down."

"Man up, woman." He grinned. "Okay. You're the kickboxer. I'm a street fighter. I'm trailing you one night, and you notice. So, when I try to grab you, what are you going to do?"

He reached out to grab her shoulders. Kati backed for an instant, but when he reached for her again, she threw a roundhouse kick to his side. He blocked it with a lift of his leg and lobbed a faked punch. She ducked and threw another kick, but Reece stepped close, and her kick went past him. He brought a punch to her face and another to her chest, both barely touching her, and then he grabbed her waist.

Kati frowned. "You were expecting the kick."

"Of course. I know you. You favor the right roundhouse. I knew it was coming and kept the weight on my right leg so I could block the kick with my left and still come after you with a punch. I also looked for cues to tell me what you were going to do next. The second kick was easier. I just stepped in close and let it pass, and I was still able to throw my punches."

"All right. But next time we're in the gym, try that again."

"I know your second go-to, also."

"Reece Jernigan, you will find you've met your match if you keep egging me on. What does this have to do with the prayer meeting?"

"Because when you told me what Miss Eleanor said, I knew you were going to embrace it or back away. Babe, you're whole hog into something or not in at all. And that's what scares you right now."

She stared at him. Yes, if she did this, it would take a lot out of her. "What I need to know is if God wants me to do this or if it's just Miss Eleanor."

"And you've prayed about it?"

"Of course, I have." Kati glanced upward. "I've tried."

"Are you asking me if you should go tonight?"

"No, I…"

"Because I think you should."

She growled, and Reece laughed.

"Why?"

"Because if Miss Eleanor called a special meeting, it's because she feels God's leading her to. And, Kati—"

"Yes?"

"Too much is happening right now. A soldier goes whether they're tired or not."

"Who said I'm a soldier?"

"You entered the Army when He called."

She nodded, glanced upward to heaven again, and closed her eyes. "I know."

Reece tugged her into his arms. "This is your gift. Remember, the weapons of your warfare are mighty through God to the pulling down of strongholds. You'll get through this. Your prayers avail much. Think of that. That's scripture. Whatever you and the others pray about tonight will be worth it. And remember that Elias was a man like us, and he prayed that it might not rain, and it didn't rain for three years and six months. And he prayed again for it to rain, and it did. Go. Expect miracles."

Kati pulled free. He was right. Of course he was

right... So, why was she having such a hard time?

***

Patriot arrived at the hospital near the time Kati had told him Chloe would be taking her dinner break—all conditional, she'd told him, on what emergencies they had tonight. He asked the first person he saw in scrubs which way the ER workers came out for break, and she'd directed him to this hallway. One glance inside the door to the ER showed a lot going on. He leaned back against the wall, crossed one arm over the other, and waited.

He wasn't sure why he'd told her he would be in touch. It was better for her, for them both, not to be in touch, but he couldn't forget the pressure lifting off his shoulders that night at the beach. Couldn't forget her. He'd told her stuff he hadn't told anyone else, things he was ashamed of, things that had sliced into him, into who he was.

Her whole demeanor that night had touched him, the way she'd listened, the things she'd said, the way she looked in the moonlight, hair blowing across her face. And he loved how she jumped in to help others, even, as he knew, if it was dangerous.

Finally, she came through the doors, talking and laughing with another person in scrubs. When she saw him, she skidded to a stop, her sneakers making a short screech on the polished floor. The other worker, fortyish and male and fit, stopped beside her and glanced at Patriot. His gaze jumped between them. When neither of them said anything, the man arched a brow, then walked past them down the hall.

Patriot straightened. "I brought a couple of sandwiches and some chocolate. Some water."

Her eyes rounded. "Uh...Okay."

No smile this time, but what did he expect? "Is there a place we can eat privately?"

"Yes. Sure."

She waved a hand in the opposite direction from where her coworker had disappeared. Patriot moved beside her, holding the bag from the local sandwich shop, and waited for her to lead. She walked in front of him in silence until she came to a door that led outside to a small enclosed area. Tables and potted trees dotted the patio.

The night sky hung overhead. It was dark and private. *Good.* He took the water and the sandwiches out and then handed her the Dove chocolate bar.

"I'm hoping to buy a little grace here—with the chocolate bar and sandwiches."

"You need it." She unwrapped the Dove bar and bit into it.

He felt that. The decision to come tonight, and the decision he'd made to try and arrange a way to see her—asking Alan to grease the skids as Patriot joined the volunteer fire department—had worked in two areas. First, he'd needed to get out. Sheltering inside for weeks felt like being a sugar glider on an exercise wheel. And yes, he needed to talk with her. He'd waited two days past the fire-safety meeting. She hadn't been happy to see him that day, and any plans he'd had to talk with her had vanished when he'd seen her face. She'd almost bolted from the meeting.

The Dove bar was disappearing fast.

"Dessert before dinner?" He couldn't keep the amusement from his voice, thinking of her face that day in the car—covered with powdered sugar.

"Long night."

"All right then. You deserve it."

She finished the chocolate, took a drink, and sat back. Realization hit him. Not only was she tired, despite the laughter with her colleague, but she was having trouble transitioning out of the ER. Had something happened tonight? At any time, her work would be demanding. He volleyed their need to talk with her emotional level.

"Look, if this is the wrong time, just eat, and I'll take

off."

Her hand jerked. "No. Please."

"We can do this later."

Her eyes met his, the question in them. If he left…no, he couldn't say for sure when he could do this again. She knew it, too.

"Give me a couple of minutes."

His eyes searched hers. "Okay. But eat some real food." When she frowned, he smiled and let the amusement come though again. "Please."

Her eyes narrowed, but she pulled the sandwich toward her.

He did the same. "I have all night, but you don't."

She glanced at her watch, grimaced, and took a bite. "Italian?"

"You said it was a favorite."

He won a half smile, and then he let the silence stretch out as they ate. His sandwich disappeared in a hurry, and he spent a few minutes studying her. He had come in the middle of the night, had spent time losing anyone who might be tailing him. If anyone was. However, was it right seeing her again? Even using the explanation as an excuse?

She finished her sandwich, drank some water, and raised her head to catch his look. "What is your name, anyway? Is Travis your real name?"

"Yes, but stick with Patriot. I haven't earned the other back yet."

Her brow scrunched. "And you don't owe me anything. I'm sorry that I read more into that time at the beach than I should have. My fault. You have whatever grace you need."

Is that what she thought? And yet that had been his first thought. To let her think exactly that. And he could still go with it. She'd given him the out.

He lifted a brow. "That easy? You let me off that easy?"

She chewed her lip and nodded. "Yes."

Her voice sounded stiff, in control, not like the girl on the beach—the one filled with laughter and warmth. But it was that ease and that vulnerability that cinched his desire to know her more, to let her know the truth. She ran to save people, gave grace when none was due. How could he do less?

He leaned forward. "Chloe, I do owe you—an explanation and more." He hesitated. The table made a divide between them.

Standing, he put out his hand. A beat passed before she took it. He pulled her to her feet and over to a spindly tree that stood in a shadowed corner.

"I'm sorry about that day at the church. If there had been another way...but I couldn't take a chance. If someone was watching, I didn't want them to think there was anything between us. Even Kati and the others inside. If anyone said anything to the wrong person, it could endanger you, and I couldn't do that." He drew his fingers along the softness of her jaw. "And your crazy smile that day. I loved it, and it scared me to death. If anyone saw it...I had to act as if you were no one special."

Her look was hesitant, wary.

He wanted to erase it. "That night on the beach was God sent. The release of having someone, having *you*, to talk to, to hold. To laugh with." Something had come alive within him that had been dead too long. Hope, maybe. Love? He couldn't go there yet, but... Unless he'd misread her smile that day. He tilted his head, wondering.

Only it didn't matter. He had to stay away from her.

He dropped his hand. "But it can't happen again. We can't see each other—until this is finished."

Her eyes searched his, as if she wondered whether she could trust him. *Yes*, he wanted to say, *you can*, but his gaze dropped to her mouth. The moonlight played over her hair, touching her cheek and her lips. He hesitated. Her lips parted, and, good night, he wanted to kiss her again. He drew his eyes

118

up to hers. Waited a moment, then lowered his head. She didn't move, didn't pull away, and he covered her mouth with his.

It's okay. You can trust me. But the words were only in his head. He felt a tentative response and tightened his arms. Would she understand? Her hands slipped up his arms, caught his biceps, and she leaned in. He turned his head and sought to deepen the kiss.

What was he doing? What was he thinking?

He drew back but stood holding her. She'd misinterpret his actions if he didn't control himself, didn't step away. "I don't want to hurt you now, didn't want to hurt you then, but I had to pretend you meant nothing to me. Do you understand?"

Her head dipped in assent. "Yes. I...Reece said something similar, but..."

Thank you, Reece.

"Good. Because we can't see each other after tonight." He swallowed. "Not until this is finished, and I have no idea how long that will be."

She said nothing, just lifted her face to him. He groaned. So much for control. This time he didn't try to temper the kiss. Her body melded into his, and heat poured through him. He wanted to hear her laugh again, see her smile.

The door across from them opened. Light sliced to their corner and across them. Chloe stiffened and tried to back away.

He held her close, hiding her head against his chest. "No. Stay here."

"Oh! Sorry!" A woman's voice. The door closed. The darkness circled in again.

"No one should see us together, even here." He thought about her friend in scrubs and brought his head back. "You never know who might say something. You'd be in too much danger."

***

Kati stepped next to Reece and intertwined his hand with hers. The night sky held a half-moon, bright enough to illuminate the jogging path and the field in front of them.

"Maria is new to the program, but I'm sure she heard the rule about no one-on-ones."

Reece leaned against the lone pine and pulled her against him. He scanned the area next to the fellowship hall, about twenty yards away. "I never thought I'd be playing nursemaid when I took this job."

Kati laughed softly. "Hey, Luis just wants to make sure he doesn't get kicked out of the program and end up back in prison."

"Yeah, like Maria's going to seduce him."

"Babe?"

His head bent to hers. "Hmm?"

"You might be losing your discernment about women."

"You think? We'll have to discuss that later."

"Umm." She snuggled into him. "You're doing a lot you'd never thought you'd do."

"Yeah."

She lifted her head. "Tell me about that."

"About?"

"How discontented are you in what you're doing these days?"

"Don't worry about it. I'm fine."

"Says the macho man."

"I'm fine."

"You said the other day you'd rather be on the streets again."

"I need a Joshua to do that. Jesus sent out the disciples two by two. Unless you…"

"Hey, that's your gift. Unless you need a bodyguard."

He grinned. "I might take you up on it."

Kati leaned against him then put a finger to her mouth. "Here she comes."

Maria stopped at the corner of the fellowship hall and looked around. The pole light near the parking lot scattered yellow past where she stood, outlining long, curly hair and a shapely figure. Her head turned their way, and she stared in their direction.

Reece tightened his arms around Kati. "What are we supposed to be doing out here?"

"Not sure. Making out?"

"You talked to the man. What did he say?"

"Ad lib. Just be where we can keep an eye out."

Reece grunted. "Luis should have told her no."

"They had some long affair, I think. Six months or so, and he said she tried to kill him when it was over. Said she had a temper to match his."

"So, he's the one needing the bodyguard?"

"Uh-huh. Sounds like it. Anyway, he was captain at the time, and he swears it was all about the prestige to her."

Reece chuckled. "At least with Becca, he knows it's not that."

"And he did ask how Maria got into the program."

"Same way he did. But it was a tentative okay. She's on probation—a little stricter than others."

"Shhh. Here comes Luis. He's not sure why she wants to see him. If she's changed."

Maria stepped toward him, her hands moving as she talked. Kati grinned. They couldn't hear well, but Maria's animated way of talking gave them some information. Luis stood out of her immediate space, but in a moment, Maria moved closer. Her manner altered, and she touched her hair, pulling it between her fingers.

"Uh-oh," Kati breathed.

Maria's head tilted as she talked. Luis shook his and shifted backward. When Maria reached out, he moved his arm from her grasp. Luis's raised voice drifted toward Kati and

Reece.

"Can you tell what they're saying? It's in Spanish."

Reece lifted a finger. "Wait a minute. Yeah, she says she's changed, but Luis is not buying it. Now she's questioning whether he's changed. Good thing you don't understand this. Her language is spicy, and you were right. The woman's coming on to him."

"Ha! I knew it."

"She's upset that he's not interested."

"Good for him."

"Uh-oh. He's telling her about Becca."

"Is that a good idea? If she's the jealous type—"

"Maybe he wants to put an end to this now."

Maria's hands moved wildly, and she leaned forward, spitting words at Luis. Luis pulled his head back. Words ricocheted between them, their voices rising. Kati tightened her hand on Reece's arm.

Maria's hand shot up and connected with Luis's face. The sound echoed across the distance. Luis stilled, but even from where she and Reece stood, his thinned lips and balled fists were evident.

Reece grabbed Kati's hand and dragged her forward. "Hey, man, what's up?"

Maria spun their way, nostrils flaring, mouth wide. She spewed words that Kati couldn't understand. Luis said something hard and clipped, and Maria crossed one arm over the other and pressed her lips together.

From the look of Reece's tight jaw, it was a good thing Kati didn't understand Spanish. No one said anything for a moment.

Kati tried a light voice. "Hey, Maria. You two know each other?" Maria's glare at Luis said a lot. Kati forced a smile. "I know you're new, Maria, but these types of tête-à-têtes aren't allowed."

"These what?"

"One-on-ones."

"What about you?" Her chin lifted in Reece's direction.

Kati chuckled. "Reece and me? Oh, we're staff, and we're married."

Maria's look bounced from one to the other, then shifted to Luis. Her eyes narrowed. "Well, I just wanted to get reacquainted." She snorted. "But some people think they're better than others."

Luis's eyebrows pulled together. "*Mira, mamá, no empieces con tus cosa—*"

"Luis." Kati put a hand on his arm, then turned to Maria. The woman's angry expression almost put her off. "Maria, come with me. Let me introduce you to the girls you haven't met. And then let's hang out a little and get to know each other."

The woman's brow lifted. "Sure. Whatever." She threw a glare in Luis's direction and moved next to Kati.

They walked in quiet for a while. Kati struggled with what to say, wanting to move past the previous scene.

Maria cleared her throat. "So, Luis says he's got a woman. Is she in this program, too? In the dorms?"

Kati turned to look at her. Why had the question sent a strobe-like flash of warning through her?

Chapter 10

Be sober, be vigilant; because your adversary the devil walks about like a roaring lion, seeking whom he may devour.
1 Peter 5:8 NKJV

Chloe threw her scrubs in the washing machine, then stumbled into the kitchen, took her usual chair, and put her head in her hands. Between the gunshot wound, the auto accident, and the child's 105 temperature, she'd need some time to wind down this morning. She stared at the clock: 7:45. The last twelve hours had strained every technique and bit of knowledge the ER team had.

But she smiled as she passed Publix on the way home. No stopping there ever again. Warmth spread through her. Had she read too much into Patriot's appearance at the hospital the other night, too much into his kisses? On one hand, how much did she want to believe she hadn't? On the other, she wondered if it could ever work.

She'd thought it could work with Alex.

But Patriot was different. Stronger physically, outwardly focused, with a desire to help others. Alex had often left her with the feeling that she needed to pull him up by— well, not his bootstraps, because he never wore boots—but by his toes and keep him going. Only she hadn't been able to do that.

And Patriot... Her stomach felt sick. Could she live through that again? Although Patriot's case had been extreme. Besides, he was headed back to Colorado when this was all over. She just needed to wrap those emotions in a tight ball, get hold of herself, and forget his kisses...

Yeah, forget. Like that was going to happen.

Chloe swallowed and pushed up from the table. *Get your mind back on breakfast and then sleep.* Sleep had been next to zero the last couple of days, and she needed it. A smoothie would help. Bananas, strawberries, blueberries. She pulled them from the refrigerator, along with almond milk and vanilla extract. Oh yeah.

She caught sight of her phone shimmying, snatched it from the table, and slid her finger across the text notification.

It's Patriot. When's a good time to call?

Her heart flipped. Really? She pulled in her breath. He'd said he wouldn't call. It was better that way, and three days later…

She texted a return message: Now is good. Or anytime later today or tomorrow.

Her heart sank a little at the *tomorrow* entry. She'd never get to sleep if he didn't call. *Call now. Call now.*

She waited a minute longer, then grabbed the fruit and almond milk and began fixing her smoothie, flipping a glance at the phone every few seconds. Before she started the blender, she sat and stared at her phone.

Nothing.

Awww.

She rose and turned on the blender, glanced over. Was the phone moving? Vibrating? She flipped the blender off.

"Hello? Hello?"

"Hey."

His voice warmed her, and every insecurity vanished.

"Hi."

They were both silent for a moment, then he chuckled. "You just get in from work?"

"Yes."

"Having donuts this morning?"

"What?" She huffed. "I'll have you know I'm doing my usual smoothie."

"Healthy? I'm impressed."

She giggled "I'm a healthy eater. No matter what it

looks like."

"If you say so. Listen, I need to let you know about GreasePaint."

She stood. "Why? What's wrong? Is he okay?"

"He's jake. Sorry. I mean he's fine. He's joining the program at church. Just got approved. It took a little longer than usual to okay him, but they're letting him in provisionally. He's not a believer but has agreed to all the rules and stipulations."

"That's good, isn't it?"

"I think. If he's really finished with the gang. He and his dad are not getting on, so he needs a family to feel part of right now. And structure. But I want you to be careful when you see him."

"Why? He seemed nice."

"Nice, huh? You interested? He thinks you might be."

"Interested? In him? That's crazy. He's a kid, anyway."

"The kid can still be dangerous. And don't let on that we...that you know where I am or who I am. As far as he knows, you saw me that day when we pulled him from the pond and no more. He doesn't know I'm living here, although some of the other residents have probably figured it out."

"But he's your friend."

"For now."

Chloe could feel the frown between her eyes. This was not the conversation she'd expected. She sighed. "All right."

"Chloe?"

"Yes?"

"It's good to hear your voice."

She closed her eyes, the circling warmth started inside again. "And I'm glad you called, even if..."

"Even if it's business?"

"Yes."

"I wanted an excuse to call. I'm glad I had one."

She smiled at that. She was glad too.

"But I need to go."

She groaned, and he laughed. "Eat a donut for me."

"I don't do donuts—"

Laughter sounded again even as the phone clicked off.

"—all the time."

***

Patriot placed his phone on the table and stood with his head bent. The smile on his face faded. He'd kept the conversation short for both their sakes. He'd already fought his desire to see her.

He faced the window.

Three years hiding. Three years of guilt and cowardice. Sure, being a firefighter took courage, and he loved the job— more than he'd thought he would—but he'd still hidden out in Denver. Never let anyone close. Or family know where he was. And family meant a lot to him.

Chloe meant a lot. Suddenly, deeply.

He stared out the window, chewing on that thought. Something clicked inside him. He had a reason to move forward. God had given him a reason.

In Denver, it had felt like riding a tilt-a-whirl, spinning round and going nowhere. Because that was not who he was. Running, hiding. That was not who God made him to be. What had Chloe said? He'd forgotten who he was in Christ.

Yes.

He had.

Outside, men and women made their way across the campus. Campus? Where had that description come from? Well, it was partly right. The church grounds encompassed the dorms and classrooms. Being on the second story gave him a good view of the surrounding area.

He watched a woman walk toward the jogging trail. Definite curves, definite swagger, and lots of dark, curly hair. His eyes narrowed as the woman looked around, then suddenly sprinted past the clump of trees toward the street beyond. He managed to catch a glimpse of her red shirt before she disappeared behind more trees farther away.

What was that about? Should he tell Reece someone had escaped? He chuckled. Probably what it felt like to some of them. But they could walk free at any time. Nothing to keep them here but their word. Well, no. A few had come from court, where a judge had given them a choice between this place or jail. And those were the ones he worried about, the ones Reece worried about. But they were a minimum. Like GreasePaint. No, he had to get used to thinking of him as Gary Lovett. Most of their residents, though, came because they'd had an experience with Christ, because they wanted to turn their lives around.

He straightened and moved back into the room.

All right, Lord. It's time to stop hiding. If we're going to draw j-beck out, I need to get out there.

He walked to the bureau, opened the drawer, and pulled out the SIG Sauer and his shoulder holster. As he headed down the stairs, he called the Sheriff's Office. He and Reece had come up with a plan, but now it needed to be put into operation—if the Captain gave his okay. They had to decide the best way to leak the information to j-beck and then let him think the whole idea was his—because no way would the gangsta show himself unless he thought the idea was his.

***

Chloe stood on the church steps in the darkness. The Wednesday evening service would end soon, and she'd slipped out just in case… Daft might be a good description of herself if she expected Patriot to be out here. Just because he was before…

Okay, maybe barmy would be a better word, because if she could ever step into this caldron again, she didn't know when. The relationship with Alex had looked like it was going

128

someplace—until he'd committed suicide.

She'd wanted to die, too, after Alex.

But she'd found God instead.

She bit her lip. And Patriot had tried to end his life. But Patriot had known God when he'd tried to kill himself. Her shoulders slumped. How could that happen?

She sighed. She knew. *Satan comes to kill and steal and to destroy.* Of course, the Bible used the word "thief," but Chloe was not ignorant of the Enemy's devices. She'd studied the Word of God, been in Bible class and in the prayer group for too long. She was under no illusions. The Christian life was not an easy life. Satan fought against them. And he had attacked Patriot multiple times.

But he hadn't won. God had.

She smiled, stepped farther into the dark, and leaned against the building.

A car turned off the road, dousing the headlights, and drove slowly through the parking lot.

Strange. A parent early to pick up their kids? Well, the portable building didn't have a light on it, but someone would turn on the floodlights when the service ended.

The car stopped, and the light from the pole lamps caught a package flying from the window, like someone throwing a shot-put. Then tires screeched, and the car tore off.

Chloe's gut tightened. What was that? The package looked slightly larger than a bowling ball. She started to walk down the steps but stopped. *Wait, Chloe. Think.*

A second later, the package burst into flames. Her hand went to her mouth. No. Not again. She turned and ran into the building.

"Reece!" The whispered urgency conveyed itself to several parishioners. They looked her way. Reece walked over.

"There's a fire outside."

His brows shot up, and a couple of people rose from their chairs.

"No, no. Smaller. Not the building this time."

Reece strode to the door and out. Chloe followed, with others behind her.

The fire had already engulfed the package and looked like a bonfire now. Someone mentioned getting a hose. Reece waved everybody back just as Patriot trotted around the corner of the building.

"Reece, what—"

"Wait." Reece stopped the man with the hose. "Let it burn out. Don't mess with anything. Chloe, what happened?"

She pulled her gaze from Patriot's and looked at Reece. "A man, well, a person, pulled in from the street and tossed something out of his car, and it burst into flames."

"You saw it?'

"Yes. I was on the stairs."

Reece turned. "Patriot, where were you?"

"Jogging path."

Reece nodded. "You put up those cameras we talked about?"

"Sure did."

"Good. Let's get them down and call the police."

***

Lynn heard Rich moving around, and she rolled over in the bed. Was it morning already? "What time is it?" Groggy. Surely it was too early for him to be going to work.

"Eight."

"Really?" She tried to clear her head. Wow. She was usually up by this time, fixing him breakfast if she had nowhere to go or a late wedding appointment. Weddings took so much planning.

He leaned down and kissed her head. She turned toward him and tried to smile. He laughed. "Stay in bed. You look like you need it."

"You're in a good mood."

130

"Got a call from the office. Something I think I've been waiting for."

She tried to focus. Her husband could claim hunk status anytime, and she liked looking at him shaved and dressed. "Oh? That's good."

"Yes, it is. Stay in bed. I'll see you tonight."

"Okay." She rolled over, pulled the covers higher and closed her eyes.

***

The sound of sirens was instant and loud. Kati threw a glance at Reece and then another out the window. Flashing lights flew past. Three cruisers. Reece jumped from the desk even as Kati whipped out of his office and raced past China.

"Kati, you and China stay here until we know what's going on."

But Kati had her hand on the doorknob. She threw it open then stepped aside to let Reece go first and followed him. He glared at her but said no more.

The three cruisers tailing Rich's Porsche fishtailed into the dorm's parking lot.

Reece stopped her with a hand.

She grabbed it. "What's going on?"

"An arrest, maybe. Stay here."

She nodded.

Rich and his partner jumped from his Porsche and strode toward the dorms. Three deputies leapt from their cruisers, guns drawn. One whirled their way and motioned for them to stop.

Kati's heart did an erratic flip. What were they doing here? Why hadn't the Sheriff's Office called? Many men and women in the dorms had a rough relationship with law enforcement. Their anxiety levels would soar like a solid hit on the High Striker game at the carnival.

Rich pounded on Luis's door. "Sheriff's Office! Open

up! Sheriff's Office!"

Residents came to their windows. Doors flew open. The deputies gestured for the others to stay where they were. Women from the dorms rushed outside. Gary Lovett stood in his doorway.

The door Rich had pounded on opened. Luis stood in jeans and a T-shirt. He stared at Rich, and then his eyes slid past him to the deputies with their guns drawn.

"Luis Ramirez, you're under arrest for the murder of Marcos Suarez."

The jerk of surprise that shot through Kati mirrored itself in Luis's face. The female detective stepped next to Rich, and Rich grabbed Luis's arm and turned him around. He pulled handcuffs from his jacket pocket and put them on.

Prayers tumbled from Kati's mouth, unprompted, under her breath.

The other detective was talking at Luis even as Rich turned him around and led him forward. Luis's face had slackened, but he said something to Rich. The detective merely shook his head.

The others in the dorms stared. Kati's heart clenched. *Father, we need You.*

Reece dropped her hand. Heat burned off him.

Kati knew the feeling. "Why didn't he call us? Let Luis surrender? Or have him come to the office and arrest him there? Not this public display of force."

Reece said nothing. Everyone watched as Rich led Luis to the cruiser.

Luis's gaze met theirs, his eyes questioning. Reece shook his head. Raw emotions cut across Kati's heart. She prayed that Luis had really surrendered to Christ, prayed that God would give him miraculous peace during all this. He'd been so careful with the meeting with Maria. He did not want to go back to prison.

Reece stepped forward.

Rich held up a hand. "Stay out of this, Reece."

"You know I can't. Can I talk to him?"

"At the jail, after he's booked."

"I'll be there. With a lawyer."

God, surround Luis now. Lead and guide him. Keep him safe. Kati glanced up at Reece. *And keep my husband, too. Don't let him flatten Rich.*

She ground her teeth. She'd like to do it herself.

The sheriff's cruisers left, one with Luis inside. Rich and his partner headed to Rich's car.

Reece stepped in front of them, his jaw tight. "You had to do it this way?"

"What way would you have wanted? I don't owe him anything. You and this whole church act as if he's something special. He's a murderer."

"He's a new creature in Christ."

"Maybe he is. Maybe he isn't. Doesn't mean he gets a free ride for his crimes."

"What do you think this will do to Becca? To you and Lynn and Becca?"

"Lynn understands. She stands behind me. Becca..." His voice hesitated. "Becca will be glad to know what he is...at some point..."

"She, unlike you, already knows *whose* he is."

Rich walked past him to the car.

Reece followed. "When we talked about this before, you said you had no proof. Now you have?"

Rich turned to look at him. His gaze traveled to the women near the dorms. "Let's say an eyewitness came forward." He turned and slid into the Porsche, and they pulled away.

Kati did a slow turn. The men and women from the dorms still stood outside, but her eyes moved to Maria. The woman ducked her head, whirled, and made a beeline for her room.

Chapter 11

Wherefore take unto you the whole armor of God, that ye may be able to withstand in the evil day, and having done all, to stand.
Ephesians 6:13

"Miss Eleanor?"

Pastor Alan's voice echoed the knocking sound. She opened her eyes. The dream disappeared. Nothing to worry about. If God wanted to show her something, he'd give it to her again or show her another way. In the meantime...

"Miss Eleanor?"

She pushed herself up from the recliner as the knocking repeated. "Alan?"

"Yes."

She made it to her front door. Afternoon sunlight lay on the wooden floor, having penetrated the door's beveled glass. The pastor had only come to her house unannounced three times before. Once to check on her because she hadn't answered her phone after repeated calls, and two other times for emergency prayer needs. The man's wife, Daneen, had undergone a mastectomy a few months ago and was still dealing with chemo.

Miss Eleanor unlocked the door and opened it. "Are you okay? Is Daneen?"

He stepped in as she moved backwards. "Daneen's fine." But the lines between his brows deepened.

Sleep vanished completely.

"Have a seat." She waved at the old, comfortable couch and returned to the recliner. She sat erect on the edge of the seat. "What is it?"

"I need a prayer partner. Luis has been arrested—for murder."

The words hit hard. *No.* He was their poster boy, of course. Wrong of them, but to have him come "home" to the church after three years in prison, to have him so obviously changed...

"This...this can't be recent."

Alan shook his head. "No. Reece tells me it's for the murder of the man that headed up the gang when Luis joined them. We're going back some six or seven years. Reece says Luis told him it was self-defense."

Miss Eleanor's shoulders relaxed. It wasn't good, but it was defendable—if it was true, and she hoped it was. "Okay."

"Rich came to the dorms with three other deputies, pulled up with sirens blaring to arrest him."

"Oh no. He couldn't have done that differently?"

"I don't think he wanted to."

"Did he think how that would affect the others? The ones that have come from prison and are trying to go straight? To have a 'friend' from church blow in there and arrest one of them? They're not much for law enforcement, anyway."

Alan's slight grin was the only light she'd seen from him so far. "Understatement."

"What else?"

"I tried to call you. Sorry if I woke you."

"Afternoon nap. No problem. What else?"

"Becca. While I was calling you, I heard Kati calling Becca."

Miss Eleanor leaned in. "Oh my. Oh my. That is going to create..."

"A huge problem in that family."

"And Luis?"

"Reece is at the jail, talking with him, I hope. This will be hard on his faith."

"We need prayer."

"Yes."

"Bow your head."

He grinned as he obeyed, and she shook her head. *Sorry, Lord. I don't mean to take over...* And yet. The need and drive in her was immediate. Right now, shooting through her, energizing her. The Holy Spirit setting a fire in her that she'd felt so many times before. When He came like that, she couldn't do anything but give in.

"Dear Father, we come to You once more. In Jesus's name. The name that is above every name, the name that has power over all the power of the Enemy. We come to You and praise You for Who You are, knowing that nothing is too hard for you. Your Word says that when the Enemy comes in like a flood, You will raise a standard against him. Jesus is the standard, but You also use us. For whatever reason, You have chosen to allow us to enter the battle, to stand in the gap, so, Father, we do. We stand in the gap together, Alan and I—and others I feel sure—between the forces of evil and your people. Direct us, direct our prayers, and send the angels we need to fight the battle before us."

***

Kati wanted to growl. Dennis had come by after work to talk with Alan, and he'd given her a quick nod, almost one of dismissal. Too bad *stubborn* was her personality description. She wasn't leaving unless Alan asked. The man had a sick wife at home, and he'd been here too long today, with Luis in jail. So many people calling. He didn't need an unscheduled meeting.

Dennis took a seat across the desk from the pastor and glanced Kati's way. "I hope you have a few minutes, Alan."

"I do, but if this has to do with the new building, I'd like Kati to stay."

Dennis lifted a brow but turned to Kati and smiled. "Of

136

course."

Kati slipped into the other empty chair, glad she hadn't left with Reece. He'd gone to play basketball with some of the dorm's residents. Most needed an outlet after today.

She and Reece had stayed late, anyway. Maria had disappeared after Luis's arrest but before anyone could talk with her. Reece had gone over her application and entry forms and wondered what they'd missed when allowing her into the program. Still, he'd told Kati to withhold judgment. Rich had not confirmed that Maria was his witness.

Kati shoved those thoughts away and turned toward Dennis. *Give the man a chance, girl. Alan says he means well.*

Dennis leaned forward, his chin jutting. "Alan, I just want you to think more about what we've said."

The man's voice carried its usual persuasive tone. Kati watched Alan's tired face. She knew how much sway that tone had whenever she'd attended the board meetings with Reece—because usually she and Reece and a few of the others made up one side, while Dennis and his team made up the other.

Politics.

In the church.

She pressed her lips together. No wonder Reece found meetings so…impossible. She'd rather be kickboxing or doing anything besides just listening…

I didn't call you to just listen.

She straightened, glanced at Pastor Alan. His focus hadn't drifted from Dennis, and Dennis was pressing his point.

"Have you thought how much this community needs a big church? Your influence would be that much wider, too. We can double the numbers with the right building, the right promotions."

Kati bit her tongue. Why didn't they just present their sides to the church and let the congregation vote? Kati had made that presentation before, but the idea was tabled in committee. Not that committees were all bad. You needed them, but did there need to be so much hassle? It seemed like most folks left their Christianity at the committee room door.

Pastor Alan stretched back in his chair. "I'm not opposed to a big church. You know that. But I'm not wanting to change the ministry we have here. It seems to me that you, Roger, and a few others are wanting an uptown church. Our residents aren't going to feel comfortable with that."

Dennis leaned forward, sharp chin tight. "That is the beauty of this whole idea. Separating the ministry to these ex-gang members and ex-cons from the real church. We'll build more dorms and another church across town. We can do that ministry there. In fact, someone suggested Reece head that up. He's an ex-gang member. He understands these others. Then you could hire an assistant pastor for the church here." He whipped around to Kati. "Reece would go for that, wouldn't he, Kati? He never really wanted to be assistant pastor, right?"

Uh-oh. She wouldn't step into that one. "I'd have to let Reece answer for himself."

"Well, think about it, Alan. You can have a big church and this ministry to gangs. It would work perfectly."

I didn't call you to just listen.

Kati straightened again. What was she doing here? What was she supposed to be doing?

Pastor Alan steepled his hands. "Dennis, in all the meetings we've had over the last few years, you've never expressed opposition to what we were doing ministry-wise."

Kati prayed silently. *Lord, Thy will be done. Thy Kingdom come. We don't want man's plans, but Yours. How can this man talk about the* real *church as if the men and women here that have accepted Christ and are trying to turn their lives around are not as good as he is? The Pharisees didn't want Jesus to eat with Zacchaeus either and didn't like that Mary washed Jesus's feet with her hair. You love people, Lord, no matter where they come from. Let him see that.*

She sighed and lifted her head. Pastor Alan's eye met hers, and he smiled.

"I'm not against it," Dennis said. "It's just that this has

been my church for ten years, and I don't know half the people here anymore. And to tell you the truth, I don't want to know them. I want my church back." Dennis stood.

Pastor Alan closed his eyes for a moment, then opened them again. "Sit down, Dennis. Let's talk."

"There's nothing to talk about. Look what happened today. You have a man arrested for murder. *Murder.* Right here at the church. It's all over the news. I had people calling me from North Carolina and Texas telling me about it. You know how that felt?" His hand swiped through the air. "You need money to rebuild. Roger and I and a few others are willing to work together to make that happen, but within certain guidelines. And those are to separate the church from the ministry. We don't really care how you do it. Just do it."

Kati continued to pray. *Thy will be done...*

Pastor Alan stood, too. "Dennis, I'm sorry you feel this way. I never knew. I wish you'd said something earlier."

"It doesn't matter." He waved a hand in dismissal. "No one thought it would take off like this. Most of us thought that after the initial, you know, how people get excited about something new...we just thought it would blow over."

"Who is *we?*"

"Not important. Roger and I and a few others."

"And yet you've both donated heavily to the IronWorks ministry."

"Of course." He stepped toward the door. "But that's what we want to make clear. That kind of money won't be coming your way if we can't separate these ministries. And let the government get involved. That's what they do. Support this kind of stuff. Let us give our money to build a church we can be proud of. Not one where half the congregation are ex-cons or people from the streets."

Kati raised her head. She could still feel the oil of the Spirit as it poured over her. She swallowed, not wanting to break that and not being able to stay quiet either. "That would be my husband you're talking about."

Dennis had swung toward the office door. "Ah, Kati, you know I don't mean Reece. We know he's changed. It's these others we're not sure about."

"But he was on the streets with Joshua for three years. Discipled for three years. In direct ministry. Like the disciples were with Jesus. Three years. These men and women deserve the same. For us to invest our time and effort and love in them for a certain amount of time so they can learn a different lifestyle, so they can learn that God is faithful."

"I'm not arguing with that, Kati. I just want them to do it somewhere else."

***

Patriot sat at a table in the bar, back to the wall. Good position to watch anyone that entered. He wasn't in the Gordones' territory, but close enough they'd hear of it. One man had eased out the door not long after Patriot had entered. On his way to let them know, Patriot guessed.

He took time to order a drink that now sat in front of him untouched. The lead bartender edged over to his phone and made a call, and Patriot was busy calculating if his need for a contact here might cost him more than he planned.

A few minutes later, a young woman stepped through the door. Her eyes trailed over each patron. She strolled toward the bar, then turned and sidled up to his table, head cocked, come-hither smile on her face, and wearing a dress tight enough to display all her assets in case he was interested. He wasn't.

Lord, please move her on.

He made the appeal to the One who had kept him in other situations. Occasionally while undercover with the gang, he hadn't made the appeal. Later, he always wished he had. Three years later, the regret still surfaced.

"Buy a girl a drink?"

"Sorry. I'm waiting for someone."

140

"I guess they're late, huh?"

"They'll be here."

"But you could use company till then?"

He narrowed his eyes. "No."

She slid into the chair across from him, holding the smile, and Patriot straightened. Was she what she appeared or a diversion? Someone to keep his eyes away from coming trouble? He volleyed that ball a moment, then stood, pulling bills from his pocket.

"Here. You'll have to get your own drink." He started to walk away, but she leaned her head back.

"A kiss for Sammy."

He stopped, his gaze meeting hers. A glance around the room landed on the lead bartender setting up a glass. The man gave a slight nod and turned away. Patriot leaned down and kissed her. She did it well, seeming interested but not touching him. He pulled back.

Her hand grabbed his. "Sure you got to leave?"

He let a regretful smile appear. "Yeah. Another time."

She shrugged, dropped his hand, and grabbed the money he'd left. "Your loss."

The kind of loss he'd take any day, thank you.

When he climbed into the truck, he stuck the folded paper she'd slipped into his hand into the ashtray, wiped his mouth, and wheeled onto the road.

***

Rich pushed open the door of the church offices and stopped.

Luis stood just inside, reaching for the door also. Heat went through Rich. He'd heard the man had made bail already. His jaw tightened. Even the judges in this town gave Luis preferential treatment. A murderer—out on bail.

Luis said nothing, although Rich didn't miss the tightening of the man's fists before they relaxed. They stared at each other.

"Out already?" Rich forced the words. All he wanted to do was put a fist through the man's face.

Luis nodded.

To his left, Rich's peripheral vision caught Reece coming to his office doorway. No surprise there. One gang member to another. But his conscience hit him. No, Reece would do what was right whenever he could.

He forced his attention back to Luis. "Pleading not guilty won't help you."

A movement from the other office told Rich Pastor Alan had come to his doorway, too.

Luis stepped back, his eyes never leaving Rich's.

The reason Rich had come—added information on last Wednesday's fire—dropped as he faced Luis. "Well? Where's the gloating? You were always good with it."

"I was, Detective."

Rich snorted and shook his head. He started to pass Luis and head to Reece's office, but Luis stepped in front of him. Rich stopped, straightened. If something else was coming, he'd welcome it.

"I was, Detective. Very arrogant. You know. You remember. Jail does something to a man." A slight smile flitted across his face. "You know that. You wanted me to go there. You know what else changes you? Jesus changes you."

Rich made a sound in his throat. Like he was going to buy that. Everyone else had. Not him. "Jesus changes people, I agree with that, but my problem is with you."

Luis's eyes narrowed for a moment. "*¿No me crees?*" He swung his arm toward Reece, then Pastor Alan. "And yet you have these men of God to vouch for the reality of God's life in me."

"You've fooled a lot of people."

"But not you, huh?"

"Not me."

Luis's mouth worked. "I can't say much to change that,

but it is true that Jesus has changed me. I plead guilty."

Rich drew his head back. "What are you talking about?"

"Your statement, Detective. Yes, I am out on bail, but I pled guilty." His head swung Reece's way. "Your brother will tell you."

Rich's gaze pivoted to Reece. He could see the man's anger. Reece was not happy with this whole conversation, but he nodded at Rich.

"You heard him."

Rich couldn't contain the emotion. It had raged inside too long. *"You admit it?"* His voice shot up two decimals.

At Luis's nod, volcanic anger blew apart the relief that the truth had come out. He slammed his fist into Luis's jaw.

Chapter 12

Though I walk in the midst of trouble, You will revive me;
You will stretch out Your hand Against the wrath of my
enemies, And Your right hand will save me.
Psalm 138:7 NKJV

Luis fell back, stumbling against the receptionist's desk. Alan shouted.

Reece grabbed Rich from behind and dragged him away. "Get hold of yourself."

Swirling blackness surged in front of Rich, and Reece's voice was a growl in his ear. His ears rang. Rich blinked to clear his eyes. Alan stood in front of him, and Luis half lay against the edge of a desk, holding his jaw, eyes smoldering.

Rich caught Reece's arm. "All right. Let go."

The beefy arm tightened a moment. "You're sane?"

"I'm okay."

The arm loosened.

Pastor Alan stepped forward, blocking his view of Luis. "We're not used to seeing you like this. Something going on we don't know about? Something personal between you and Luis?"

Rich pulled free of Reece's hold. What had happened? He'd wanted to pummel Luis for a long time, but as a law enforcement officer, he'd put that aside. Or so he'd thought. What had just happened?

"Rich." Alan's voice was insistent.

"He admits it. He killed my brother-in-law."

Everything in the office stopped. No one moved, then

Luis stepped around Pastor Alan.

"Your brother-in-law? *Qué*?"

"You heard. My brother-in-law. He left my sister, and she divorced him after he got involved in the gang, but he and I stayed close—as close as could be under the circumstances. I had to arrest him once, but then he disappeared." Rich's focus narrowed on Luis. "And you took over as *capitán.*"

Reece turned toward Rich. "You need to listen to him."

"Like everyone else has? And be deceived?"

"He admits to killing Marcos but hear him out."

Rich crossed his arms. Luis rubbed his jaw again. "Go ahead. What are you going to say? That it was self-defense?"

Luis nodded, and Rich shook his head.

"Your brother-in-law, Detective, was a nasty hombre. He liked to beat up his women." Rich snorted, but Luis continued. "I showed some interest in one *chica bonita*, and he took her, but he treated her worse than the others. He beat her bad one day in front of me. I was hacked off. He knew it. Laughed. But then I let my mouth go, and he is on me so fast. We're fighting, and the whole gang is watching and shouting. But he has a gun, and when he gets me down, he pulls it and shoots me. Only the gun doesn't go off. He can't believe it, and he looks at it and then he points it at me again, but now I have my knife out, and I shove it into his chest." Luis stopped a moment, looks at all three men. "He pulls the trigger anyway. It goes off, but his aim is bad because of my knife. You understand? He tries to kill me, but instead I kill him."

Rich stared at him. "Not the story we have from an eyewitness."

"Your eyewitness lies. Others were there. They will tell the truth."

"We'll see." Luis's words echoed in Rich's head, but waves of blackness pulsated through him. He needed to get out of here, needed to get someplace where he could think straight. Rich turned toward the door.

"Detective."

Rich threw a look over his shoulder. "Ask your sister."

***

Chloe stepped from her car before the church office still wondering why Reece had asked her to stop here on the way to work. She glanced around. Patriot had mentioned doing night patrols at the church. Wouldn't it be nice...

She shook her head. 6:00 PM. It wasn't even dark. Daylight savings time was in play. And she'd seen Patriot just five days ago during that excitement with the firebomb at Wednesday night's service. Right. Could she even count that one minute before Reece dragged him off?

As she opened the outer office door, a mumble of voices from Reece's office met her, but the door was closed. Odd. She knocked and heard Reece's, "Come in."

When she opened the door, Patriot swung his head her way. She stopped. He was sitting in front of Reece's desk, one ankle crossed over a knee, dressed in jeans and t-shirt and, wow, did he look good.

She didn't realize the surprise and grin in her heart had spread across her face until a movement from Reece brought her focus his way. His eyes reflected his amusement.

He pointed to the chair next to Patriot. "Have a seat."

Patriot winked and turned back to Reece.

What was he doing here?

What was she?

Chloe dropped into the other chair and smoothed the top of her scrubs down. Did she have to be in scrubs again? Hadn't he seen her in scrubs enough?

Reece leaned back in his chair. "I could have called, but I thought some face-to-face might help us."

Chloe tried to keep the blush from climbing into her cheeks. Was she so obvious? Had he done this for her? She snuck a sideways look at Patriot. Had Patriot asked for her to come?

Reece crossed one arm over the other. Tattoos on both arms bulged as he did. "The Sheriff's Department looked at our video from that Wednesday night service, but could not get a good view of the subject's face. He seemed to be wearing the same clown hair as the man Patriot chased the other time. And his face was pale, although they couldn't make out any features. One tech suggested the subject might be wearing make-up. We do know the make of the car was the same, although again, we couldn't get the license plate. Chloe, is there anything else you remember from that night?"

She stared at Reece a moment. Okay, girl, concentrate. "Besides what I told the deputy?"

"Yes, sometimes a few days after an event images surface that you didn't remember before."

Chloe nodded. "I did think about what you just said. Clown hair. Fuzzy hair. That's all I could see, the hair against the lights in the parking lot. My attention was on what he was throwing out the window."

Patriot leaned toward her. "What did it look like before it caught fire?"

"A package. Like a brown paper bag wrapped around something."

He put a hand on her knee. "What something?"

Could she concentrate with the heat his touch generated? "I...uh...Something long." She held up her hands. "About ten or twelve inches long. Four to six inches across? I'm just guessing. It's an impression. It was so fast."

Patriot removed his hand, sat back. "But it hit the ground and exploded?"

"Well, it burst into flames. I said explosion then, but there was no noise, no boom."

Patriot glanced at Reece. "So, something that just caught fire. He could have lit it right before he entered the parking lot. Put something fire retardant on the passenger seat so any sparks don't singe the seat. Then he tosses it out the window, and the bag catches fire sending up flames. Did they get the info back from the fire department yet?"

"No. You know the timing on stuff like that. It takes weeks. That's why I wanted to talk with Chloe again. You stopped this guy the last time, and Chloe caught him this time. I'm thinking he'll try something different next."

"Which means we'll need to be on our guard."

Reece nodded. "But do we think this is the same person that used so much accelerant burning down the church?"

Chloe looked between the two men. "You think this is two different people or groups?"

"MO's are different, but let's don't jump to conclusions yet."

"But who else would have a feud against the church?" Chloe couldn't see it.

Reece glanced at his watch. "Let me call Kati before she leaves for work." Chloe started to stand, her eyes darting to Patriot. But Reece waved them both back down. "Stay here. I'll take Alan's office. He's gone home."

Quiet settled as Reece walked out and the door closed behind him.

Patriot looked her way. "We did need to see if you remembered anything else, and I thought this would be good to have you drop by so we could talk, but no one's fooling Reece."

Chloe glanced at the closed door and back. "You think he left us alone on purpose?"

"Pretty sure he did."

She lifted a brow. "Really?"

Patriot laughed, stood, and drew her to her feet. Her arms slipped around him, and his head lowered. She could lose herself in his kiss. Or forget the fire and everything that had gone on since, everything except him and the gentle pressure of his mouth....

The door opened. "Well, well." A voice interrupted.

Patriot drew free of her hold, and Chloe spun to see

Dennis in the doorway, his brows drawn close together.

He glared at Patriot. "You're one of the men from the dorms, aren't you?"

Patriot said nothing. Dennis's glare turned into a scowl, and he turned on Chloe. "What are you doing here? With him?"

Chloe bristled. "What do you mean *with him*? And what business is it of yours? What are you doing here?"

"I came to see Reece." His gaze flew back and forth between them. "But that can wait." He made an abrupt turn and left. The outside office door shut forcefully.

Chloe's hand sought Patriot's. "What was that about?"

"You didn't catch the meaning?"

"Well, maybe I did, but I didn't like it."

"Neither did I. For a moment. He thought I was one of the men from the dorms, and he didn't like seeing you with me." He enclosed her hand in his and drew her close again. "But in one way he's right. Most of the men and women here are regenerated—they're new creatures in Christ, but the scriptures tell us we are all being renewed day by day. No one is perfect. They're subject to falling, like we are. It pays to be careful."

"But…"

"I'm not saying don't have compassion, don't love as God tells us to do. That is what we're about as Christians. I am saying have wisdom, use caution as you step forward with people. Have their backs but let someone else have yours." He smiled and slipped his hand to the side of her face. "But…enough talk."

***

Rich shook his head. The blackness fractured as he drove away from the church. *Was he sane*, Reece had asked him, and for a moment he hadn't been. For a moment, he wasn't himself.

Jesus, what happened?

He stopped at a diner, ordered coffee, retired into a corner, and prayed. The tightness in his head eased and the darkness cleared.

Rich blew out a breath.

He'd hit Luis, and if the man wanted, he could press charges. Well, he'd know if Luis did if deputies showed at his house. But first...

His sister?

What was that supposed to mean? What could Tammy know? He and his sister were close. If she knew anything, she would have told him a long time ago. And she'd never said anything.

He'd inherited the Porsche from his grandmother, and it was practically the only thing he and Tammy had ever fought over. She had wanted it just as much as he had, but his grandmother had left it to him and left Tammy an equivalent amount of money to make up for it. He'd leave it to his nephew if the car made it that long.

He left the diner and headed her way. As he approached the front door, it swung wide. His nephew squealed and threw his arms at Rich. Rich swung him up and around and remembered Luis playing with Manuel. He shoved the memory away. It didn't matter. But something inside him felt sick.

Rich shook his head. Too many things these days.

Maybe Tammy would ask him for dinner, and he'd have a few minutes to play with Jaron. He set the boy down. If so, he'd better call Lynn. Tammy waved him in.

When he finally sent his nephew to play in his room, Rich stood at the counter, watching Tammy throw a salad into a bowl to go with the rotisserie chicken. Whole-wheat rolls sat on the counter, ready for the oven. She had no problem including him and had asked about Lynn, but a text to his wife had brought a *no, but thank you* reply. She wasn't feeling well, so she was glad he could eat there.

He leaned forward. "Tell me about Marcos."

She glanced from the salad to him. "Marcos?"

No wonder she was surprised. They'd been divorced two years before Marcos disappeared, and that was five years ago.

"Do you know anything about his death?"

Her hands stopped. "What would I know?"

He watched her, feeling as if he was interrogating a subject.

She set a tomato on the counter and straightened her back. "You're giving me that cop look. What's going on?"

"Luis told me to ask you about Marcos's death."

"What? The man you think murdered him?"

"The man who admits to killing him."

Her eyes widened. "He admits it? After all this time?" She stopped, frowned. "Marcos is dead. For sure?"

"It's what I've told you all along."

"I know. I...there's always..."

"Yeah. But it's been too long."

"And now Luis has admitted it." She stared at the floor. "Not sure how I feel. How should I feel? He was my husband." She lifted her gaze. "This is what you wanted, isn't it? To know. You should be dancing in the streets."

"Should be."

"What are you talking about? You've wanted this for years." She threw a look over her shoulder. "After Marcos left us, you swore you'd pull him in for something, but you weren't able to. Couldn't get anything to stick, anyway. And then he disappeared. We both said good riddance, but when you found out Luis took over the gang, you thought Luis killed him. Only no *body* ever turned up." She tilted her head. "I thought you'd be ecstatic. You could never prove Marcos was dead or that Luis murdered him, but now..."

"Do you know anything about how Marcos died?"

"I told you, no. If Luis says he killed him..."

"In self-defense."

She took a step back. "In self-defense?"

"Yeah. Why would he tell me to ask you?"

"I have no idea."

Past her shoulder, Rich caught a movement in the doorway. His nephew stood there. Seven years old now, he would understand some of what they were talking about. He must have heard the intensity of their voices and come down to check.

Tammy whipped around. "Jaron, go back to your bedroom awhile longer. I'll call you for dinner."

The boy's eyes shifted back and forth before he made a slow turn and disappeared down the hall.

"You know, I've never told him anything about his father except about the times you two were in high school together. I don't want him to know this. Not at this age."

Rich nodded. They were getting nowhere anyway. As he moved to get dishes from the cabinet, his mind flipped through the scene at the church and Luis's words. He set the dishes on the counter, turned to Tammy, and studied her again.

So many small remembrances tumbled across his mind. Ones he hadn't paid attention to back then. Pain shot across his chest, followed by anger. How had he not seen it? In his own family? He was a deputy then, making almost nightly domestic violence calls.

He gritted his teeth, pushing the words out. "Why didn't you tell me Marcos beat you?"

She'd picked up the tomato, and it slipped from her hand, bounced on the countertop, and hit the floor. Her face and stance, as well as the splattered tomato, witness to what he'd asked.

The fire inside him, so close to igniting these days, boiled higher. "He did, didn't he? That's what Luis wanted me to ask you about."

Her face reflected the indecision and, for a moment, fear. It startled him. She had no reason to fear him, and she knew it. He'd been there for her when their parents died, when

Marcos left her, when Jaron was born…

Unless it reminded her of Marcos. He'd witnessed the man's temper numerous times, especially after the doctors had diagnosed Marcos with high blood pressure and it had disqualified him from military service.

He banked his own emotions. "Tammy."

She put a hand out, almost to ward him off. Tears filled her eyes.

"Hey." Surprise shot through him. He stepped past the squashed tomato and pulled her to his chest. "Why didn't you tell me?"

"I couldn't."

"*Why?* I would have done something. You know that. "

She looked up and forced a smile. "I was afraid you'd kill him."

"I would have." He didn't have to think about it. That was his first reaction—although hopefully, he would have tempered it. Or God would have. He had a momentary flashback to the church and his fist connecting with Luis's jaw.

"Uh-huh." She gave his arm a squeeze and stepped back. "There was just you and me. I couldn't lose you, couldn't have you end up in jail. You know how you are. You grab hold of something and don't let go. That makes you a good cop but is scary in relationships. Marcos…I know at one time he was your best friend, but there was this side of him you didn't see. He was evil."

Rich walked to the kitchen window and stared out. "I should have known, should have seen." He'd been too busy with his own life, his job.

"No, that's crazy. Everyone that's abused knows they have to keep it secret."

Rich flinched at the word. Abused. He'd always wanted to protect her, and he hadn't. And he'd wanted to turn Marcos from the way he'd chosen, get him out of the gang, and he hadn't done that either. From the moment he'd realized Marcos was dead, the anger had started—against Luis, against

God. Talk about irony. If he'd known about the abuse, he'd have beat Marcos until he looked like the tomato on the floor—squashed.

Rich rubbed his fingers across his forehead, willing the pressure away. "I wondered why you seemed so stoic after Marcos left, why you never cried." Of course, they both knew by then how much Marcos had changed.

"I was happy he left. I wasn't sure why or where he'd gone, but I was deathly afraid he'd come back." She stopped, and Rich felt her eyes on him. "I didn't want him to come back."

And for so many years he'd been angry at God because Marco had left, because the divorce followed, because Jaron was without a father. Rich had tried to step in, be there for his nephew while all the time blaming God. He felt physically sick. If Marcos hadn't left...

Usually the cycle of abuse didn't end. Tammy and Jaron would both be living with it still.

He wanted to sit down, to put his head in his hands, wanted to throw up and then ask God to forgive him.

"Rich." Tammy's voice stabbed through the ache inside him. "You need to think about this. Luis's story might be true. If he said it was self-defense, maybe it was."

***

Rich stared through the windshield. Tammy's words washed through him like rain sheeting the car. Hitting and sliding. If Luis was telling the truth, then he—Rich—had believed the lie the woman had spun. Not that he hadn't realized she had an axe to grind. He could hear it in her words, but the story seemed plausible, and Rich had been looking for something, *anything*, for years.

What else had he been wrong about?

The car rounded the corner, and he saw the house lights and Lynn's Jeep in the driveway. Relief washed over him. She was home.

He needed to bounce this whole scenario off her. Anything he felt unsure of, he usually kept to himself. But in doing so, he knew he kept part of himself from her, too. He'd been angry at God because of his parents' death, Tammy's divorce, Marcos's death, and he didn't know how to rid himself of that.

But he needed someone with a level head. And that was Lynn. His perfectionism, her levelheadedness. He smiled. He'd married right, anyway.

He heaved a sigh as he wheeled into the driveway. He didn't want to present the cop persona he put on so often, but the other person—the one who just wanted to come home, grab his wife, and—he drew a deep breath—hopefully, one day a son or daughter. The man who wasn't perfect and the one who was tired of worrying if the next person he approached might put a gun in his face.

The one who might have made a huge mistake.

**

Pastor Alan's voice sounded soft after the staccato ringing of her phone. Kati struggled with the sheets and tried to sit up. Reece growled at her and turned over.

"Alan, what did you say?"

"I need you to call the prayer team, and I need you and Reece to pray, please."

Amazing how fast sleep could leave. "What's wrong?"

"I'm at the ER with Daneen. There's been a…problem. Maybe just a reaction to the last chemo, but she's in a bad way."

"Reece and I will pray right now, and I'll call Miss Eleanor—"

"Kati." The tone of his voice stopped her.

Next to her, Reece turned back her way. The light from the electrical gadgets in their bedroom reflected in his eyes.

She hesitated, then, "What?"

"I got a call from the hospital across town. Miss Eleanor's been admitted."

***

Rich pulled the Porsche into the dorm parking lot at the church. His watch showed almost 6:00 PM, and the residents were crossing to the fellowship hall for dinner. Some heads turned his way; no one waved.

He walked across the short lawn to Luis's door and knocked. The memory of the last time he'd pounded on the door swept him. He grimaced but straightened. He and the Lord had gone over this last night. He'd been sure for years that Luis had killed Marcos, and now he had a witness. It had driven him the other day. Not right, letting the emotions drive him. He'd tried never to be that cop—the one that lost control. But it had taken a long time in prayer to say he'd messed up. But when he did, the tightness around his head finally eased. Like some huge clamp releasing its grip.

Yes, he'd had an eyewitness. Yes, Luis admitted his part. But now Rich wanted truth.

The fact that his witness had disappeared, well, that was another reason he was here.

The door flew open, and Luis stared at him. Neither said anything.

After a moment, Rich cleared his throat. "How about a steak dinner instead of whatever they're serving over there?" He indicated the fellowship hall.

"Why would I do that?" Luis's eyes were hooded, suspicious.

"Because I'm ready to listen to your story."

Dark eyes searched Rich's face. "You talked with your sister?"

"Yes."

Luis studied him a moment longer, then glanced

toward the Porsche. "And your partner?"

"Is not here."

Again, the hesitation, the examination. Rich waited.

Finally, Luis's jaw gave a jerk of assent. "Then okay. I will let you buy me a steak."

***

Kati paced the cardiac waiting room and turned as Reece walked in with their dinner.

He set the bags down and handed her a water. "How is she?"

"They're going to move her to a room."

"Already?"

"You know how they do things these days, but they're going to keep her for a day or two because of her age."

"A heart attack. A stent. And they move her to a regular room within twenty-four hours?"

"Yeah." Kati looked at the subs that he drew from the bags and grimaced.

"You need to eat."

She slugged him playfully. "You mean you need to eat. Go ahead. I'm not sure I can."

"You've had nothing today."

"I know, but..." She flopped into a chair, glad the room was empty except for themselves. "Reece, what is happening? We're getting pounded again and again."

He stared down at the sandwich, then set it on the small table beside them. "You know why. We have an enemy. He's organized an all-out attack against us. Think of it—the church, the IronWorks ministry, the prayer warriors."

She stared at her hands. "But Miss Eleanor has always been on top of things. I mean, we have prayer every week."

"Yes. But we can't depend on one person to fight our battles. Now wait. I know you and the rest of the prayer team are fighting. And even many not on the prayer team. But look—first the church fire, then this idea of Dennis's, then Luis is arrested. That was another blow as big as the fire to some. We have residents who had a growing respect for law enforcement, mostly through Rich's relationship with them, now seeing him as untrustworthy. Then the prayer team's attacked. You can't tell me Miss Eleanor said something to you about stepping into her position if she hadn't felt the need, if the Holy Spirit hadn't prompted her. This heart attack? She might not have known it was coming, but God did." His eyes met hers.

Kati sighed. "She's ninety-two."

"Uh-huh. And think of the individuals, the families being hit. Becca is reeling as much as Luis, I'm sure."

"You believe him, don't you?"

"That it was self-defense. I do, but will a jury?"

"And Isabella and Manuel. Rich and Lynn leaving the church. And Dennis's family. I mean, even though the man irritates me, he's one of us."

"And those in the dorms. They're wondering what's happening. We're teaching them that God is on their side, and they're watching everything explode."

Kati frowned. "A well-coordinated attack."

"Yes. You know we keep up our weekly training and sparring at the gym, but if either of us has a match, we take it to a whole other level of training." She caught the spark in his eyes. "I like watching you prepare for a kickboxing match. Your intensity, your concentration, your moves—they all improve. You step up your game, but look at us—we didn't know someone had called a match, didn't know we needed to step up the game. God, I'm sure, was trying to tell us, but we were complacent, blind."

Kati wanted to punch something. He was so right. "Miss Eleanor has talked to us recently—even talked about training. Or teaching. Only we weren't listening to what she said. God told her to start teaching us to war, but I think most of us were content to just go on the way we've done it before.

158

I have been, anyway."

He curled his fingers around her balled fists. "Miss Eleanor and your group have been fighting with a disadvantage. The last three years have been relatively quiet. We've won the battles easily. But now...you're right. This is war. I'm thinking of that scripture about how the violent take it by force."

"Really? Miss Eleanor mentioned that."

"From the mouths of two or three witnesses..."

She punched him. "Yeah. I get it. 'From the days of John the Baptist until now, the kingdom of heaven suffers violence, and the violent take it by force.' That's what you mean?"

"Yeah. Matthew 11:12. There's two ways people look at that. One is that Satan is attacking the Kingdom of God—like what we're seeing right now. And the other is that *we* take the Kingdom by force, too. We fight for it in this world. It doesn't have to do with our salvation. We're saved because of Jesus's sacrifice, nothing else. But we're still in this world, and we represent his Kingdom, and we're being attacked. We must fight back. Just like in the ring. You don't stand there and let someone pummel you. You fight. You use your weapons."

"You're wanting me to take up the mantle, aren't you?"

One side of his mouth lifted. "You're a warrior, Kati. That's why Miss Eleanor wants you, why God wants you. He's put that in you. You're a fighter. We all have different gifts. This is yours."

"I know I need to step in while Miss Eleanor is in the hospital, but..." She stood to face him and flung out her arms. "I need to hear God's voice. I need to know I can do this, with everything else that's going on. I want a baby, Reece. *We* want a baby. You said you did. Then there's my work here at the hospital, and the anti-trafficking group, and the IronWorks ministry. And you. I don't want *us* to get lost in the midst. How can I do it all?"

He tugged her down onto his lap. "I've never heard you this uncertain."

"I'm having a tough time saying yes to this."

He nodded. "I understand."

"Do you?"

"How long was it before I said yes to being assistant pastor?"

She leaned back. "I forgot. You did struggle with that. But, Reece—"

"Still struggling with it. I'll support you in whatever you decide, but I think you've forgotten something."

"Yeah? What is that?"

"Grace. The thing that's gotten us this far. God said his grace is sufficient. He said it to Paul, and since he's no respecter of persons, he says it to us, too. His grace is sufficient, and his strength is made perfect in weakness. The only thing you need to decide is—do you want it?"

Chapter 13

*Stand therefore, having your loins girt about with truth, and
having on the breastplate of righteousness; And your feet
shod with the preparation of the gospel of peace; Above all,
taking the shield of faith, wherewith ye shall be able to
quench all the fiery darts of the wicked.*
Ephesians 6:14–17

Lynn picked up the dinner plates, smiling at Tammy,
who leaned over to Jaron and whispered to him.

"Oh." His head bounced up, and he looked at Lynn.
"Thank you, Aunt Lynn, for the dinner and the cupcakes. They
were great."

Lynn set the dishes on the counter. "I thought you'd
like them."

"I loved them."

"I think your mom did, too."

Tammy grinned. "Anything I don't have to cook
myself, I love. But your cooking is excellent."

"Ha! I'll let Rich know you said that. Sometimes I
think I could throw anything on the table, and he'd inhale it."

"I understand that. He always ate like a lion devouring
his prey."

"Still eats like he's eighteen instead of—" She stopped
and listened.

Pounding sounded from the front door.

"Hmm. Wonder who that could be." She walked
toward the living area.

"Whoever it is, they sure seem impatient."

"Yeah. Hope they don't beat my door down."

She walked to the front but glanced out the small
window near the top of the door. Three men stood outside.

161

They wore jackets despite the warm weather. Tattoos climbed their faces, and patches covered their jackets.

She moved back from the door. Rich had described gang members to her, and these looked... She peeked out the window again even as one glanced up at her. The pounding on the door increased. Lynn backed up a foot. *No, not opening the door to whoever they are.*

The pounding stopped, and someone yelled, "We know you're in there. Open the door!"

Definitely not.

She headed to the kitchen. One of the men bellowed again.

What were they doing here? What did they want?

"I'm calling Rich," she told Tammy. "There are three guys out there that I don't like the look of." The rattle of the doorknob echoed through the house.

Were they trying to force their way in? Dread shot through her.

Tammy stood. "Who is it?"

"I don't know. They look like gang members. Take Jaron and go upstairs." She pointed to the other side of the kitchen. "They don't need to see you. Use that doorway and take the hall, then the stairs to the second floor."

Tammy's eyes rounded. Jaron stood, too.

"Mom?"

"Shh, honey. What are you going to do, Lynn?"

"Like I said, I'm going to call Rich. And I'm getting a gun."

"You're getting his gun?"

Hammering and yelling came again.

Lynn glanced back through the doorway. "Mine really. I know what I'm doing. Rich bought it for me and took me for shooting practice more times than most parents take teens for driving practice. Go upstairs."

She watched them disappear, then went to a cabinet, stretched upward, and pulled down a lockbox. She rolled the combination lock. When it clicked open, she lifted the gun out.

The knocking and yelling increased, along with pounding on the living room windows.

Glass shattered. Lynn darted to the living room, keeping the gun pointed toward the floor. Shards of glass littered the hardwood floor. Her heart slammed into overtime.

One of the men stood in front of the window. He laughed when he saw her and turned to the other men. "The babe is back. Guess that popo knows how to pick 'em." He pulled a gun, aimed it her way. "Open the door, Delilah."

Two other men joined him at the window. Lynn bit her lip. Her insides shook. She hadn't called Rich. Her phone was in the kitchen.

What was she going to do? If she let them in...

The man shouted at her again. *No, she couldn't let them in.* Tammy and Jaron were upstairs, but the gang acted like they had no idea about that, even though Tammy's car was in the driveway. Did they think it was hers? And could they see she held a gun? Yes, it was down by her side, but... Maybe they couldn't see it. It was bright outside, darker inside. Maybe...

She had to do something.

Jesus.

She couldn't think past His name. *Jesus.*

The man's next words were filled with expletives. He waved his pistol.

She turned in slow motion, stepped toward the door, then whirled, lifted her gun, and fired. All three dropped to the ground. Lynn sprinted for the kitchen, grabbed her phone, went through the kitchen's second doorway and up the stairs to the second floor.

They'd barricade themselves in, call 911, call Rich...

Please, Lord.

***

Even though the steak was excellent, the conversation had been uneven. Rich hadn't expected much else. They'd kept the discussion to Becca and Lynn, Isabella and Manuel. Now he settled back as the waitress cleaned the table and studied Luis.

The transition from family to the real issue took a minute. He steeled himself to hear the story again.

Luis waited. Rich permitted himself a half smile. There was still enough of the ex-gang member—or Luis's own hubris—across the table that he was going to let Rich approach the subject, and Rich had to swallow his own pride to do it. He and Luis had more in common than he'd thought.

"So, tell me what went down with you and Marcos again."

"I told you before. Why don't you tell me who your eyewitness is and what he said. Or is he a she?"

"Why would you think it was she?"

Luis smirked. "Because my...you would say 'mistress'...showed at the dorms a couple of weeks ago."

Rich straightened. He lifted an eyebrow. "Your mistress?" The woman had not mentioned that, of course.

"While I was captain of the gang, *si*. She showed up at the dorms one day and said she wanted to talk. She wanted to start our relationship again."

"And you're saying you refused?"

Luis glared at him. "Of course. You may not believe that I have changed in many ways, but even you should be able to tell the feelings that I have for Becca are real."

Rich studied him. "So, Marcus tried to kill you, but you killed him instead?"

"*Si*. I would not have been stupid enough to try that. He had too many lieutenants guarding him. I was defending myself."

"And why didn't the lieutenants take you out then?"

Luis shrugged. "It is a question that. I have no answer. Marcos was not...liked. More about himself than the gang. Perhaps they wanted a new leader." His eyes suddenly lit. "Or perhaps they were afraid of my knife."

Rich's gaze met his, and after a moment he snorted. He'd been waiting for the arrogance to come through, but Luis had known it, known Rich was waiting for anything that indicated the ex-gang leader still hovered inside, and he'd given it to him. Only they both knew it wasn't real.

He handed his credit card to the waitress when she returned, and settled back again. "So, tell me about this mistress. Why would she want you in jail for murder?"

"Even you, gringo, have had a few women hang on longer than you wanted." Luis grinned. "But have you ever told a Latino *mamá* she was no longer wanted? On a good day, you could get yourself killed."

"So, she tried to kill you?"

"*Sí.*"

"And having messed that up all those years ago, she decided she would just come and join the program here and try again?"

Luis shrugged. "I'm not sure why she came, but I do know she wasn't happy when I told her about Becca."

"Another woman in her place. You warned Becca?"

"Of course."

Rich started to say something, but his phone rang. He glanced at it, started to turn it over then frowned and answered it. "Richards." He straightened. "What? Who is this?" He listened a moment, then pulled the phone back and stared at it. He lunged from the table and headed to the door.

As he swung it open, Luis appeared beside him. "What's up, man?"

Rich popped the lock on his car. "Stay here. Call someone from the church to pick you up."

He climbed into the Porsche and hit the One-Call button for dispatch. "2012. Code 8. I received a call from the captain of the Gordones. He's setting fire to my house with my wife in it."

Dispatch recapped. "2012. Code 8. Fire at your address. Persons, your wife, inside. Go ahead."

He gave the address and the information again even as he started backing out. Luis grabbed the door handle and yanked it open.

"Stay here," Rich barked.

Luis flung himself into the car. "No way, man. They're waiting for you."

Rich threw the car into drive. He needed to call Lynn. Get her upstairs and away from the doors and windows, tell her to get the gun. He spun out of the parking lot, heart doing an erratic drumbeat.

His gaze jumped to Luis and back to the road. "Call Reece. Have them pray." His voice grated. "What are you doing, anyway?"

"You need backup."

Rich hit Speed Dial for Lynn's phone. "You're on probation. Besides, you don't have a gun."

"Give me the pistol strapped to your ankle."

Chapter 14

And take the helmet of salvation, and the sword of the Spirit,
which is the word of God: Praying always with all prayer
and supplication in the Spirit, and watching thereunto with
all perseverance and supplication for all saints.
Ephesians 6:17–18 KJV

Kati walked to the back of the property, along the jogging path to the pond and the stand of trees. Scary to think of the white supremacist gang reorganizing. Why were people so hateful? Prejudice? She shivered, thinking of Patriot and GreasePaint and her husband in the middle of a gang vendetta. Reece had told her they wanted Patriot dead.

Patriot and Luis, and maybe Rich Richards, too.

She'd cringed when he'd said that.

But had they wanted more than that? Why meet at the church? Rich thought it was because of Luis. Yeah. They hated Luis. Because he was Mexican.

She shook her head. So did many others. Good people who hated others of different races and heritage. *How can you love me*, God asked in the Scriptures, *if you don't love those I created?* And God created all—all races, colors, and languages.

Wow. Think about that. He loved King David, who was an adulterer and most likely a rapist—how would Bathsheba resist or fight off the king of Israel? No way—and then a murderer, sending her husband to the front lines of the battle to be killed. If God loved that man enough to restore him…

Which was what it was about. God, the great restorer, the Savior of the world. Look at all the people that had come through the church's program during the last three years. Restored. Loved. Most still walking in the light of His Presence.

She stopped and stared into the pond waters. Dark but clear. Yeah, the muck on the bottom was dark with decaying vegetation, but the water itself was clear. When the sun hit it during the day, you could see the clarity.

You trying to tell me something, Lord?

Where people saw the bottom of the pond—skin color or race or culture—God saw the clear water of the person he had created, the person he loved, the person who could be redeemed through Christ's death, burial, and resurrection.

A bird darted past her. She glanced up. Evening cooled the day's warmth, settled the day's noises. The only sound now was birdsong—a multitude, it seemed. She smiled. One to the left, one right, one in the tree overhead.

I know You're talking to me, Lord. Why aren't I ready for this? I mean, stepping into Miss Eleanor's shoes. Are you kidding me?

She swallowed and looked past the trees. The blue of the sky had faded. A touch of gray, of silver and edged at the bottom with pale peach. Kati took a deep breath.

Aw, Lord. It's not about me anyway. I know that. I'm such a mess. If You want me to do this, though, I need to know it's You. Not Miss Eleanor, not my husband. But You.

It was getting late. She turned and headed back to the sanctuary. Music poured out when she opened the doors, washing her. She winked at Reece as he went by talking on the wireless radio. Making sure the security team was in place. Now more than at other times. He'd mentioned beefing up the volunteer group.

This Wednesday's evening service was more packed than Sunday's. News of Miss Eleanor and Daneen had traveled fast.

She slipped into a chair next to Chloe. They hadn't seen each other much lately. Their shifts had changed. She missed her. Chloe seemed to have a straight line to heaven when it came to knowing what to do in the ER.

She gave Chloe a smile and began to sing with the others.

The song ended, and Pastor Alan stepped forward. "We're going to do more praise and worship. Don't worry. But I know you've heard about Daneen. She's holding her own, which we're both grateful for. And you've probably heard that Miss Eleanor had a heart attack."

A buzz went through the congregation. He held up a hand. "She's in a different hospital than Daneen. I've done some running back and forth today. It's amazing how God can keep you going. And how people can help." He looked around, smiled at Kati and others. "Miss Eleanor told me to let the congregation know *everything* going on, and you know that was an order."

People laughed. Kati's heart lifted. Miss Eleanor was one of a kind.

"And so, let me say that in relation to a new church building, we've run into a roadblock. The insurance company tells me that the church building and classrooms were only insured for part of their worth. This is my fault. When I took over ten years ago, I did not look closely at the insurance papers. The amount seemed adequate at the time. Of course, since then we've added the offices and the nursery, windows, siding, and other improvements. The offices and nursery were add-ons and not covered. However, those are being worked on already, thanks to all of you. Here's the problem. We don't have enough insurance money to rebuild the sanctuary at today's prices, much less a bigger one."

Quiet followed the announcement. A movement distracted Kati. Someone slipped into the chair on the other side of Chloe.

Patriot leaned toward her and whispered, "Reece told me I might want to be here." He slipped a hand around Chloe's.

Kati lifted a brow at her friend, but Chloe just smiled.

Pastor Alan cleared his throat. "As I said, this is my fault. Something I wish I'd thought about before now. But in this, as with Daneen and with Miss Eleanor, I have to trust God. He's fixed too many of my messes for me not to believe he can do it again. Not that I am excusing myself. It's only that while running from one hospital to another today, I realized how much I mess up even when I desire to do right. God gives grace when you need it, and I need it. Right now."

"You've got it, Pastor!"

"His miracles are greater than our goof ups!"

"Thank you. You don't know how much I appreciate all of you. God tells us to come boldly to the throne of grace that we may obtain mercy and grace in time of need. I need both. You know, I got home about midnight last night and started praying for Daneen, for Miss Eleanor, for the buildings we need, for our ministry here, and for all of you—well, I just couldn't stop. I think I was praying more in desperation than in faith. Anyone ever do that?"

Oh yeah. Kati grinned even as others murmured agreement.

"That's what I thought. Well, God pulled me up by my bootstraps and told me I was not alone. *You* are not alone. Jesus is with us. He allowed this fire *not* to consume us but to purify us. Satan had a plan for evil, but God will use it for good. He told me to *hold on*. And then he said..." Alan picked up a paper from the podium and waved it. "I had to write it down.

"There is no situation, circumstance, or predicament, no shortage, deficit, or lack, no evil, sickness, or problem, no plan, subpoena, or attack. There is no enemy, force, or dilemma, no shadow, verdict, or malady, no slander, accusation, or gossip, no wilderness, desert, or tragedy. There is no weapon fashioned in the forges of hell by our enemy that is strong enough to succeed in bringing us down." *

"Yes!" someone yelled.

Alan's face split into a grin. "Listen. There's more. There's no tongue of judgment loud enough to drown out the roar of God's angelic armies sent to deliver us. Isaiah 54:17 says, 'No weapon formed against us shall prosper; and every tongue that shall rise against us in judgment we will condemn. This is the heritage of the servants of the Lord, and their righteousness is of me, says the Lord.'" *

People stood all over the sanctuary, clapping.

Someone whistled.

Pastor Alan waved for silence. "God reminded me that we have angels stationed around us. The Psalms tell us that angels excel in strength. They do His commandments, hearkening unto the *voice* of His Word. Have you spoken His Word aloud lately? Have you read it? Do you know that angels are innumerable on the earth and in heaven? In fact, Revelation 5 says there are millions of angels about God's throne. Millions. Here on earth, angels sometimes take on human form. Did you realize that? Hebrews 13:2 tells us to make sure we are hospitable to strangers because some people have entertained angels and were not even aware of it." *

He lifted his Bible and waved it. "It is a remarkable thing God has done, giving us this Book, with His words all throughout, and telling us to keep our eyes on it, to hide it in our hearts and speak it out loud in faith! God's Word should be our top priority."

"You know what's next? Prayer. The effective fervent prayer of a righteous man avails much. Now I just told you how I messed up. I don't have my own righteousness, but because Jesus died for me, I have His. He was made sin for us so we might be made the righteousness of God in Him. How about it? Are we going to pray fervently? Not just talk about it. Do it. Tonight."

"Yes!" Kati yelled, then clamped her hand over her mouth.

Chloe laughed and shouted, "Yes!"

"I'm not ready to give up on my wife or Miss Eleanor

or our church. Are you?"

A chorus of "No" echoed in the sanctuary.

"Okay then. Kati, do you want to come up here and lead off?"

Kati jolted. *Now, Lord? Now?* She stood slowly.

"Go on, Kati. Go," Chloe encouraged her.

God, he's right. You're the Creator. You can do anything. What have I been so afraid of?

Reece walked from his position next to the side wall and took her arm. He pulled her into the aisle. His grip hurt. She glanced at him in surprise.

He leaned forward. "Go pray, Kati, and tell Pastor Alan that the Gordones called Rich to tell him they're going to burn down his house—with Lynn in it."

She twisted and stared up at him.

He walked her to the front, leaned over again, and whispered, "They'll be waiting in ambush for him. And he's got Luis with him. We need a miracle. More than one."

He turned, walked back to where Patriot sat, and motioned to him. As they disappeared through the back doors, Kati felt the wash of the Holy Spirit. She was praying before she took the first step to the platform.

Pastor Alan handed her the mic, and she continued in prayer. "Lord, thank You that we're here today. That You're a protector of those that trust in You. I feel Your Spirit." She stopped and kneeled. "The Enemy comes to steal, kill, and to destroy, but you have come to give us life and life more abundantly. I see the Enemy's hand, Father, and I intercede. We intercede." She swept her hand out to the congregation. "Where two or more are gathered in Your name, You are in our midst. Here we are, and we ask that You move even now. We stand against the Enemy and everything he is trying to do. Reece has said three lives are in danger. Right now. Maybe more."

A gasp came from some in the congregation. A couple of people stood. Some moved into the aisle and knelt, too.

"But you just had Pastor Alan tell us how good and powerful you are. You have us here for a reason. We ask for protection around these three, Father. And anymore that may be in danger. Send Your angels. Do not let the Enemy win. Drag people from death's door today."

Pastor Alan's prayer rose with hers. Voices throughout the congregation climbed.

She'd been slow in accepting her assignment. The Enemy had been at work in her life, and she hadn't seen it. Miss Eleanor had said that Satan had already mounted an attack and his forces were at work. Now people she knew and loved were in danger.

What was she waiting for?

She stood. "We're putting the Enemy on notice. No longer are we sitting back. No longer are we arguing with God's call on our lives or on this church body. We are running toward the battle and facing the Enemy, standing in Jesus's name. No one will die today. Do you hear me?" She sent her voice into the unseen world, against the Enemy. "No one will die."

***

Miss Eleanor shifted in the bed. Why couldn't they make hospital beds more comfortable? Or the pillows?

She felt agitated and didn't know why. *I feel sidelined. I can't get up with all this stuff attached to me. I can't pray.* She stopped. *That's not right. A lie of the enemy. I can still pray. Doesn't matter where I am, what I feel like.*

She huffed and bowed her head. "Father, I come to You in Jesus's name. You know what needs to be done, who needs to be saved, who needs help. Send your angels now."

Footsteps sounded nearby. Air whooshed past her. She tried to concentrate.

"Sorry to wake you. Here's your medication for tonight."

She lifted her eyes, tried to push the irritation away. An interruption wasn't necessarily a terrible thing. It could be God.

The nurse standing in front of her was male. African American and...maybe Indian? She wasn't sure. It was hard to ask these days. She didn't want to offend anyone.

The young man stepped to her bedside. "My name's Rodney. I'll be your nurse for the night. I just need to check a few things right now." He held out his hand with a small cup in it. "I brought your meds so you won't have to wait for them."

His voice had a slight accent. Indian from India. The machines made background music for his voice.

She smiled and reached for the cup. "So, you're my nurse. I'm glad to meet you."

He grunted and moved to the machines, checked them. "How are you feeling?"

"I'm feeling great. In fact, I'm feeling good enough to get out of here."

"That's what we're here for. To help you get better and back home."

"I have a lot of people praying for me, so I think I'll be leaving tomorrow."

He stepped back to her bedside. "That's okay if you believe that."

"You don't believe?"

"I believe in science."

"I believe in science, too. Some of it. Seems like it changes over the years, though. I've been around a long time and seen a lot of changes, but God is the same yesterday, today, and forever. He never changes."

***

"Rich! Oh, thank You, God."

Lynn's high-pitched voice tightened his gut. "Are you

all right?"

"There were men here. They tried to get in. Broke a window. I...I got my gun. They look like gangsters, and they're still outside somewhere."

His heart skittered. "How many? Did you call 911?" He'd made the call to her as soon as he'd slapped the siren on top of his car.

"Three, I think. I haven't called. It happened so fast."

His mind flipped back and forth, emotion and adrenaline washing through him. *Focus on what's necessary.* "How do you know they're still there?" Although if they wanted him, wanted him to watch his house burn, his wife burn, they would be there. Waiting. Watching.

"The car is across the street, an older Altima a couple houses down. Rich, Tammy and Jaron are with me."

"What?" Waves of emotion rose, curled, crashed. "What are they..."

"They were here for dinner, but then these men came..."

"Okay. Listen. We're on the way. Backup's en route. The fire department's rolling."

"The fire department?"

"Lynn, get Tammy and Jaron and get upstairs. Wait for us." He had to let her know. "There could be a fire."

Her gasp was audible. "Rich—"

"Wait for me or the deputies or the firemen. Don't leave the house. The men you saw will be waiting for you. You understand?"

"Yes, I—"

"You've got the gun?"

"I have it. I shot through the window when they tried to get in. I wanted to call you, but I couldn't stop to do it. We're upstairs, barricaded in."

He made a sliding turn around the next street. J-beck and the others had tried to get in, but Lynn had frustrated their plans. A jolt of pride at what she'd done sped through him. But no wonder they called and planned to burn down his house. The idea of them getting to Lynn, though, formed icicles in his veins. He shook himself.

"Rich?"

"Yeah?"

"I love you."

He sucked in a breath. "I love you, too. Hold on. Tell Tammy and Jaron to hold on. We'll be there."

"All right."

"I have to go. I have to get dispatch."

He pushed the End button, stared at the road ahead, hearing her words. He forced his mind back to where he was. He'd driven halfway home without seeing or concentrating.

A look at Luis showed the man had his head bowed. Praying. Good. They needed a miracle. Or two.

Chapter 15

Our God is a consuming fire.
Heb 12:29

Chloe knelt on the floor near the platform. All around her people prayed and worshipped. Some stood and praised God for His faithfulness. Her eyes closed, she listened, coming into agreement with the prayers around her, with the praise. God inhabited the praises of His people. And they needed Him. She could feel the danger. The first time she'd experienced it so strong. It frightened her. An enemy trying to bring death and destruction, but it stirred her, too. They needed to stand against him. She needed to.

The effective, fervent prayer... She leaned forward. "God, save these men. Save them. I don't know what's going on, but I feel it, Lord. Thank You for using me. I come against and stand against everything the Evil One is trying to do to stop this ministry, to stop Rich and Luis. Save them. Save Lynn. Don't let the Enemy win. What he means for evil, use for good, as Your Word says."

An impression formed in her mind. Patriot's face.

"Lord, I don't know what this means, but save Patriot, save anyone who might be involved in this. You're a consuming fire. Let Your Presence be with him."

The memory of Patriot saying he was going back to Denver washed over her. The sense of loss swelled. How could he mean so much in such a brief time?

She realized she'd stopped praying. Where had that come from? No, she wasn't going to think about it now. She wasn't getting sidetracked. A blaze ignited inside her. Patriot needed prayer now, and the others. Her stuff could wait.

***

Patriot swung up onto Truck 9 as it prepared to leave. The call had come into the station just as he and Reece veered into the parking lot. He'd run into the bay and been greeted by the lieutenant. They could use him. Good. He'd planned to go. Engine 9 pulled out of the bay, followed by Truck 9, another engine, and a command unit. They'd have fifteen firefighters on the ground.

He pulled on his turnout jacket and fastened it.

Their unit should be the first to reach Rich's house. They were closest. If so, their unit would have command. He hoped to go in with the lieutenant for any rescues. Rich's wife, and now they were saying two others—a boy and his mother— were inside. Patriot's heart jumped to overtime at the news. So like the other.

Help us reach them, Father.

He'd worked a couple of fires with the company over the last two weeks and trusted he'd shown he knew what he was doing. The captain and the lieutenant knew he'd taken rescue courses in Denver and been involved in rescues. He wanted to be in on this one.

As they pulled onto the street, Reece's SUV drove in behind them. The man couldn't help in any official capacity, but Patriot coveted his prayers.

***

Rich slid the Porsche around the corner into his street and spotted the Gordones' car to his left. A short distance past it, smoke rose from the back of his house. Lynn and Tammy and Jaron. Everyone he had in the world inside. His stomach clenched.

A movement caught his eye. He slowed, stopped. "Get down. Someone's on the right of the house."

Luis dropped lower. "I need the other gun, man. They aren't going to just let you waltz in there."

"I'm going to drive up to the front door." Rich handed his gun to Luis. "Take this one. Cover me."

Luis took the gun. "The firefighters are on their way. And the police." A fractional pause. "And there's someone on the left side."

Rich twisted his head around in time to see a shadow whip behind the house. He pushed Speed Dial on his phone. "Come on, Lynn. Answer."

"Rich?"

"Where are you?"

"Upstairs in the main bedroom. Where are you?"

"Here, but we have company outside. Stay where you are." He put down the phone, stared at his house. The fire had consumed the church within minutes.

They needed backup now.

"We need to take care of these guys."

Rich sent Luis a glance. "Got a way to do that? One on either side and one missing in action. Backup will do that if they get here. I've got to let dispatch know there's three people inside and that you're with me."

He hit the mic button, talked with dispatch. Was the woman even listening? Did she get that his family was in danger?

She repeated the status. "2010's en route. 2040, 2015 responding. Fire is rolling. Stand by."

He wasn't up to an argument.

"That's negative. If 10's not here in one minute, I'm going to get my family."

"Stand by 2012."

Rich shut off the radio.

"She's not happy with you."

"Feeling's mutual."

What was taking so long? Dispatch should have had someone en route as soon as he'd called it in. Black smoke swelled against the faded sky, and flames clawed along the roof. He hit Speed Dial again. "Lynn, get the others and get downstairs, but stay inside, away from the windows."

"Okay, but we barricaded ourselves in. It'll take a few minutes."

"Barricaded—all right. Get moving. Fire's at the back of the house."

"We can smell it. Rich?"

"Lynn, just move." Pressure pressed against every nerve in his body.

"Jaron dropped the leg of the desk on his foot when we were moving things. We might have to carry him down."

No.

"Okay. Take down the barricade. I'll get up there."

"Rich, don't—"

He dropped the call as flames exploded past the roof. Smoke spun skyward. He had to get in there, get them out. The church had gone up in minutes.

No sirens. Where were they?

He turned to Luis. "All right. I'm flooring it up to the house. I'll roll out, hit the door. You cover me."

Luis's mouth lifted. "You got it."

Rich shot him a look. The man was feeling the adrenaline hit.

"When backup gets here, drop the gun on the floorboard. Put your hands in the air. Say I dropped the gun while getting out. That's all they need to know."

Luis slid a look his way. "Go, man."

Rich hit the accelerator, and the Porsche surged forward, tires spinning, screeching. They flew toward the house. Rich slammed the brakes just before they hit the front door. He jumped out, crouched low, and darted for the door.

Shots sounded over his head.

"Hey, j-beck. You want me?"

Behind him, Luis's voice carried all the challenge and bravado the ex-gangster had ever had. "You gonna hide behind a fire and a wall, *basura?*"

Rich grabbed the doorknob. Locked. The key…

"Well, well, we got two for one." J-beck's voice sounded on his right. "Hear that, guys? The cholo is here, too."

"You think to insult me, *chusma?*" Luis hollered. "You set fire to a woman in her house? *Eres un conbarde.* Coward!"

Movement from the left caused Rich to drop to his knees. A bullet whizzed past. Luis's return fire, went left then right, and then he scampered to the front of the car.

"Go, man. Get inside."

Rich had wanted the ex-gangster inside the car. But even as the thought came, Rich leaned back and kicked—the adrenaline pumping through him helping to shatter the lock. The door flew open. Shots rang out. Bullets implanted themselves in the walls. Something hit his leg from behind, and he crumpled.

Luis hollered then fell silent.

Pain tore through Rich's leg as he tried to pull himself inside. The silence bothered him. Was Luis down? J-beck trying to figure his next move? Where was backup?

Luis groaned, then cursed and scrambled forward. He shoved Rich out of the doorway and slammed the door shut as more bullets splintered the wood.

Sirens wailed in the distance.

Yes.

Rich closed his eyes. The fire in his leg mimicked what he smelled in his house. Smoke hovered over them. "Give me the gun, Luis. Go get my family."

"Can't, man. I'm hit."

Rich's heart dropped.

Luis collapsed beside him, and Rich glanced over. A dark stain spread across the man's shirt.

Jesus…

He shifted closer to Luis, dragging his leg.

"Sorry, Rich—"

"Shut up." He pulled up the T-shirt. Blood. Lots of it.

"Where's the blasted entry?" He wiped some blood aside, saw a hole, and put his hand over it. Pressed. "How many times I got to do this for you?"

Luis tried to laugh, coughed.

"Don't move. Hear the sirens? They're here. Hold on."

"They'll walk into a trap."

"With the Gordones?" Rich pushed past his own pain. "Without BearTrap, they're cowards. Like you said. Bet they ran when they heard the sirens."

Luis grunted.

Rich pulled himself higher, kept the pressure on Luis's wound. Where was Lynn? He couldn't go up. His heart squeezed. *Jesus, I need You now.*

"Lynn," he yelled. Nothing. "Lynn! Get down here!"

Lights pulsated through the windows. Sirens screamed. The smell of smoke hung over them. He glanced toward the stairs. The fire's black signature curled across the ceiling.

Luis coughed again. His breath came in short gasps.

"Hold on. As soon as the perimeter is clear, they'll find us." Rich glanced toward the stairs and gritted his teeth against the pain in his leg. "Lynn! Tammy!" Where were they? Surely they'd heard the shots...

His heart sank. Yeah, they'd heard the shots and ducked back into the room, if they'd come out.

Luis gave a feeble laugh. "Good thing I say my prayers this morning."

Rich forced a smirk, his head counting off the number of problems they had, his ears searching for sounds of Lynn or Tammy or Jaron. "You should have been a little more specific. Like no GSWs. No gun shot wounds."

The door flew open. A person in a firefighter's turnout gear stood in the doorway. Others pressed in behind him. They stopped.

The wash of relief that crashed through Rich made him shaky. He pointed to the back of the house and the stairs. "My wife, sister, and nephew. Upstairs. Hurry."

The lead man said something into his radio. Another firefighter dropped down beside Luis.

Rich cleared his throat. "He's got a chest wound. GSW."

A third firefighter pushed through the door and knelt beside Rich.

"Layout of the house?" the lead man asked.

Rich pointed over his head. "Kitchen that way and family room next to it. Master bedroom's that way, but she said they were all upstairs. Three of them. One child. Hurry." He indicated the stairs once more.

The lead firefighter spoke again into his radio, then pointed to two firefighters behind him. "Take the downstairs." He pointed to the other man waiting nearby. "Travis, you're with me. Upstairs."

***

Patriot stared at Rich and Luis. His heart slammed. What had happened? Outside, the Gordones were gone. If that was who the deputies were looking for. And, according to Reece, it was.

Patriot glanced at both men again. They wouldn't know him in his helmet, turnout gear, and airtank. Ambulances were outside.

Save them, Lord.

He turned and followed the lieutenant. Why hadn't the three upstairs come down?

The rest of the crew would attack the fire from outside for now. Shouts filtered through the door and told him they were unrolling hose and that the ladder truck stood ready.

As they reached the second floor, black smoke met them, slashing their visibility. Heat combined with the roar of the flames. He looked down the hall, where the outside wall was already engulfed, fire burning like a boiling pot of orange light above a broken window. The ceiling crackled and buckled in places.

Two doors led off the hall, both closed. The lieutenant indicated the closest and tried the knob. Locked. He shook it, then pounded. They hadn't much time.

The lieutenant stepped aside. Patriot moved forward and clipped the Halligan-type entry tool he carried into the doorframe. A moment later, the door fractured around the lock. He shoved it, but it caught on something. He pushed harder, and it gave.

Blankets mounded behind it. Okay. Probably to keep out the smoke. Someone had shoved the bed to one side. A dresser stood beside it. The room in disorder. The closed door and blankets had kept the smoke and heat to a minimum. He checked the blankets and bed. No one. A door to the left led either to a bath or closet. Patriot made a motion to the lieutenant, indicating his intent to check it out. He moved forward and opened it.

Three people stood together in the bathroom. One with her arm around a young boy. The woman in front had a pistol trained on his gut.

Travis stopped.

No one moved. They stared at each other. Then the woman's eyes widened and her shoulders slumped. Her relief mirrored his. She dropped her gun hand to her side.

The lieutenant stepped up beside him, spoke into the radio, then pointed to the boy and his mother and indicated for them to follow him.

The mother shook her head. "Jaron hurt his foot."

The lieutenant moved past Patriot, lifted the boy into his arms, then gestured for the mother to follow.

Patriot glanced over his shoulder. The firefighters outside would prop an extension ladder to the window. The lieutenant set the boy down next to his mother and motioned for them to stand against the wall. He slid the window open and pushed out the screen, letting smoke and heat out. The extension ladder slammed up against the outside wall.

Patriot looked at the woman with the gun—Rich's wife?—and motioned for her to hand him the gun. She wasn't going down the ladder with a loaded pistol. She nodded and handed it to him. Good. No one wanted an accidentally discharged gun—either because of carelessness or the fire. He crossed to the firefighter who had reached the window and passed him the gun. He handed it to the other firefighter on the ground.

The lieutenant lifted the boy and transferred him to the fireman on the ladder. He gestured to the mother.

When Patriot rotated back to Rich's wife, she still stood in the bathroom doorway. He walked over and took her arm. A loud crackling sounded above them. The ceiling buckled and fractured. He thrust the woman back into the bath as part of the ceiling collapsed. Showers of sparks and smoke billowed upward.

The woman gasped, igniting a spasm of coughing.

He grabbed a towel and threw it over her head. "Breathe through this." He hoped she could hear him and understand. The gases and heat were deadly.

The lieutenant jerked his head around. Patriot Travis looked across the burning rubble to where he stood. They were effectively cut off.

"I'll get the mother out. Then we'll move the debris." The lieutenant jerked his head toward the first woman. But even as he said it, the snapping and sudden popping from the ceiling once more warned them.

Patriot pushed Rich's wife farther into the bathroom as another section of burning ceiling tile dropped from above.

They weren't going to get to the window, but a small pathway to the hall door remained. Could he get her out that way? They needed to move now.

"I'll carry her out."

The lieutenant looked across at him. Even past the smoke and the helmet, the man's frown was evident, but he nodded, then turned to help the other woman through the window.

Patriot did an about face. "I'll carry you down. Lean against me and give me your right hand. Let me lift you. Don't help."

He didn't give her time to think. He grabbed her right hand and draped it over his shoulder, wrapped his arm around the back of her right knee, and lifted her body onto his shoulders. She was tall and solid, and his SCBA tank didn't help. He stumbled a moment then regained his footing. He had her left wrist with his right hand to keep her safely in position, leaving just his left hand free.

A couple more towels hung on a bar. He grabbed them and tossed them over her. "Hold one of these around your head."

He passed the fiery rubble and headed for the hall. As he stepped from the room, burning fragments rained down around them. He spun away, holding tight to the woman. She had no protection from the flames or the burning wood and plaster. He stumbled back against the wall, and she screamed.

Her fear mixed with the roar of the fire overhead. Patriot righted himself and scanned the hall both ways. He couldn't see for the smoke. Which way? He'd just spun around. Which room had they come out of?

"Which way?" He yelled at her, but she didn't answer, didn't seem to hear him. Dread shot through him. He had to get her out of here.

Just go the way that seems best.

He took a step. Stopped.

The voice in his head didn't sound right. How many times while undercover had he just gone without God's leading? Without prayer? He regretted everyone.

You have to get out of here. You don't have time to wait.

But he didn't move. He tightened his grip on Rich's wife and prayed.

Lord, which way?

Nothing.

He twisted his head back and forth.

Lord?

A noise behind him caused him to turn. Another firefighter was standing there. Not someone from their unit. They must have sent another unit to help. The man pointed to the right.

Travis's heart swelled.

Thank You.

He placed his left hand on the wall and progressed to the stairs. Visibility lightened as he neared them. He took a deep breath and edged down. The living area had emptied, and he exited the house.

Cool, fresh air met him.

Sirens still screamed.

He set Rich's wife down. She stumbled but threw off the towels. Travis saw the black burn spots on them and on the back of her jeans.

"Thank you. I..." She shouted over the noise, then coughed. "Thank you."

An EMT reached out to steady her. "Let's check you out."

But she shoved his hand away. "Where's my husband? Where's Rich?"

The EMT pointed. "Two men are being loaded into the ambulances, but we—"

She twisted that way. Rich, on a stretcher, was arguing with the man and woman trying to get him into the ambulance. Reece stood next to him. Lynn shoved the EMT aside and ran to the vehicle.

Travis pulled his helmet off and turned to thank the other firefighter. No one was there. He jerked his head around. The lieutenant stood to his left, pulling off his helmet, too.

"Where's the other firefighter?"

"What other firefighter?"

"The one from the other unit."

The lieutenant's brows rose. He looked toward the street. "The second and third due just arrived."

Travis stared at the additional engines. Firefighters piled out. No one wore turnout gear like the one he'd seen.

He looked at the house. Where was the other man? He took a step toward it.

The lieutenant grabbed his arm. "What are you doing?"

"Someone's in there. From another unit."

"No one's in there. The other companies just arrived. No one's had time to get inside."

Travis looked toward the street. He didn't understand that. What if the lieutenant was wrong? What if... He stared at the trucks in the street, looked again at the lieutenant.

The man shook his head. "No one's in there, Travis. You and the girl were the last ones."

Chapter 16

Who makes His angels spirits, His ministers a flame of fire.
Psalm 104:4

Miss Eleanor didn't feel right. She knew that. She'd felt better yesterday. Ready to get out of the hospital, in fact. Today her heart didn't seem to be doing the job it was supposed to after the stent. She pushed the button on her hospital bed and sank back onto the sheets. But it was nice to be alone for a while. Visitors had worn her down.

"What's going on, Lord?" She frowned. "What's happening? To me? To the others? You know. I'm tired. I hate to admit it, but I am. You have a whole congregation there at New Life. Use them. Use Kati and Reece and Alan. Becca and the others. That whole congregation. They're not there just to sit on those pews. Put them to work. Call them to work. Praying and loving and reaching out to others. Rich or poor. You love them all. Call them. Use them."

The feeling of warmth inside, of being loved filled her. God was good. She had no physical family left, but she had the family of God, who cared and supported her. And she had God—the God of all flesh, the Creator of the ends of the earth. She sighed and smiled.

"Eye has not seen, nor ear heard."

"Talking to yourself or praying?" Rodney stepped into the room with a smirk.

"Just communicating with God."

He went to the machines near her bed. "You think you can do that?"

"Oh, I do it all the time. God has made a way for us to come close to Him. That's why Jesus died. So we could be reconciled to God."

He pulled a bag from his pocket and exchanged it for the empty one hanging near her bed. "And why would we need to be reconciled? What does that mean?"

"Reconciled? Well, at one time, man walked with God, but that was before man sinned. God is perfect, and when man sinned, it separated him from God. We're all separated now until we ask Jesus into our life."

The man's mouth thinned. "If there is a God, a God of love as I've heard, then why would a little sin separate us from Him? What makes Him the judge, anyway?"

"Well, He's the judge because He's the Creator. He made us. He wants a life with us, but He's pure and holy and can't live with us when we've sinned, so He made a way past that. He came to earth so He could fix it, but He had to die to do it. To fix all the wrong things we've done. He came in the form of a man—we call him Jesus—and then He died for the sins of the world. Only God could do that. Die for all the sins. And then He rose again because He was sinless. It really does make sense if you just think it through."

"Seems strange to me."

"Here. Look in the drawer there. See that little Bible? It's really the New Testament with the Psalms and Proverbs. Take that and read it."

The man turned it back and forth. "I don't know."

Miss Eleanor chuckled. "It won't bite you. That's mine. Someone gave it to me a long time ago. A Gideon. They give out Bibles, you know."

He frowned and slipped it into his pocket. "Never heard of them." He walked toward the door. "You need anything?"

"No, I think I have everything I need. Just thinking about heaven."

He laughed. "Well, a better place to be than here, I guess."

"Much better." She closed her eyes as he left. *I'll pray*

for you. But she didn't say it. She just lifted his name up to God. *Lord, can You bring him into the family, please? I'd like to see him up there with us one day.*

***

Kati couldn't believe how the anger had exploded in her. A real eruption like the volcano that had hit Pompeii. Not the intermediary ones. Because that was what happened when she heard the Gordones had put both Rich and Luis in the hospital, that Luis fought for his life.

How dare the Enemy try to kill them when she—no, they, the whole congregation—had prayed specifically that it would not happen.

She paced the waiting room, glad the others had gone for dinner, glad she had the time alone with God. "Lord, I'm way beyond thinking I know everything—especially when it comes to You, but You did say to come and reason with You. Well, I'm doing that. We prayed according to Your Word, and I am standing on that. In another place, You tell us to come boldly before Your throne so we can receive grace and mercy in time of need. Well, we need that, too, Lord. Help us. Help Rich and Luis. Help their faith and their physical conditions." She dropped into a chair and bowed her head. "You said the thief comes to steal and kill and destroy, and You came to give us life. So, I intercede for Luis. For his life. Only You can do the miraculous. We need that now. I ask it in Jesus's name."

She rose again, paced again, stopped, and swung around. "And I'm standing. Having done all to stand, You say, then stand. I just want to let the Enemy know—I'm standing!" Her voice rose.

As she started back the other way, Reece stepped into the room, grinning.

She stopped and scowled at him. "What is that look for?"

"I wondered how long it would take you to get mad."

"Yeah, well."

He stepped up beside her, ran a hand down her cheek. "I don't think God is pleased when we let Satan run all over us. He wouldn't have given us weapons if we weren't supposed to use them. Daniel prayed, but he had to wait—to stand—for twenty-one days until the angel fought past the Enemy's forces to get Daniel his answer." He stopped suddenly. "But you know all that."

Kati stared past him. "Yeah, and it also tells us there are angelic and demonic forces. That they are real."

"Uh-huh." He grinned again. "I like it when you take up your sword."

"The Sword of the Spirit. God's Word. I wouldn't know it so good if it wasn't for you—always after me about studying it."

"What are husbands for?"

She laughed. "Did you get in to see Luis?"

"If Rich hadn't been there, I probably wouldn't have. You know, I tried my best gangster look, and that nurse wouldn't budge until Rich came out."

"That, mister, is because we nurses are made of steel when it comes to our patients."

He caught her arm and tugged her to him. "I got that impression. Next time, I take you with me."

***

Luis groaned, and Rich lifted his head. For the last three and a half days, the congregation had soaked Luis in prayer. And for the last day and a half, Rich had been here after insisting the doctor release Rich from his own hospital room.

And it was time Luis started communicating.

The ICU unit was clean, cold, and quiet except for the background noise of the machines attached to Luis's body. Rich had had surgery himself and spent two days with all the attachments, and didn't envy the man—except he had an idea that the machines along with excellent doctoring had kept Luis alive. Gunshot wound to the chest, bullet lodged in the chest cavity, collapsed lung—the man had a lithia of things that had needed tending.

A miracle he was alive.

Ahhh... Rich shifted in the chair and bowed his head again.

Thank You.

He'd done a lot of praying the last couple of days. More than in the past year. And still he needed a nudge to recognize God's hand.

I have a long way to come back, Father, after being so angry for so long. Forgive me. Help me come back.

He moved his crutches, pushed down the pain shooting through his leg, and leaned forward. Luis had been restless for a while.

"You gonna wake up, man?" Rich made his voice an imitation of Luis's. "Your woman is waiting to see you."

Luis stilled. The seconds ticked by, and finally an eye opened. Rich grinned. The eye closed, and Luis's lips moved. Rich struggled to his feet and limped to the bedside.

"Thought...I'd died...but you're no angel."

Rich chuckled this time. "Right. I'm here to harass you."

Luis groaned, turned his head away. He lay still a moment, then moved his head back. "Becca?"

"In the waiting room. They won't let anyone in but for fifteen minutes every four hours." When Luis said nothing, Rich leaned over. "I told them as law enforcement, I needed to be here when you woke up." He paused, put an arrogancy in his voice he didn't feel, and said, "But I really needed to make sure you lived. I'll never have a moment's peace if you die."

An eye opened again. Past the pain, a glint of amusement showed.

Rich nodded. "Okay, lay here. I'll get Becca and slip

her in." He grabbed his crutches and headed out the door. He'd dealt with the nurses on both shifts, and if he had to deputize Becca to have her sit at Luis's bedside, he would. Unofficially, of course.

Becca, Lynn, Kati, Isabella, Manuel, and Pastor Alan looked up as he came into the waiting room. Wow. The faces sometimes changed, but the numbers stayed the same—or larger. A few people sat at the other end, but for three days, this spot had been occupied by many from the church. "He's awake. Barely. He wants to see Becca."

She jumped up, started to sail past him. He put a hand on her arm, and she glared at him. It would take some time before he got a smile from her again. "If anyone says anything to you, tell them I sent you to sit with him in case he has something to say about the shooting. That I needed a break. You got that?"

"Yes." She yanked her arm free and went down the hall.

He sighed and hobbled to Lynn. She patted the chair beside her. "How are you doing?"

"I'm fine." He tried to hide the grimace as he sat down. He had some pain pills somewhere...

Reece entered the waiting room. "Of course he is."

Rich shuffled his crutches around, lowered himself onto the chair, and scowled.

"How's Luis?"

"Awake. Or was. He wanted Becca."

"Not your adorable face?"

"Reece." Kati put an arm on her husband's arm. "Rich has been here since they released him from his own hospital bed."

Reece winked at her. "And looks like it."

Alan chuckled. "He does look like food and a cup of coffee might help."

"Now there's an idea." Rich glanced at Lynn.

"No, let me go." Kati stood up. "Isabella, you and

Manuel come with me? I'll get us all some lunch, but I need help carrying it."

Isabella rose but threw a glance at Rich. Her smile had been missing, too. He had a lot to make up for. "My brother is doing better?"

Rich nodded. "The doctor has not been by today. Maybe while Becca's there. Luis is holding his own. He did more than grunt today." Rich gave her a smile. "Good sign. But day three after surgery can be hard, they say."

***

Travis stopped and stared out his window.

Rich was out of commission, but the captain had stepped up and agreed to the plan. Set up the sting and the SWAT team. Put himself out there. They'd use the girl again. Pass information through her to j-beck.

But would he believe it?

***

"The doctor said you might get out of here tomorrow."

"Yeah." Luis grimaced. "To another room, another floor."

Rich laughed. "And did you think they meant you'd go home?"

"The food here is terrible."

"But not the pretty nurses?"

"You do not mention pretty nurses to Becca."

"Ha. Only because she'd accuse me of making trouble."

"*Señor problema.*"

Rich shifted on his crutches, felt the nudge of the Holy Spirit. "I have been that in your life."

"Because I am Mexican."

Rich frowned. "That was never a factor. My parents

brought me up better than that. People are people. You have good, bad, and ugly no matter the skin color or culture. Look at the Gordones. White Supremacists that live out their hate." He shook his head, gave a lopsided grin. "I just pegged you as a murderer."

Luis stared at him. "And I was."

Rich grabbed a chair, pulled it forward. "Look, we need—"

Luis waved a hand. "While I'm here in the hospital hooked to everything, I think I hear God. You are in that chair every time I open my eyes. Last time I was in the hospital, before I went to prison, Becca was there. Now you. God gives me time to think. I was angry when you arrested me. I killed a man, but I was angry at you. If I hadn't been shot, hadn't ended up here, I wouldn't know how *loco* that was."

Rich frowned. "You know, I'm prepared to believe your story. Self-defense is not murder."

"I killed a man." He closed his eyes a moment. "The courts—"

"It might not go to court. The witness has disappeared. You said you had others that would tell a different story. The DA might drop it."

"I plead guilty."

Rich rolled his eyes. "Yeah. I'll have your lawyer file a motion to vacate."

"You would do that?"

"Yes. I guess if I chased you down all these years, I can do something on the other side."

Luis's mouth curled. "Your woman stopped by earlier."

"She's grateful you saved my life by shoving me into the house and slamming the door—and you were shot while you did it."

"Jesús did a miracle. My God is a miracle worker."

"For both of us. We should be dead."

"You go against the Gordones with no backup. You are

loco, too."

"I had you."

"And a gun I never shoot before. I wanted the little one at your ankle."

"How did you know I had one?"

"You think I'm stupid? Even when I carried my knife, I had a wingman."

"You had a gun?"

"Of course. As a gang leader." He sighed. "Not today." Rich grinned again. "You'd still like to carry one—like Reece."

"It would have been good with the Gordones."

"Did Reece know?"

"That I carried one before? Of course." Luis closed his eyes. His face smoothed.

Rich glanced at the monitors, hesitated, then headed to the door.

"Rich."

He glanced back.

Luis struggled to lift his head. "Wait."

Rich hobbled back.

Luis tried to lift himself again and groaned. "Your brother-in-law." The words pushed from his lips.

Rich leaned closer. "Lay still. I'm here."

"I'm sorry."

"What?"

"I'm sorry I killed him."

Rich straightened and frowned. What to say to that?

Luis eased back against the pillow. "Forgive me. Self-defense or not, I killed a man. Your sister's ex-husband." Luis pointed upward. "I have asked Him to forgive me. Now I ask you."

Rich's breath caught in his throat. His heart stalled, flipped, and started again. After a second, Rich placed a gentle hand on the other man's shoulder. "I do, Luis. I do."

***

Travis turned the corner of the hospital hallway into the waiting room and stopped. The room was full. He hadn't expected this many people. Everyone looked his way. Those he knew, and those he didn't. He gave a half smile and fixed his eyes on Chloe. She stood talking with Isabella and Manuel. She was in scrubs, heading for work.

As he was.

She nodded at him as if she could read the request in his eyes, put a hand on Isabella's shoulder, turned, and walked his way.

He took her arm and drew her around the corner, out of sight of the others.

"Hey," she said.

"Hey yourself. I wanted to see you before you went on duty."

The smile and light in her eyes radiated through him. He returned it, letting his eyes take it in, then dropping his gaze to her mouth. He leaned forward for a quick kiss, but she turned her head and leaned into him. His arms closed around her, wrapping her like a winter coat.

After a minute, she pressed a hand against his chest. "We might get thrown out of here."

"You think?" The amusement jumped then faded, and he dropped his arms. "I just needed to come by…"

"Oh?"

He couldn't tell her. She'd worry. "Yeah."

"You working at the firehouse tonight?"

She'd clued into something quickly.

"Why do you think that?"

"I don't know. You're volunteering, right?"

"Hmmm."

"You'd tell me if you were doing anything dangerous, wouldn't you?"

Wow. She was always right there with her questions.

"Chloe." He stopped.

She frowned. "What's going on?"

"Nothing. That you need to know about."

"That doesn't make me feel better."

He shook his head, gathered her close again. "Don't ask."

"Travis."

He smiled. "That name means something coming from you."

"I can call you that?"

"Yes."

"Good because that's how I think of you now. You know what it means? What Travis means?"

"It means something?"

"Yes. Crossing over. That's what it means. Crossing, crossing over. And that's what you've done." She touched her chest. "I feel it."

Strange that she should say that. He'd felt it too after he'd carried Lynn out of the fire. He leaned forward and kissed her. "I have to go. I'll call you later."

"But—"

"Hey, you two." Rich's voice separated them.

Travis dropped his arms, wrenched his eyes from hers, and stepped away. "How's Luis?"

Rich grinned. "Making it. Better yet, the doctors say they'll move him from ICU tomorrow if he keeps improving."

Travis nodded. "Good to hear." His focus shifted to Chloe, then back to Rich. "I have to go."

Rich nodded. He put a hand on Chloe's arm. "Chloe, help me give Becca the news about Luis. You know how our relationship is right now."

Chloe's eyes narrowed, and her gaze held Travis's a moment more, then she swallowed. "Okay."

Travis touched her arm, a feather touch, then turned and strolled purposefully down the hall.

Chapter 17

*Trust in the L*ORD *with all thine heart; and lean not unto
thine own understanding. In all thy ways acknowledge him,
and he shall direct thy paths.*

Prov 3:5–6

Chloe watched until he turned the corner. Why was everything inside her diving to the lowest depths? Like a submarine heading to the bottom? She lifted her gaze to Rich.

"He'll be all right. He has lots of backup."

What? He needed backup?

She couldn't speak, couldn't move.

Rich shifted toward the waiting room door. "Come inside. Lynn's here." He waited for her to step forward and limped in after her.

Chloe felt him behind her, heard the scrape of the crutches as he followed. Pain went through her—for him, for the wound he'd suffered, for Luis. His had been a fight for life. Her whole insides shook. What if something similar happened with Travis? What if…

Lord God…

It was hard to pray.

"Lynn." Rich tilted his head toward Chloe and turned toward Becca.

Chloe stared after him. Of course. His request for her help with Becca had been a ruse so she'd let Travis leave. Her focus stayed on Rich for the moment. He was actively seeking Becca out even as the young woman glared at him. As Luis' fiancé and Lynn's kid sister, Becca had a right to be angry with Rich, and yet…

She turned to Lynn.

200

Lynn lifted a perfectly arched eyebrow and scooted over on the hard bench. "What's up?"

"Travis...Patriot...is doing something dangerous but wouldn't tell me what."

"Probably better that way."

Chloe glanced around the room, her stomach so tight she felt sick. What was he doing that he needed backup? "Can we pray?"

"Sure." Lynn bowed her head.

Chloe hesitated. "We all prayed for Rich and Luis the other day, but—"

"But you don't understand why something happened to them?"

"Yes. It's easy to share platitudes with others. Not so easy when it's people you care about."

Lynn squeezed her arm. "I understand that. But it doesn't lessen their truth. That God often has bigger plans than we do. We don't understand perfectly. We won't until Jesus returns. One thing I've come to realize since we started this ministry is that we are in a battle. We hear it over and over. But do we believe it? Luis and Rich were hurt in a natural battle, and both have been fighting spiritual battles, too. We can't expect to get through this life without problems and pain until Jesus returns. Then the battles will be over and the war won. In the meantime, we fight."

Chloe grasped Lynn's hand.

Lynn's head bowed. "Lord, thank You that You're always there even when we don't see it. Thank You for saving Rich and Luis. For saving Tammy and Jaron and me. Our house is gone." Lynn stopped, swallowed. "But You're bigger than our house. I know you will restore. And thank You for whatever You're doing with Rich and Luis. Restoration in both lives. I don't know everything that's going on, but I see peace in my husband's eyes again, and I thank You for that."

"And Father, You see the situation that Travis is in. Whatever it is, Lord, keep him safe. Surround him with Your

201

protection and Your angels, and let him accomplish what he needs to. In Jesus's name. Thank You."

Lynn lifted her head. "You know that God is good. You can trust Him. You have to—for yourself, and if you want a relationship with Travis, or anyone, you'll need to let go and let God." She smiled. "Another platitude, but true."

"Is that what you do?" Chloe nodded toward Rich.

"Of course."

"What's going to happen now?"

"With Rich's leg?"

"Yes."

"It's not good. From what I understand, the bullet went straight through but hit his femur. He has a femoral shaft transverse fracture." She smiled. "A lot of big words to us without medical knowledge."

Chloe groaned inwardly. "They did an intramedullary nailing?"

"There. I couldn't have said it. They say they have great success with it." She glanced at Rich. "Of course, being on his feet so much..."

"He needs to rest it."

"I know. Now that Luis is better, I'm going to make him go home. Do what he promised the doctor he would do. He just felt it was his fault. If Luis hadn't been with him—"

"That's what no one understands. What were they doing *together*?"

"I know Rich appears hardhearted, but he's always been fair. I think...he wanted to hear Luis out again and really listen."

Chloe smiled. "That's good to hear."

"He hasn't said much about his leg, but I know him. It's huge. He's just not letting himself think about it right now, just like he's ignoring the pain." Lynn shrugged. "Maybe he'll make captain. Then he won't be on the streets, and his leg won't matter that much."

"You look at the bright side."

"There's always a bright side. I love my husband. I love God, and I trust Him. But don't let that fool you. I have my down times just like anyone."

Chloe straightened, pulled her shoulders back. She needed to quit being the baby of the bunch here. Her faith needed to be in the God she proclaimed. She took a deep breath and looked around the room. It had lightened, the colors brighter than before.

She leaned toward Lynn and hugged her. "Thank you."

Chloe settled back in the chair, rested her head against the wall behind her and let God's peace fill her. A few minutes later, the sound of footsteps in the hall brought her head back up. She opened her eyes.

Reece jogged into the room. His gaze flicked from one to the other, hesitated on Chloe, then settled on Rich. He gave a jerk of his head. Rich settled his crutches under his arms and moved across the room.

As they went out the door, Reece's low voice drifted back to her. "He just arrived. The SWAT team's in place. He has the..."

Chloe's heart skipped. She straightened in the chair. Was he talking about Travis? He had to be. But why the SWAT team?

She ran her tongue over her lips. They'd just prayed. Praise God they had just prayed. She closed her eyes, breathed deeply. *I trust you, Lord. I trust you to keep him safe. Thank you.*

***

Travis pulled back. The bartender wasn't the same, and the place was empty except for a couple of men sitting at a table by themselves. No one at the bar. No couples. No smell of food or even the overarching smell of cigarette smoke.

He tapped the mic on his watch just as someone shoved him from behind. He stumbled forward, caught himself, and whirled, ready to meet a knife, but instead the girl fell against him. He caught her. The two men at the table leapt to their feet, headed their way.

How had they made the girl? She'd been good passing the note. Or so he'd thought.

J-beck stood in front of him, another gangsta with him. The other two now behind his back. Four. Total. No, the bartender. Five. And the girl wouldn't help. She'd looked healthy before. Now... He didn't see any blood, but he couldn't take inventory.

His eyes held j-beck's. The others wouldn't make a move until he told them. He moved the girl aside, ignoring her. He had to, or neither she nor he would survive.

"You didn't think I had this place covered? That someone wouldn't tell me she passed you something? Got it on video."

"Maybe she did. What's that got to do with our deal?"

"You've got intel on some ice the Feds are watching?"

"That's what you asked for. I give you that. You go your way; I go mine." Travis nodded at the girl. "And hers."

J-beck frowned. "She's not part of the hammer."

"You brought her here."

"You thinkin' to elope?"

"'Get out of jail free'?" Travis shrugged. "It's what we agreed to. You get the intel. I walk away. No paybacks."

J-beck let the smirk widen across his face. "Maybe that's why I brought the girl."

Travis felt his stomach cave. The girl was a problem he didn't need, but he couldn't leave her. The mic better be working, because he'd need help getting her out of here. She hadn't said anything, but now she grabbed his arm.

"You don't do this right, j-beck, and no one will trust you. You're trying to take BearTrap's place, but he had respect. You let this go south, and everyone will know."

"And how will they know? You still on the pig's payroll?"

"I'm not on payroll. But you think I came here without putting out the word?"

J-beck's face contorted, and his hand flipped out. "Hand over the burner."

Travis hesitated. He'd given SWAT enough time to set up. He hoped. If j-beck had men outside, they'd been taken out. The man had a skeleton gang compared to what they had three years ago. And he had five inside.

He moved slowly, pulled the SIG from his underarm holster, handed it over. J-beck grinned. The girl sucked in her breath. The gangster at j-beck's side chuckled. The men behind him laughed.

Travis shifted to his left foot, put his weight on his right. He might need that fraction of a second...

"You think I'm worried about props? I'm thinking I'll have some when you're whacked."

"Like Luis? You janked up. Again." *Anytime, guys. Let's do it.*

"But not with you."

Travis saw the gun rise, and he threw himself sideways, taking the girl down with him. The guys behind him yelled as the gun went off, and then the door crashed in. Shouting came from all areas.

"Police!"

"Stop!"

"Put down the weapons!"

"Police!"

Something flew over his head. A boot trampled his hand. He pulled himself on top of the girl, shielding her. Doors slammed. Glass shattered. More yelling.

"Don't move!"

"Put your hands on your head!"

Travis waited until it began to calm. Someone leaned over him. He let his gaze travel to the boots then looked up.

A man in SWAT uniform raised a brow. "We've got five targets, but we need you to identify."

Travis rolled off the girl and rose.

The girl groaned. He helped her to her feet. "You need an ambulance? An EMT?"

"Not sure." She wobbled. "We were almost killed."

"I had a blank in the first chamber."

Her eyes rounded, but then she smiled.

Travis glanced over at the men being held and froze. Four. Only four. "Where's the fifth?"

"This one tried to escape." A member of the team shoved j-beck out from behind the others.

And Travis couldn't help himself. He grinned.

***

"Chloe?" He walked slowly to the truck. She'd answered the phone. Another blessing.

It had taken hours of testimony and paperwork to clear everything up. He'd texted her earlier to let her know he was okay, that j-beck was in jail, and that he'd come by later. Her shift had ended before he finished. Sleep tugged at him, but he wouldn't go home until he saw her.

"Yes?" Her voice rose higher than usual.

Warmth circled through him. "Are you at home?"

"I stopped by the church to take an early run. I hadn't heard from you, so…"

"I'll head that way."

"Good. I… Someone else is here, too."

"I think Reece is usually there by now. He gets in early and stays late."

"No. I think it's Dennis."

"Dennis? What's he doing there?"

She laughed. "No idea."

"Well, do me a favor. Stay away from him."

"What? Why?"

"Chloe, please just do it."

"All right. We'll talk when you get here."

206

We'll talk. Oh yeah, they would, but not about Dennis. In fact, *talking* had not been on his agenda. He grinned then sobered. She did like to be informed. He put his phone down.

He'd sleep for days once he saw her. No, he'd call his family. Maybe take Chloe by there. Or no. His brothers's teasing would be over the top. Maybe later.

It was over.

Hundred-pound dumbbells lifted off both shoulders—and off his mind.

He put the truck in drive but sat for a moment.

What?

An irritating worry tickled inside. No, more like a wasp dashing itself against a windowpane. He picked up the phone again.

"Reece, you at church? No? Okay, I'm on my way to see Chloe. She's jogging, but she said Dennis is there. Any idea why he'd be there this early? Yeah, me too. Meet you there? All right."

***

Chloe reached the end of the path and decided to jog around the temporary buildings for a longer jog this morning. For some reason, the night shift in the ER hadn't worn her out. Of course, Travis's earlier text—that he was fine—had sent waves of joy through her. And now he was on the way.

She almost whirled around. Dancing instead of running could work now. She grinned. Dancing on the beach. She hadn't realized how tight her muscles were until she'd seen Travis's text.

She stopped, rubbed her head. But that meant...he'd be going back to Denver soon. Her heart did a little flutter, hip-hop thing. She pressed her lips together. What did that mean? The cold sliding through her body shook her.

No.

She wouldn't think about it now. He was safe. That

was enough.

For now.

She rounded the building and hit the parking lot.

A car was parked on the street past the church and near the dorms. Dennis had been standing at the back of the car, reaching into the trunk, when she'd driven around the bend from the other direction. She wouldn't have noticed him if he'd hadn't spun away and walked to the driver's side. The movement had caught her attention. He wore a ball cap with unruly hair sticking out, and she'd never have thought "Dennis" except for his distinctive sharp chin. But there was nothing past the dorms except a tree-covered vacant lot. What was he doing here?

And who cared?

She squinted against the morning sun. Perhaps she shouldn't have said anything to Travis, because if it wasn't Dennis, she'd feel foolish. It certainly wasn't his car. An older model she'd never seen before.

Glancing at her smartwatch, she noted her number of steps and the time: 7:35 AM. They served breakfast to the dorm residents from 7:00 to 8:00. If Dennis expected to find anyone around, he was too early and at the wrong end. The dining hall was at the opposite side of the property.

She glanced toward the car again.

No, it couldn't be Dennis.

The man, whoever it was, appeared from the hidden side of the dorms. The car's trunk stood open, and he tossed a bag into it and headed toward the driver's door. Just before he climbed in, he stopped and looked around. His eyes met hers and widened.

The man wore a ball cap over unruly hair, but his face looked like a skeleton. Ash white with dark sunken eyes and black lips.

Chloe stopped, unnerved.

He climbed into the car, did a three-point turn, and came her way.

High alert. Instantaneous. She jerked upright and began to run.

And knew at once she'd made a mistake.

Chapter 18

Fear not, for I am with you; be not dismayed, for I am your God; I will strengthen you. Yes, I will help you, I will uphold you with my righteous right hand.
Isaiah 41:10 NKJV

Instead of running to her car, she should have headed for the dining room. Toward people. Now she faced a bare parking lot, no lights in the offices, no one else jogging.

The car's engine revved behind her. Close. Too close. Her mind blanked.

She couldn't outrun the car. Her feet tangled, and she stumbled forward, twisting away even as the car's front edge slammed into her. She screamed and tumbled across the pavement, her head slamming on the hard surface.

Everything stopped, but then the sound of the car's engine and the screech of tires brought her head up.

No. No. Don't come back.

She tried to shove herself to her feet, but all she could do was roll. The car was on top of her. As she shoved away, the stench of the engine overwhelmed her. The blaring of a horn, and then a tremendous crash pounded her ears. She lay still, her insides shuddering, not knowing what was happening, whether he was coming back…or he'd hit something. The ground shook. She tried to hold her head.

"Chloe." And someone knelt beside her.

Travis? She wasn't sure. She huddled even farther into the ground. Her head spun. Pain pulsed through it.

"Chloe, I need to look at you." She heard the beep, beep, beep of him dialing. Heard another voice answering.

Then a third voice. "Put the phone down."

She felt the man next to her still. Travis. Yes, she was sure now. She swallowed the relief as fear rose again. Whose was the third voice?

"I said put the phone down."

The sound as Travis set the phone on the ground left her mind yelling, No!

"Get up and get her up, too."

Travis's hands slipped under her arms. "Pretend you can't get up," he whispered.

"Get up!"

"I think something's broken." Travis stood. "The car hit her."

Chloe twisted to see the other man, raising her head for a moment. A young man. *Not Dennis*. Holding a gun, and his hand shaking. One of the white supremacist group? But at the throbbing in her temples, she eased her head to the pavement.

Another car pulled into the parking lot. Her heart jumped again. Reece!

The young man cursed.

Silence dropped over them except for the growl of both car engines.

Then a car door opened, and a pair of well-worn hiking boots stepped to the pavement. She couldn't see anything else. But it wasn't Reece. Not with those boots.

"Get back in your car and get out of here," said the man with the gun, His voice ramped up two notches.

Lord, we need Your help.

"Get out of here."

"Okay. Okay. But I need to tell you that my wife has already called 911, and she's praying. So..." said the new arrival.

Chloe couldn't see more, couldn't lift her head again, but the swirl of anger that rode in the young man's voice shook her.

"My name's John, by the way. John Jergenson. This is my wife, Sharee, and our two children."

He had children in the car! Alarms sounded inside her head.

"I'm going to let her drive off, but I'll stay if you don't mind."

"You'll stay?" The man's voice jumped.

Lord, he's losing it. Please help him. Protect us.

Travis's foot edged forward.

"Yes. You see, I'm not sure which of you needs rescuing. Can my wife and children leave?"

The cursing sounded like a yes. The car eased forward. The hiking boots turned toward the young man again.

"Stay where you are!"

"Okay. Can I ask what's going on?"

"No!"

Chloe saw large tires and the bottom of a black SUV turn into the parking lot. The young man's legs twisted that way, and Travis jumped. He slammed into the man, and the gun spun across the pavement. The person in hiking boots sprung forward and grabbed it.

Chloe cringed. *Don't let it go off.*

Travis and the young man crashed to the ground, rolling, grunting. Swinging.

She tried to pull herself up.

"Wait." The man with the hiking boots—John something—dropped beside her. "My wife did call 911. Wait until they get here. Are you bleeding anywhere?"

"The gun?" Reece stood over them, hand out, tattoos climbing from his thumb up his muscled arm.

John Jergenson looked up. His eyes narrowed.

Chloe cleared her throat. "It...it's all right. He's the pastor, the assistant pastor."

John rose. He glanced down at Chloe once more, then handed the gun to Reece. In the distance, sirens sounded.

Reece turned toward the lurching bodies. He stepped back and sent a well-timed kick to the young man's side. The man sprawled forward, flat on his face.

Travis staggered to his feet.

When the other man rolled over, Reece aimed the gun at him. "I think you'll wait right there for the police."

Travis turned toward Chloe. She pushed herself to a sitting position, then to her feet. John reached for her arm, steadied her. She saw Travis's truck now, plowed into the front side of the other man's car. She threw her gaze back to him.

He caught both her arms. "Are you okay?"

"You wrecked the truck?"

"Had to when I saw him try to run over you."

She wrapped her arms around him. "It wasn't Dennis."

"No."

John's voice reached her. He'd turned away to talk on his phone. "I'm fine. Yes. You called 911? Did you ask them to send the fire department? Well, call back. There's a fire at some buildings here. Yes. Okay."

Chloe pulled back from Travis's arms. His gaze vaulted past hers to the dorms. Bright orange flames and black smoke spiraled upward at the far end.

***

Miss Eleanor thanked God for letting her come home. Some people needed the hospital, and maybe she had too, but she'd needed to come home more.

She took a deep breath.

Remember that young man, Lord. I've asked for his salvation. In Jesus's name. And I know You want everyone to come to a knowledge of the truth. So, do that for him. Please. And Kati. Let her know You're calling her. Give her the strength when she needs it. I know she's worried about filling my shoes. Ha! I'm no one special. You and I know that. You have prayer warriors all over. Those that stop and pray when needed. Your army. Draw her. Keep her and Reece safe. Keep Alan and Daneen safe. You need to heal Daneen, Lord. Alan needs her. I feel his need. And grow the ministry. Help the men and women there that are seeking You.

She signed, leaned back in the recliner, and breathed in. *You're here, Lord.* She closed her eyes, smiling, absorbing the shimmering Presence. The room filled with a gentle humming.

Glorious really.

It made her want to lie on the floor on her face. Humble herself in His Presence. She guessed if she got down there, He'd give her the strength to get back up.

She smiled at that and glanced upward. "If it's okay with you, though, I'd just like to go lay down in bed." The Presence seemed to warm, bathing her in a luminous light. She smiled again, rose, and walked to her bedroom.

***

"Rich, please. Let me help." Lynn tried to hold onto her patience.

He struggled with his shirt, balancing on one leg. He'd put the crutches against the wall, and they'd toppled. She'd left them there. They'd arrived at the rented apartment, and she could see his exhaustion, but his pride was fighting her.

"Wives are allowed to help their husbands, you know. It's written in the contract." She gave a saucy smile, and he scowled. "Please."

"Okay. Okay." He dropped his hands, but the growl was still in his voice. She kissed his cheek then pulled the T-shirt over his head.

"The shoes," he mumbled.

"I know." They were the hardest things right now. "Lay down, and I'll get them."

He maneuvered onto the bed and stretched out, his eyes closing. His face slackened. She touched his cheek then untied his shoes and slipped them off.

"You want to sleep?"

The nod was so short it seemed like sleep had already

overtaken him. She ran her finger down his cheek, walked to the other side of the bed, and took off her shoes. A moment later, she lay next to him.

He was here. Even if all she did was listen to him snore that would be enough for now.

"When you're awake, I'll tell you about the baby."

His eyes opened, and he slid her a sideways glance. Blue looked into blue.

She grinned. "I'm sorry. I couldn't keep it to myself another minute."

He struggled to turn her way, but she put a hand on his shoulder. "No, don't move."

She lifted onto her side and grinned down at him. "I'm pregnant. Eight weeks. The first couple of tests were negative but I knew. The doctor says that happens sometimes, but she and I are pretty sure of the date. Well, I am anyway." Her smile widened.

"You're sure?" His voice was rough.

"Yes. Are you happy?"

He put an arm out, slipped it around her and drew her down next to him. "Yes. You know I am. We've waited a while."

"But your mind is already working, isn't it? Don't worry. Your doctor said six months, and you'll be up and around doing your usual. But no marathons."

He grunted.

"And don't worry about the job. If you don't make captain, God will provide something."

His head turned her way again. "Captain?"

She couldn't help the whole grin thing. "I'm already praying about it."

He said nothing. She moved to look at him.

"Two new positions?" he asked. "A father and a captain at the same time? You don't think you're overdoing this?"

"Well maybe the captain thing will come a little later."

His eyes closed.

"Rich?"

"You know I don't deserve any of this. You, a baby..." The roughness in his voice cracked.

"Being alive?"

He cleared his throat. "Yeah. And Luis alive."

She rolled on to her back but clasped his hand. "God is good."

He took a deep breath. "Yeah, He is."

***

They walked from the restaurant, across the street and onto the beach. The glow of sunset smeared across the skies and reflected in the water. The back and forth rush of waves met them.

He'd brought her here three days after the man had tried to run her over, because... Well, it's where he realized how special she was.

When they got to the water's edge, Travis picked her up and swung her. Chloe laughed, and he lowered his head for a kiss.

It was over.

Finally.

Joy-filled adrenaline pumped through him. She was okay—cuts and bruises and still the occasional headache, but the doctors said that would disappear. A mild concussion. They'd kept her overnight. And the firefighters had extinguished the small fire at the dorms. Started with fire logs, it hadn't had time to do much damage. And j-beck was in jail.

Travis held her as they stared at the waters, the luminous waves hypnotizing in their beauty. "You're sure you're up to a walk?"

"I'm sure. Three days cooped up is all I can take."

They kicked off their flip-flops and walked along the shore, wet sand and foam under their feet.

"So, are you going to owe for the truck?"

"The rental agency and I are discussing it."

She turned to look at him. "Discussing?"

"I think we'll work something out. It's not a total loss."

"But they can't rent it."

"No. I might have to take it off their hands."

"You don't seem worried."

His head shifted her way. "I'm not letting anything worry me right now."

"Me either." But something tightened in her face.

"The look on your face says otherwise."

"You're going back to Denver?"

"After the trial."

Her gaze darted away. She studied the waves. Wind circled them and tugged at her ponytail, pulling strands free.

"What's wrong?"

"I…it's nothing. We can talk later."

Usually that would be his line. But whatever was bothering her, he wanted to know. She'd referenced a couple of things over the last few weeks. That day in the parking lot and that evening at the beach.

"Chloe, if we're going to get to know each other, we have to be open. Not just me with you, but you with me. It's a two-way street."

She swallowed. "Okay."

So why was she looking at him like he'd transformed into a grizzly?

"I'm trying not to think about you leaving."

Oh. Okay. He could address this. "I'm not going to just disappear. I—"

"You talked about leaving as soon as you could. So I just wondered…"

What had she wondered? He pulled her into his arms. "I'm not just leaving, and saying 'it was fun,' and never seeing you again."

She stared at him as if trying to pull out the truth of

what he said.

He laughed. "I think I understand the donuts now."

"What?"

"You stop when you've had a whirlwind night at the hospital. And eat through the stress. I know what you need. You need someone to turn to, to listen to you. God didn't make us to be alone. That was part of my problem. Remember?"

She chewed her lip but said nothing.

He tilted her head up. "We're never alone, really. I forgot that when I first went to Denver, but I was running, hiding. In fear. I'd almost died from the knife wound. My faith was in tatters. It took God saving me that night to get me back into the Word. Studying the Bible as I'd done years ago. Spiritual healing to go with the physical healing."

She was studying him, eyes searching his.

"But I was also talking about us. I want to be here for you. Or at least a phone call away. You thought I'd just run off?"

"I wasn't sure—"

"Did something happen before? With someone else?"

She stared past him, rubbed a hand over her mouth. "I was engaged."

All right. That shouldn't be a surprise, but his heart caved, anyway. She'd cared for someone deeply...

"Alex was in the army, and after he came back from overseas, he had problems. Like so many others, and he wouldn't talk about it. He was paranoid, thought people were spying on him, out to get him. I would listen to him, but no matter what I said, it never helped."

"He had PTSD?"

"Yes, but wouldn't get treatment. One evening, though, we had a long discussion. A good one. I thought. But as I look back, I realize it was one-sided. Me doing most of the talking because he wouldn't. I thought it helped. I told him Christ could make him whole. He had a superficial belief in God, but I didn't think he knew Jesus as Savior. Things seemed better after that. We started planning our wedding. One day he didn't make an appointment, and he didn't answer his phone. I went to his house. I had a key..." She stopped and cleared her throat. "He was in the living room. On the floor. He'd shot himself in the head."

Travis swallowed. He didn't know what to say. He could see the scene from her point of view. Feel the shock and horror. The helplessness. He'd always seen his own attempted suicide from his perspective. The view from her eyes shook him.

"When you said you'd tried to take your life..." She stopped, took a shuddering breath. "I thought I'd helped Alex that day, but I hadn't. Which is why when you shared what you did, I was afraid I'd mess up again."

"Chloe, you didn't." He whispered against her hair. "What you said that night was just what I needed. It put a period on all that God was saying to me, had said to me."

"I didn't know. You never said anything. It just made sense that you'd want to get away from here. I failed Alex. Failed to meet whatever need he had. I didn't know with you..."

"It's not your fault that your fiancé killed himself. I'm sorry for that. Sorry for you and him. But you can't blame yourself. You're not God. You can't fix everybody."

She pulled the loose strands of hair away from her face. "I only feel confident in the ER."

"That's because it's your gift. God gives each one of us a gift, you know. Yours is a gift of healing."

Chloe waved her hand impatiently. "No, that gift—it's talking about miraculous healing."

"Who says it's not miraculous? I've heard Kati say how she depends on you in the ER, that you save lives because you automatically do what needs to be done. That God directs you."

"She said that?"

"Haven't you ever thought about it?"

"I've felt that way sometimes. Like He's directing, telling me what I need to do. I don't talk about it, but I go home, and I think about what happened and wonder."

"And you couldn't think about what's happened with us and know that I care?"

She hesitated. The sun hovered near the horizon. Rays of light fingered the sky above it and glazed the waters below. "I...guess I was afraid."

"Because Alex left, and in the worst way. By committing suicide."

"Yes."

"But from what you've said, it wasn't you he was actually leaving, but life. And you're not a professional counselor. Which I'm sure he needed, along with a real commitment to Christ." He stopped for a minute, tilting his head and studying her. "You thought I would leave?"

"I wasn't sure."

He touched her cheek. "Crazy girl. I have plans—of you coming to Denver and staying with a nice grandmotherly type I know. Then I'll fly back here for visits. Stay with my parents. Everything on the up-and-up. Let's get to know each other."

"Really?" Her voice jumped.

He almost laughed at her expression. Instead he bent his head and let the gentleness of his kiss answer her. He wasn't leaving her, even if his job was in Denver. They'd put the plans into action, and let God do the rest.

Chapter 19

*And God shall wipe away all tears from their eyes; and there
shall be no more death, neither sorrow, nor crying, neither
shall there be any more pain: for the former things are
passed away.*
Revelation 21:4

Kati walked into Reece's office and put her hands on
her hips. "You're giving up being assistant pastor and going to
head up the IronWorks ministry instead of Pastor Alan and the
board?"

Reece leaned back in his office chair. "Yeah. Well, I'll
still have a board. You heard?"

"Alan just mentioned it. When did all this happen?"

"Sometime over the last few days."

"And you didn't want to talk to me about it?" She
leaned across the desk and punched his nose with her finger.

He drew back. "I'd planned to. It just got back
burnered with everything else."

"Hmmmp."

"I was pretty sure you wouldn't object. I'll be home
more." He lifted his brows, grinned.

She kept the frown for a moment longer then smiled.
"I'll love it." She rounded the desk and sat on his lap. "So,
who's Alan going to get as assistant pastor?"

"Alan said it's the couple that's been in Indonesia.
John and Sharee Jergenson."

"Do you know them?"

"Haven't had more than a chance to say hello. I know
he was here before, and a lot of people respect him. I know he

didn't run when Chloe was in trouble."

Kati nodded. "Courage. A definite plus. But the deacon board is in disarray."

"Losing Dennis and Roger Cummings together is hard."

"They both stepped down and left the church, but I feel sorry for Dennis, you know? It's not his fault his nephew took what Dennis said and decided to…well, set fire to a few things."

"To see if he could add to the general chaos? He just bungeed off what the Gordones did in that first fire. Thought he'd try some small ones of his own. Wanted to help us see how right his uncle's views were."

"Yeah, well, that wasn't right. And he could have killed Chloe."

"Tried to, I think. Once you step over the line, it's not hard to take the next step." Reece rested his elbows on his desk and joined his hands. "One of the things we stress at the ministry. Satan entices you to something little, but you know it's wrong. If you give in, next time he'll tempt you with something bigger. Most of them know how true it is, but now they recognize the temptation and see where it could lead."

"You'll do good heading that up." She snuggled into his neck. "Long day?"

"Long enough. Let's go home."

"Sounds good." She stood.

Reece grabbed his keys. "One more thing. Alan's decided he wants women on the deacon board, so those two spots will get filled by women."

"He's really asking for trouble, isn't he?"

Reece chuckled. "Sometimes, I think Alan thrives on trouble."

"And how are we going to rebuild?"

"With this last attempt to burn down the dorms, people have stepped up, money's coming in. What the enemy means for evil…"

Kati grinned. "Yeah. God will use for good." She watched as he locked the client files. "What about Lynn and Rich? I wish they'd come back."

"They might. Give the Lord some time."

The front office door opened. Kati turned. Who...

A younger man with slicked-back hair and piercing eyes stepped through the doorway. He waved a small book. "I need to talk to someone about what's in this book."

Kati glanced at Reece, then walked over to the man. "Can I?" She put out her hand.

He frowned, hesitated, then handed the book to her. She opened it and turned to Reece. "It's Miss Eleanor's little New Testament."

The man put out his hand now, wanting it back. "She gave it to me. She was in the hospital. I work there. She mentioned this place." He glanced around. "She said I could call her at any time, but I haven't been able to get in touch with her, so I just decided to drive over here."

Kati handed him the New Testament back and slipped into a chair.

Reece pulled his chair around the desk and waved to the man. "Have a seat. Throw us your questions, and we'll do our best to answer them."

***

Alan strolled up the walk to Miss Eleanor's house. She'd lived here as long as he'd known her. Her house was painted white with green trim. Azaleas planted near the house bloomed in profusion. An older home, wooden. A rarity in Florida these days. Termites liked wood, so they used construction block. He took a deep breath.

She hadn't answered the phone. He'd told her he would call for a couple of days just to check on her and that Daneen would be by with some food. But Miss Eleanor hadn't answered one, two, three calls.

He knocked, and after a minute he used the key she'd given him years ago. Just in case...

Alan stood over the bed and looked down at her. He'd known, of course. God had let him know before he got here. She looked peaceful. He grabbed the sadness and sense of loss and forced a smile.

Yes, she looked peaceful. She could finally rest, was finally home, was dancing on the streets of gold. He chuckled then. Yeah, and hugging all those who had gone before her. And looking for Jesus. Wouldn't that be a reunion?!

Ahhh. He needed to call somebody. He needed his wife. He took another moment to pull himself together, to walk to her beside and pick up the little book she'd shown him numerous times. Her prayer book. He flipped through it slowly, the warmth inside him growing. So many names, so many healings, saved marriages, salvations... Years' worth of names. He flipped to the back. Looked at the name and the date and lifted a brow in surprise.

Three days ago.

The entry showed a trembling hand. *Rodney. Nurse. In need of salvation.*

He smiled. Pocketed the book. Someone had to keep up the prayers. Her small New Testament was missing. She usually kept the two together. Well, he'd find it later.

Miss Eleanor had given him funeral plans the day she'd given him the key. A planner. That's what she was. The funeral paid for. All he had to do, she'd told him, was make sure everybody knew it was a party. Because she would be having a party in heaven, and she wanted to look down to see the party on earth. They'd better sing and shout, because that was what she'd be doing.

He chuckled again. "Yes, ma'am. We'll have a party."

The End

"...Well done, thou good and faithful servant..."
Matt 25:21a

Miss Eleanor has made numerous appearances in the Spiritual Warfare Series as well as in the Dangerous Series. I have patterned her after my mother, Elaine Knadle, a missionary and prayer warrior who loved her family, and after Clara (Grandma) Talley who I knew for many years. I know both these women are rejoicing in heaven today with the King of Kings and Lord of Lords, their Lord and Savior, Jesus Christ.

While writing *FIRE*, I came across a blog post by a long-time friend. When I read it, it hit me as exactly what I thought Pastor Alan would say when Satan threw everything he had at the church and the ministry and expected it to go under.

And, of course, it didn't because our God is greater. Greater is he in you than he that is in the world. Sometimes people are wounded in the fight, sometimes they even die, but God is greater, his promises are greater. We may not understand why things sometimes happen the way we do, but we do know we win the war!

So, I asked my friend if I might use his blog post, and he gave me permission. Here's the post, the exact way he wrote it (I edited it a little in the story to fit).

*THERE IS NO...
         *Blog post by Robert Kerce, Oldsmar, Florida

"There is no situation, circumstance or predicament,
no shortage, deficit or lack,
No evil, sickness or problem,
no plan, subpoena or attack,
There is no enemy, force or dilemma,
no shadow, verdict or malady,
No slander, accusation or gossip,
no wilderness, desert or tragedy...

"There is NO weapon fashioned in the forges of hell by our enemy that is strong enough to succeed when we condemn it. There is NO tongue of judgment loud enough to drown out the roar of God's Angelic Armies sent to deliver us. This is our heritage as servants of the Lord!

"No weapon that is formed against thee shall prosper; and every tongue that shall rise against thee in judgment thou shalt condemn. This is the heritage of the servants of the LORD, and their righteousness is of me, saith the LORD."

(Isaiah 54:17)

"Bless the LORD, ye his angels, that excel in strength, that do his commandments, hearkening unto the voice of his word. Bless ye the LORD, all ye his hosts; ye ministers of his, that do his pleasure." (Psalms 103:20-21)

"For he shall give his angels charge over thee, to keep thee in all thy ways. They shall bear thee up in their hands, lest thou dash thy foot against a stone." (Psalms 91:11-12)

Angels are innumerable on the earth and in heaven. As a matter of fact, Revelation chapter 5 notes there are millions of angels about God's throne. Here on earth angels sometimes take on human form. Hebrews 13:2 tells us to make sure we are hospitable to strangers because some people have entertained angels and were not even aware of it.

According to Psalms 103 (above) God's angels excel in strength and do his commandments. And accordingly, the angels of God respond to believers who quote God's word, as long as it is God's Word, and not our own desperate words.

It is a remarkable thing God has done, giving us his book, with his words all throughout, and telling us to keep our eyes on it, hide it in our hearts and "SPEAK" it out loud in faith! God's word, taught by Holy Spirit, is our top priority.

But we should never let it drift from our consciousness - the fact that angels are ever present in this world and working on our behalf. "Are they not all ministering spirits, sent forth to minister for them who shall be heirs of salvation?" (Hebrews 1:14)

Playlist

Music:

https://www.youtube.com/watch?v=HcpeLDp0Foo
Run to the Father by Cody Carnes

https://www.youtube.com/watch?v=BY6VAy9y_iQ Jesus,
Friend of Sinners by Casting Crowns

https://www.youtube.com/watch?v=Z0QG3rhbIO4
Alabastar Box by CeCe Winans

https://www.youtube.com/watch?v=hVFPjlp6nkk This is
the Great Adventure by Steven Curtis Chapman

https://www.youtube.com/watch?v=1TKAN-nAsu8
My Story by Big Daddy Weave

https://www.youtube.com/watch?v=Zp6aygmvzM4 The
Blessing Kari Jobe & Cody Carnes | Live From Elevation Ballantyne
| Elevation Worship

https://www.youtube.com/watch?v=ca2mXA7kdVc
You're beautiful.by Jeremy Riddle (Bethel Church)

https://www.youtube.com/watch?v=kkHo70DeiMM All
Your Promises are Yes and Amen Pat Barrett | Bethel Music &
Housefires

https://www.youtube.com/watch?v=zmNc0L7Ac5c
Another in the Fire by Hillson United

https://www.youtube.com/watch?v=iJCV_2H9xD0
Waymaker by LeeLand

https://www.youtube.com/watch?v=lZu7mfYS_VY Well

Done, The Afters

https://www.youtube.com/watch?v=DGbQ90kYZrl   Prize Worth Fighting For, Jamie Kimmett

https://www.youtube.com/watch?v=5_alauL2xKA   Shout to the Lord, Hillsong Worship

https://www.youtube.com/watch?v=Bm5HyEtuzp0 Benny Prasad - Liberty University – 2013 (His testimony)

https://www.youtube.com/watch?v=7hiN_R2Kd3g I Need You More, Kim Walker-Smith (Jesus Culture)

Thank you!

Over the years, so many friends, relatives, other authors, reviewers and readers have blessed me. Each one has added to my writing and my life as an author, reader, mom, wife, sister, grandma, and friend. God has put some great hearts in people. I can't name you all, but my own heart is enlarged because of you.

I had two editors for *FIRE*. One helped during the writing, the other with the finished manuscript. Amy Dohman and Dori Harrell, I thank you for your expertise and encouragement. You both definitely gave the book the final "ump" it needed. Also, I want to thank my formatter, Rachel Skatvold, who always has so much patience with me as I submit my manuscript with all the front and back matter to her to make it into a finished project

Special thanks go out this time to two people, former firefighters who answered many questions for me: Former Pastor and Fire Department Captain, Ken Pippin, who is now serving the Assemblies of God as the Pen Florida Adult Ministries Director. And former Freeport, Long Island volunteer firefighter, teacher, and soon-to-be author, Jeff Keene.

Thank you both!

Even with such good help and hours of research online, mistakes can be made. If there are any errors in the fire "scenes," they are mine, or they were "creatively" used for the storyline.

Hi! I'm Linda and a Florida transplant who now lives in Tennessee. I love things like sweet tea, apple butter, the fall, Christmas, and both the mountains and the oceans.

I'm a member of American Christian Fiction Writers, Word Weavers International, plus multiple Facebook author and reader groups. and a past finalist of ACFW's Genesis contest

My work with crisis pregnancy centers and anti-trafficking groups gave me insight into, and a heart for, women struggling in today's society.

My books feature sweet romance wrapped in real-life issues women face today and have an edge of mystery and suspense. I hope to entertain but also to encourage the reader in their walk with God.

My two series, The Dangerous Series and The Spiritual Warfare Series, are each unique. Both are better read in order, but every book is a stand-alone, too.

***

I hope you enjoyed, and more importantly, were

blessed and encouraged by The Spiritual Warfare Series. It is so easy to see people as our enemies, and yet Satan and his minions are the forces behind so much of what is happening in our world today. Prayer, praise, the Word of God, and the Name of Jesus are important weapons we can use in this arena. Take up your weapons!

Reviews are welcomed and can be left on Amazon, Goodreads and Bookbub. https://www.amazon.com/FIRE-Contemporary-Christian-Romantic-Spiritual-ebook/dp/B08CWDB4QQ/

My Amazon author page includes all my books and can be found at: https://www.amazon.com/Linda-K.-Rodante/e/B012OITZ2Y/ref=ntt_dp_epwbk_0

***

If you missed the first two books in the series, here is a portion of *Warrior*, Book 1, that you might enjoy. Please turn the page.

Warrior

Chapter 1

For the weapons of our warfare are not carnal, but
mighty through God to the pulling down of strong
holds. 2 Cor. 10:4

Kati Walsh drove a gloved fist toward her opponent's face, but Terry Johnson shot an arm up, blocked her punch, and danced backward, grinning.

"Come on, girl. You're slow today."

Kati scowled. Sweat rolled down her back. Her pixie-cut blonde hair clung to her face, but she bobbed forward, arms up—protecting, waiting.

Terry jutted his chin and egged her on. "Come on. Come on. Lay into me."

"You're gonna get...too cocky...one day." Kati's breath huffed out between words.

"But not today." Terry threw a right jab that she barely countered. His leg sliced a roundhouse kick into her side.

"*Oufff!*" She doubled over. The body armor they wore wasn't much good against power punches or kicks, and as her trainer and sparring partner, Terry knew it.

He laughed. "You should have known that was coming."

The spurt of anger squirted adrenaline throughout her body. She'd take the adrenaline but keep her cool. She concentrated on the next combination. Left foot jab, jab, straight right, left hook kick. Terry parried and blocked each one with ease.

He came back with a jab, straight right, left hook, and a right spinning back kick. She was familiar with his moves and managed to block or step away from the combination, but the spinning back kick almost caught her. He laughed again as she stumbled and righted herself.

Her breath hitched, but the adrenaline rush gave her one more jolt of energy. She made a small weight shift and threw an uppercut. Her glove smashed into his jaw. He flew back, slammed against the ropes, and dropped to his knees.

She wove back and forth, gloves up, and stared down at him. "You should have known that was coming, Terry."

Too bad the spiritual demons she battled these days didn't fall as easy.

***

Reece Jernigan stood in the shadows outside the boxing ring. The Florida sun forced the building's air conditioners to work overtime, and he was glad for his cutoff jeans and the short-sleeved polo. A T-shirt would have been nice, but not in this neighborhood...

He glanced to his right, wondering why Josh insisted on khaki Dockers and a white long-sleeved shirt each day. Josh didn't have Reece's tattoos to hide, so his need for the "uniform" made no sense. At least today Josh had rolled up his sleeves and left the tie in the SUV.

A loud grunt came from the boxing ring. The woman in the ring bounced on her feet but kept her eyes on the man on the platform. He had one glove on the ropes and struggled to stand.

Reece turned to Joshua and lifted his brows.

Josh returned the look and grinned. "Well, don't make her mad, bro. Remember the pastor's wife said she might not be happy we're here to pick her up." He lifted his chin, indicating the woman in the ring. "And don't pull any of your stunts, expecting me to save your hide."

Reece snorted. "No worry there. You always leave me hanging."

"You give me no credit for extricating you from the traps you set for yourself."

"Extricating? What's *extricating* mean? No one understands what you say, Josh. How does that help me?" He turned his attention back to the sparring mat.

The woman leaned over and said something to the man. He grimaced, mouthed something, and stood to his feet. She bit her lip, an obvious attempt to hide a smile.

Reece chuckled. "Come on. Let's go get the Battle Maiden before she does another number on her sparring partner. He looks like he's asking for it."

"See? That's what I mean. Battle Maiden. You've got a name for everyone, and not everyone's enamored with them."

Reece muttered "enamored" under his breath and walked past Joshua toward the ring.

The woman's breath huffed from her chest, but her bouncing slowed. The spiky blonde hair was matted with sweat. "I apologize, Terr. I didn't mean to hit you that hard."

The other boxer rubbed his jaw, face contorted. "It's not a competition, Kati. You ought to be careful, or you might find yourself on the ropes next time—or with your face messed up."

The man straightened and threw a feinted punch. She rocked back and blocked, her eyes widening.

Terry laughed. "Gotcha, babe."

The girl frowned. "I told you not to call me babe."

Reece stepped closer. "That *gotcha* would work better if she hadn't already sent you to the mat with a real punch."

"Reece." Josh's voice cautioned.

The man glared. "Who are you?"

Reece nodded at Kati. "Came to give a ride to the winner. Looks like that would be the lady."

The woman's focus moved his way. Her green eyes studied him. "You did, did you? Then I'll have to repeat Terry's question. Who are you?"

Joshua put a hand on Reece's arm and moved up beside him. "I'm Josh Corbin. The new assistant pastor at New Life Church. Pastor Alan sent me to pick you up. He said your car was being worked on, that his wife—Daneen?—was supposed to give you a ride home, but they have an unexpected meeting. He also said you wouldn't have your phone on you, so you probably wouldn't know."

Reece grinned. No lie. Not in that outfit. The girl's eyes narrowed when she caught his stare, and Joshua's head swiveled around. Reece sobered.

"Ask him for an ID, Kati." Terry bobbed forward. "They both look suspicious to me."

Joshua dug for his wallet, flipped it open, and shoved it in her direction. "Pastor Alan did send a text to your phone. You can go get your phone and read it."

She glanced at his ID. "I don't really need this. I know your name. Knew you were coming to the church today." Her gaze slid to Reece. "And you are?"

"This is Reece Jernigan. He's the friend who brought me. He's also looking for a job..." Josh glanced around the gym, looked at them inquiringly.

Reece sent him a scowl. "Thanks for the help, *friend*, but I'm fine on that score."

Joshua's mouth hitched, and he turned back to the woman. "We can wait until you're finished." He nodded at the man, Terry, and walked back into the shadowed corner where they'd stood before.

Reece glanced around the gym before following. Yeah, he and a gym like this? Not again. Not in a million years. "What was that about, dude?"

"Just giving you something to think about besides the Battle Maiden."

Reece's look skipped back to the rink. He eyed the girl as she raised her gloves. A kickboxer. With a rock-solid uppercut. Nice.

A motor revved outside, followed by a screech of wheels. The sound circled the building, halted. A minute later, someone gunned the engine. Once. Twice. Three times. Then circled the building again.

Reece concentrated on the sound. Motorcycle. Something niggled inside him. He frowned, listened to the sound again, and then moved past Joshua toward the front door.

"Hold the fort, man."

As he neared the door, the unmistakable smell of gasoline hit him. He picked up his pace. Premonition hit every nerve. He slid in front of the doorway. On the other side of the glass, fire leapt from a burning container to the ground. The bushes and walkway in front of the door appeared wet with accelerant. An engine roared, and a motorcycle disappeared around the building's corner. Reece stared. Flames jumped skyward and raced for the building.

He turned and ran. "Fire! Fire out front! Where's the back entrance? Fire!" He sprinted toward the ring.

Josh ran up beside him. "What's going on?"

"Someone set a fire out front. Grab the girl and her partner." He hollered at the other boxers and members. "Fire! Fire out front! Where's the back door?"

Someone pointed. He threw his hand in that direction, pointing toward the back, and took off at a run. A huge whoosh came from the front doors. Someone screamed. Others hollered and ran toward the back. Those working out looked his way. He dashed across the gym. "Fire at the front doors! Get out!"

Everyone began running. Those from the changing areas appeared, pulling on clothes, alarm on their faces.

A man and a woman neared the back door.

"Don't go out that door!" Reece roared. "Stop!" His three years out of the trenches could cost them. "Don't go out that door!"

The woman skidded to a halt, and Reece grabbed the shirt collar of the man in front of him. "Let me make sure it's safe."

The girl stepped aside, eyes wide. "Go ahead."

"Out of the way!" yelled someone else.

Reece stepped in their path and put up a hand. "Wait here. All of you, wait here."

He looked past them, found Josh's tall figure along with the sparring couple. "Keep them back. I need to check outside." He slipped the Glock from the holster at his back and stopped by the door.

Motorcycle. Gasoline. An intentional fire.

It didn't leave him with a good feeling.

He stilled the noise in his head, stepped to the door, twisted the knob, and thrust it open. Nothing. He waited a moment, trying to hear over the clamor of voices behind him. Gun up, he slid his head past the door, then jerked backward.

A man straddled a motorcycle outside. One person. Brown skinned, tattoos, biker jacket, and smirk. Behind him, in the empty parking lot, the streetlight had clicked on, leaving an eerie glow.

Reece shot another look at Josh, the girl Kati, and her sparring partner. They stood in front of the others, but their eyes were on him. Terry's gaze darted to the front door and back. A wall of flames mixed with the rising smoke on the other side of the gym. Reece waved them back against the wall. Most moved, but Terry yelled at him. Reece held up the gun, sent a narrow-eyed stare, and everyone quieted.

He turned to the door again, eased his head forward. The man on the motorcycle revved its engine. His mouth showed a wide, uneven sneer before he laughed and screeched down the street.

Reece's gaze flicked right and left. Nothing, no one else. He holstered his gun and waved the others forward. They scrambled and pushed past him, but he caught Terry's arm.

"Who's in charge here? Is everyone out?"

The other man snatched his arm free. "I am. I'm in charge. It's my gym." His face had whitened. "It's on fire! Everything I've poured into it. My life!"

Reece nodded. Emotion ricocheted through him, but he moved his gaze back to the street. "Are you sure everyone's out?"

Terry's sparring partner, Kati, leaned forward. "Unless someone slipped in after you, everybody is here." She turned toward Terry, her hand resting on his arm. "I'm sorry, Terr. So sorry."

The shock on his face echoed the look in his eyes. "I can't believe he actually did it."

"He? Who are you talking about?"

Josh caught Reece's gaze. "I called 911."

"Good." Reece examined those milling around, taking in their reactions. His focus shifted to Terry. "He? There was a biker out here."

Terry's mouth opened. He swallowed. "What did he look like?"

"Hispanic maybe, but tall. Young. A gang member?"

Sirens sounded in the distance. Terry's eyes half closed. "He wanted insurance money." When he twisted back to the building, his face seemed to dissolve. "Or he said this would happen."

"This was a warning. He left you and the others alive, in one piece. Next time they might be outside waiting for you."

The girl gasped. Reece's eyes shifted her way.

The color disappeared from her face, leaving green eyes to search his. "Who are you anyway? A cop or something?"

Red and blue lights and pulsating sirens rounded the corner. Police cruisers appeared. A red fire engine rocked to its side, rounding the building. Men and women poured from the vehicles.

Reece watched the quick, decisive movements of the firefighters. "No. No one in particular. No one important."

***

Kati shifted the large box in her arms and kicked a knock-knock on the door. At least her kickboxing came in good for something, so far sharing about her faith at the gym had not. Her heart squeezed. What would Terry do now? What would the members do? She'd call soon, but she didn't want to inundate him when she knew others would be calling. She would pray and leave the solution in God's hands.

"Come in!" The voice sounded strange and stressed, but she recognized it from the aftermath of the fire and the drive home two days ago.

She tapped again with her foot, and a moment later the door flew open. Joshua stood looking at her, brows high, his face echoing the tone of his voice.

"Sorry, but my hands were full." She indicated the box with her chin.

He eyed it for a second, then reached and hoisted it out of her arms. When he stepped away from the door, he moved his chin to wave her into the room.

"Come in. Come in. Have you got your car back then?" He deposited the box onto his desk. "What's all this?"

"Yes, to the car. Thanks for asking. And this is just some office equipment that was buried in a back closet here. I thought you might need it. We haven't had an assistant pastor in years, and this office hasn't been used forever, so..."

He nodded and looked around the room. Papers and books littered the desk. Other boxes and books filled the two chairs and lined the walls.

"Although maybe you won't need..."

Josh made a sweep with his arm. "Does this look like chaos to you?"

"Can I take the fifth?"

He grinned, the stress lines easing. "Setting up home and an office and preparing for my first sermon here—well, this equals my first jump from an airplane."

"A bit unusual." Kati nodded. The congregation had talked about the new assistant pastor over the last month, but their nervousness, she realized, did not match his. "We watched the videos of your preaching and FaceTimed. We're good. Relax, Pastor."

He shot her a grateful smile, moved books from a chair, and waved her into it. "Wired into the whole congregation for a one-on-three-hundred conversation also ranked up there."

His smile was engaging, and so was the loose limbered way he moved. Like a cheetah, she decided. Long, lean, and wiry. She laughed at his expression. "That *was* interesting."

He pulled open the box and dug through it. "Looks like good stuff. How'd you know I needed this?"

"That was pretty easy when I thought about Pastor Alan and Daneen having to go out of town."

Joshua stopped, looked over the box at her. "Such a shock

for him, his brother dying like that. No warning."

Kati nodded. Sadness washed through her. "He is such a great guy. He and Daneen both are wonderful. He would be here for you if he could."

"I know. I'm not worried about that." His mouth inched up on one side. "Just a little flustered trying to get settled in."

Kati glanced around the office and identified the smell that wrinkled her nose. "You've already painted."

"Here and at the house. Reece is handy with most stuff, and he keeps me going. I'd sit and spend the time on the sermon if he'd let me."

"Ah. The slave driver. Martha to your Mary? I might have guessed that." She hesitated. During the ride back to her place two days ago, the two men's conversation had proved amusing and interesting. "Is Reece your brother?"

Joshua pulled plastic desk organizers, a stapler, tape, pens, a desk caddie, and other items from the box she'd brought. "Martha to my Mary, huh? I'll have to tell him that." The small grin showed his amusement. Then he put his head back, and his look changed. "A blood brother? No. But a friend that sticks closer than a brother? Yes."

Hmmm… Kati leaned back in the chair. Their looks were completely different—Josh tall and blond with blue eyes, Reece stockier, dark hair and eyes—so she hadn't expected them to be related, but you never knew. "That's something to say about someone."

"Yes, it is. What about you, Kati? Who are your close friends at church? Are your parents here? Siblings?"

"Friends? Let's see. Lynn Richards. You'll meet her and her husband, Detective Rich Richards. He's been pushing for a security team at the church." Kati hesitated. "And Ryann Byrd's a close friend. Although she doesn't attend much anymore. And you'll need to know Miss Eleanor, our eighty-eight-year-old prayer warrior."

"Ah. I'll need to get with Rich Richards. And you said a prayer warrior? I'll definitely invite her and anyone else that does combat in that arena to lunch soon." He sat back on the edge of the desk and crossed his arms.

His grin warmed her.

"I want to establish a regular prayer meeting to pray for the neighborhood and for unsaved friends and relatives."

"I'd love that, and we have a group who will love it, too."

His blue eyes focused on her. Wow. Could those eyes see through her? Feeling suddenly nervous, she stood.

"I'd better let you finish your work." When she started for the door, she realized that he'd left it open. Good move.

"Kati." He came off the desk then stopped. The smile reappeared. "Thank you for bringing these." He waved his hand to the things on his desk.

"You're welcome. And welcome to New Life Church."

He nodded. "Thank you again. But what about your family? Are they here, too?"

"My...family?" She tried not to stutter.

"Yes."

A movement at the doorway caused her to turn. Reece stepped into the room. His brown eyes caught hers, and a light appeared in them. He held a bag from a local deli and two bottles of water. The scent of garlic and warm bread floated her way.

"Hello, Reece." Her voice gushed. She couldn't stop it. "I see you brought lunch. That's good. I'll just go and let you two eat. Good talking to you, Pastor." She scooted by Reece and out the door. She could feel his eyes on her as she hurried down the hallway.

"What did you do to the lady, Josh?" Reece's voice followed her. "Or was it just me?"

***

Warrior by LindaK. Rodante

https://www.amazon.com/gp/product/B07HVRV2S3/ref=db s_a_def_rwt_bibl_vppi_i0

Made in the USA
Monee, IL
17 September 2020

42009077R00142